Alibi

BRANTLEY WALKER:
Off the Books

By Nicole Edwards

The Walkers

Alluring Indulgence

Kaleb
Zane
Travis
Holidays with The Walker Brothers
Ethan
Braydon
Sawyer
Brendon

The Walkers of Coyote Ridge

Curtis
Jared (a crossover novel)
Hard to Hold
Hard to Handle
Beau
Rex
A Coyote Ridge Christmas
Mack
Kaden & Keegan
Alibi (a crossover novel)

Brantley Walker: Off the Books

All In
Without A Trace
Hide & Seek
Deadly Coincidence
Alibi (a crossover novel)

Austin Arrows

Rush
Kaufman

SOUTHERN BOY MAFIA/DEVIL'S PLAYGROUND
Beautifully Brutal
Without Regret
Beautifully Loyal
Without Restraint

STANDALONE NOVELS
Unhinged Trilogy
A Million Tiny Pieces
Inked on Paper
Bad Reputation
Bad Business

NAUGHTY HOLIDAY EDITIONS
2015
2016

Alibi

A SERIES CROSSOVER NOVEL

BRANTLEY WALKER: OFF THE BOOKS, 5/
THE WALKERS OF COYOTE RIDGE, 10

NICOLE EDWARDS

NICOLE EDWARDS LIMITED
A dba of SL Independent Publishing, LLC
PO Box 1086
Pflugerville, Texas 78691

ALIBI
A Series Crossover Novel
Brantley Walker: Off the Books, 5
The Walkers of Coyote Ridge, 10
Nicole Edwards

COVER DETAILS:
Image: © Wander Aguiar Photography
Model: Lucas
Design: © Nicole Edwards Limited

INTERIOR DETAILS:
Formatting: Nicole Edwards Limited
Editing: Blue Otter Editing

IDENTIFIERS:
ISBN: (ebook) 978-1-64418-044-0 | (paperback) 978-1-64418-045-7 | (audio) 978-1-64418-046-4
BISAC: FICTION / Romance / General

DEDICATION

To Travis Walker
I wish we could all be as true to ourselves as you are.

Dear reader,

Up to this point in my writing career, with 72 books now published, I've written a myriad of storylines, ones that have made me laugh, made me cry, even made me want to stomp my feet and yank out my hair. I have not, however, written anything like this. This book … this one completely undid me. I did not expect it, even questioned it when I realized what was happening, but I've always done my best to be true to my characters, so I had to follow through.

I can honestly say, I truly hope not to live the experience again because it stole a part of me I wasn't ready to give up. With that said, I do hope you enjoy, if not so much the journey, then the love, support, and kindness the Walker family shows one another during such a heart-wrenching time.

Thanks for reading!

Nicole Edwards

Chapter One

Saturday, January 9, 2021

BRANTLEY WALKER EXPECTED TODAY TO BE A long day, starting off with a visit from Ryan Trexler and Hunter Kogan, the men in charge of running Sniper 1 Security, the largest private security firm in the state.

They were here at Brantley's request, and since this was somewhat of a job interview for the soon-to-be disbanded Off the Books Task Force, he figured it needed to run smoothly, hence the reason he was already three hours into his day and it was just now oh-eight-hundred.

He walked into the kitchen as Reese was pouring a cup of coffee.

"You only got seven miles in this mornin'. Somethin' wrong with you today?"

Brantley could hear the teasing tone, and he appreciated it. If Reese knew Brantley was stressed about this meeting, he wasn't calling him on it, but he was certainly doing his best to distract him. For a moment, Brantley's brain flipped back to a few hours ago when Reese had woken him up with that sexy mouth doing sinful things. Needless to say, it'd been one hell of a way to start the day.

"Too much shit to do," he said, forcing a smile and accepting the cup Reese passed over.

"I just got a text. RT and Hunter'll be here in a few." Reese's tone was calm and collected as usual. "We'll have plenty of time to introduce them to the team, even have time for questions. Then what's left? We get to spend the afternoon at the park with the rest of the town?"

Brantley nodded, staring into his coffee mug. "Yeah."

And *that* would be the second half of his ridiculously long day.

After he fielded questions from JJ, Baz, Trey, and Charlie regarding the fact they were no longer state employees, Brantley was going to spend the afternoon at the fantasy festival. Coyote Ridge's first one of the year.

Despite the name, it wasn't in the least bit kinky, he'd been told. It was a new festival added to the calendar this year, one meant to kick off 2021 with carnival games and rides designed specifically for the children of Coyote Ridge.

As for why Brantley was looking forward to it … well, it certainly wasn't for the games and rides. No, his reasons were a bit more selfish: he was simply looking forward to some downtime with Reese and if it meant congregating with the rest of the town, so be it.

He just wasn't sure he could get in the spirit of it today. Ever since they learned that Juliet Prince was involved in the false kidnapping scheme that resulted in JJ's house being blown to smithereens a week ago, he hadn't been sleeping much. It didn't help that they had no idea where the woman was or her next move, but something in his gut said they needed to be hypervigilant.

Brantley's watch buzzed at the same time Reese's did, which meant only one thing.

"Looks like they're right on time," Reese said. "Why don't you go out and greet 'em. I'll head to the barn, start the coffee."

Brantley nodded because he would take any direction offered. This was foreign territory for him. He had never applied for a job in his life. Well, unless BUD/S, which stood for Basic Underwater Demolition/SEAL counted. But this wasn't an endurance test that would allow his body and mind to prove his worthiness. This would require some schmoozing on his part and Brantley would be the first to admit, it wasn't his strong suit.

With Tesha, their four-legged partner, leading the way, Brantley went to greet their guests.

Stepping out onto the front porch, he steeled his spine, geared up for convincing these men that absorbing the Off the Books Task Force was the best thing to do for everyone involved. Granted, he knew they were already leaning in that direction based on what RT had told him, but they'd driven two hundred miles from Dallas to Coyote Ridge on a Saturday, no less, to seal the deal.

"How was the trip?" Brantley asked, holding out his hand to RT after the man deposited his helmet on the handlebar of the Kawasaki Ninja H2R.

"Perfect way to spend a Saturday mornin'," RT said with a wide grin, shaking Brantley's hand in return.

"I told Reese I was still thinkin' about gettin' one of those." Brantley nodded at the sportbike.

"Worth the investment," RT replied. "You're more than welcome to try it out if you'd like."

Brantley grinned. "I might just take you up on that later."

The other man strolled around, running one hand over his short hair, the other pulling off his sunglasses, revealing a pair of scrutinizing white-gray eyes.

"Brantley Walker, I'd like to introduce you to Hunter Kogan. Hunter, Brantley."

"Nice to meet you," Hunter said, gripping his hand firmly. "I've heard a lot about you."

"Don't believe everything you hear," Brantley joked.

Hunter chuckled. "Likewise." He nodded his head toward RT. "Especially if it comes from this one."

RT rolled his eyes. "Anyone who knows me knows I only speak the truth. So when I say y'all are both assholes, you can bet it's true."

Brantley laughed, feeling some of the tension dissipate.

"Reese is out in the barn startin' a pot of coffee. Y'all ready to check it out?"

Hunter's worried gaze flipped between them. "No one said anything about spendin' the day with animals."

"I guess I could clarify. *Converted* barn. No animals." Brantley glanced down at Tesha who was sitting at his feet, staring up at them, tongue lolling out of her mouth. "Well, except this girl."

Hunter turned his attention on the dog. "She in trainin'? Or can I pet her?"

"Very early stages, so she'd much prefer you did."

Hunter held out a hand, let Tesha sniff. When she gave him a slightly hesitant but approving lick, he reached down and patted her head.

"Is the rest of the team here?" RT asked, glancing around.

Brantley motioned for them to follow. "On their way. I asked 'em to be here by nine. Figured I'd give you a few minutes to look around before they arrived."

"You tell them yet?"

"No. I just told Reese last night, in fact. I didn't want to jump the gun."

RT glanced at the house, then the barn. "Reese mentioned you moved your offices to the main house?"

"We converted a couple of the bedrooms on the second floor," Brantley confirmed. "Added an exterior entrance. Gives us a little more room."

"Probably doesn't help with work-life balance," Hunter noted. "Havin' an office in the house."

Brantley chuckled. "I didn't realize there was such a thing."

"Only in the movies," RT joked.

Brantley keyed in the code to unlock the doors to the barn then stepped back out of the way to allow RT and Hunter to precede him.

"Wow. This is impressive," RT said as he scanned the interior of the barn.

Brantley glanced around, trying to see it from their viewpoint. He'd spent so much time and effort on this place, he sometimes forgot what it had once been.

Aside from the architectural design—the pitch of the roof, the Y-shaped posts that held up the rafters, and the enormous sliding door—it didn't resemble much of a barn on the inside anymore. The exterior walls had been insulated and an additional layer of wood, which he'd white-washed, added on the interior for energy efficiency. A solid, electronically controlled door had been installed for security. The original dirt floor had been covered with concrete, then stained and sealed. The hayloft had been converted, losing the original ladder and gaining a staircase. To the right of the door, a conference room had been added, and behind that, along the wall, there was a small kitchenette, a bathroom, and a storage area.

"You did this yourself?" Hunter asked, taking it all in.

"I had some help," he admitted. "The barn was here when I bought the property. Needed a little bit of work on the exterior, but not much. Replaced some wood, slapped on a coat of paint, added some security. Reese and I built the staircase."

"Impressive."

"Thanks. Honestly, I hadn't had this in mind when I did it. I was just playin' around out here, passin' time while I recovered and tried to figure out what I wanted to do with the rest of my life. Thought maybe it'd be a man cave of sorts, figured it was smart to safeguard it. Then once the governor proposed the task force, I knew it would be a good base of operations."

"Since you don't have walk-in clients, I can see that," Hunter acknowledged.

Reese appeared, setting four empty coffee cups and a steaming carafe on the first desk he came to before formally greeting RT and Hunter.

"Help yourself," Reese said. "Need cream or sugar?"

"This is perfect," RT said, pouring a cup before resuming his exploration of the space.

When RT stopped at the base of the staircase, Brantley moved closer.

"That was an afterthought," he explained. "When the team started to grow, we had to add on. Put in the staircase to utilize the loft square footage. Added the conference room."

RT moved deeper into the room. "You've got what? Three thousand square feet in here?"

"A little more with the loft, but yeah."

"Even with all this, you've got some extra room for growth."

"We do."

"I'm curious about this," Hunter said, motioning toward the row of whiteboards mounted on the wall.

"Those are our evidence boards. We start one with each case. It allows us to see the visual breakdown of what we know and how it all relates."

"Is that what this one is?" Hunter motioned toward the board at the end, which had various images taped to it as well as writing that connected a few dots.

"Yeah. We've been lookin' into a social media scam, tryin' to figure out who's behind it."

"I've heard about that," RT said, stepping closer to the board. "They infiltrate the virtual community groups on Facebook and whatnot. Pretend to be a member, get to know the others."

"Yep," Brantley confirmed. "And in at least one instance that we know of, they've attempted to kidnap a kid."

"Seriously?" Hunter's voice had deepened. "That's bullshit."

"Yeah, well, unfortunately, that's humanity for you."

"You plan to continue lookin' into it?"

Brantley met RT's gaze. "Was hopin' to."

"I think you should." RT glanced at Hunter. "You know what'd work great for them?"

Hunter nodded. "It definitely would."

Lost, Brantley stared at the pair, wondered if they were going to share with the class.

"Oh, sorry." RT smiled, looked back at the wall, and motioned with his hands. "We've been workin' on a display screen that would allow us to do somethin' similar. Ours is a bit more complex bein' that we're trackin' multiple clients at a time. It's digital and live, meaning it changes all the time as our agents update details. But it would work brilliantly for this, too."

"Display screen?" Reese asked.

"It's touch screen, like a tablet, only on a grander scale. You'd only need one because you could archive each case in a folder, open them as you need it. We've got software that would allow you to write notes, pin things in whatever order, show the images just like you would see them on an evidence board."

"JJ would go apeshit," Brantley said with a laugh.

"You said you've got a team of six now?" Hunter asked, perching on the corner of an empty desk as he sipped his coffee.

"Seven," Brantley corrected. "I've recently hired JJ an assistant."

"Potentially eight," Reese corrected. "He's made an offer to another … comm specialist, but he hasn't accepted the position yet."

"How many more are you lookin' to bring on?" RT strolled back toward them.

Brantley glanced at Reese, nodded for him to answer.

"That depends on how we structure it," Reese told RT. "As it is, we're a bit lean for a full investigative team in this area. Since our cases require us to move quickly in the sense that we're lookin' for someone who could potentially be in a life-or-death situation, we need to cover ground quickly. But at the same time, we need to maintain coverage on our workload."

"The cold cases?"

"Exactly."

"Will you continue those?" RT asked, glancing between them.

"I'd like to lend a hand to neighboring departments if we've got the ability to do so."

"So how many are you thinkin' and how much ground are you coverin'?" RT lowered himself into one of the chairs, propped an ankle on a knee, and sipped his coffee.

"I'd say a full team would be roughly ten, maybe twelve. That includes the electronics experts and support personnel."

"Ten or twelve per region?" RT clarified.

Reese looked at Brantley, then back to RT as though confused by the question. "Yeah, I guess. Are you lookin' to create more teams?"

"I'm not." RT motioned toward them. "But I figured y'all are."

Brantley hadn't discussed this with anyone, including RT. It had been mentioned, but only once. Something about creating these teams in a few major cities across the US.

"Eventually," Brantley noted.

"From experience," RT continued, "I can tell you it'd be wise to keep your electronics and support teams in one place and send field agents where they're most needed as you grow. Less on overhead that way."

"We're willin' to do whatever you need us to do," Brantley told RT. "Our only objective is to remain useful to those who need our services."

RT looked at Hunter, the men clearly having a silent conversation. When Hunter nodded, RT turned a wide grin on him and Reese.

"I'm not gonna pretend we have to get into the minutia to move forward. From the minute you showed interest, we were on board." He chuckled. "In fact, it took me all of three minutes to present it to the board and get one-hundred-percent buy-in."

Brantley stared like an idiot. He hadn't been sure what to expect, but having spent his entire career working for the government, where the wheels turned slowly when it came to decision-making, he damn sure hadn't anticipated a full-on welcome by the end of this meeting, much less just half an hour in.

"Seriously," Hunter tacked on. "We've taken our fair share of missing-persons cases over the years, but we've never had the manpower to dedicate full teams to it. However, there is one caveat."

Of course there was.

Brantley waited patiently for the bad news.

"Man, don't look like someone punted you in the balls. It's not that bad," RT said with a choked laugh.

"In my experience, it usually is," he admitted.

Hunter glanced between them, his gaze landing on Brantley when he said, "We're aware you're both accustomed to bein' boots-on-the-ground leaders"—Hunter held up a hand, thwarting Brantley's prepared argument—"which you will remain." He exhaled with a smile. "However, you'll also be considered executive management within our infrastructure. With that comes a few additional responsibilities. Financials, sales, whatnot. But you'll be assigned a personal assistant and a bookkeeper to deal with your office work. If the need arises, we can get you a spot for an office manager, as well. A complete clerical staff'll free up your team, allowing them to dedicate one hundred percent of their time to the cases."

Brantley knew JJ would be pleased with that.

"The assistant I just hired..." Brantley glanced between RT and Hunter. "If it's all the same to you, we'd like to utilize her."

"Hire whoever you see fit. You will maintain operational control." RT got to his feet. "But what Hunter's leavin' out is the other executive responsibilities. You'd be required to show up a couple of times a month for meetings, keep the board and the other teams up to date on what you're focused on and how you're spendin' your money. As well as the paying clients you're accumulatin'."

"Payin' clients? The ones we help don't usually need our services again."

"If they're lucky, that's true. But they're not the clients we're lookin' to deal with. However, we provide myriad services."

Brantley nodded, understanding.

"As for spendin', we've got a relatively foolproof budgeting system, which we'll go over so you know where your funds are allocated." RT motioned to the barn. "And if you're in agreement, we'd like to rent some space for some of our agents."

Brantley glanced at Reese, looking for confirmation he was in agreement with any or all of it.

"We can move those funds around in the budget," Reese said, which Brantley took as full agreement.

RT pulled out his phone, tapped something on it. A second later, Brantley's phone chimed, as did Reese's.

"Those are your individual welcome packets, outlinin' salary, benefits, and the like. We can discuss those further whenever you're ready. We've got the same packets for each of your current team members, with the exception of the new assistant since we weren't aware. But we can have it by early Monday mornin'. It's all covered. Like I said, we're thrilled about this expansion. And I personally think it'll benefit all of us in the end."

Brantley agreed. He knew they'd have access to resources they hadn't even had with the state. Plus, and probably most importantly, they'd have some organization. As much as he loved his team, that was one thing they'd yet to master.

When the rest of the team arrived, Brantley had regrettably informed them of the governor's decision to disband the team. He was surprised there hadn't been too much pushback. Aside from Baz and Charlie asking about the pensions they'd been promised they could keep, which he'd told them he would have to follow up on.

Once everyone had settled down, they spent a couple of hours mapping out what the new task force would look like under the umbrella of Sniper 1 Security. RT and Hunter had stayed under the guise of offering their insight, but Brantley got the feeling they stuck around because they wanted to see how the team meshed.

It'd been slow going in the beginning, what with Jessica James—known simply as JJ—having a tantrum after learning not only had her personal life gone up in flames, her professional one was in a state of chaos as well. Luckily, they'd managed to talk her off the ledge, and once she was on even ground again, it didn't take long before she was leading the charge.

As for Charlotte Miller and Trey Walker, the newest members of the task force, they were still in that awkward stage where they acted as though they had little input on the subject matter. Every so often, one or both would speak up, but it had taken Reese's continuous attempts to include them before they were contributing as true members of the team.

Unfortunately, the same could not be said for Sebastian Buchanan, a.k.a. Baz. Everyone knew the man was dealing with a personal problem, which happened to be in the form of a one-night stand that had the potential of becoming a life-long relationship. In an effort to lick his wounds, Baz had gotten shit-faced on New Year's and gone home with a woman. Turned out, that woman— Molly Ryan—was convinced she was pregnant, although it had only been a week and was still too early to confirm. Needless to say, Baz wasn't in a good place, what with dealing with that and working through his feelings for JJ.

Perhaps because of Baz's personal crisis, JJ was in rare form, taking full control of their most recent development by claiming she was in charge of the reorganization. That, of course, meant everything had to change, including the layout of the barn.

Good thing the rest of them were pretty casual about the whole thing.

"You know what? I think I'll leave y'all to this," Brantley suggested shortly after RT and Hunter had left. The absolute last damn thing he cared about was where desks were placed or who sat where.

"And just where are you off to?"

"I've got a couple of errands," he lied. "Then we're headin' over to the festival. It is Saturday," he reminded everyone. "Y'all should probably do the same."

Chapter Two

TRAVIS WALKER PROPPED HIS HEAD ON HIS hand and stared down at the beautiful woman still sleeping beside him, the soft morning light peeking in through the window allowing him to see. It was one of those rare moments, the kind where he could simply remain still, his brain not erupting in chaos, allowing him to enjoy the peacefulness.

These past few months, or maybe the past few years, had done a number on him mentally. He was dealing with so much, and it seemed every time he turned around, there was one more thing to add to his to-do list. A wife, a husband, five kids, a highly lucrative business … they all wanted a piece of him, but it seemed there was rarely enough to go around. He wasn't complaining, because he had a great life. Rather, he was just more aware of these rare moments.

Travis watched for long minutes, waiting until Kylie stirred, her internal clock signaling it was time to start the day. Because Gage had gotten up with Maddox a short time ago, Travis was going to take advantage of these few minutes he had alone with his wife.

"Mornin'," he whispered when she rolled onto her back, her arm sliding up over her eyes as though she wasn't ready for the day to intrude.

"Already?" she mumbled around a smile.

Travis tugged the sheet gently, allowing the soft Egyptian cotton to glide down and reveal one dusky pink nipple.

"What are you doin'?" she whispered, her arm sliding away, eyes opening, adjusting to the light.

He smiled, loving the way her nipple puckered as though beckoning him. "Startin' the day right."

"Kinda like you ended the day right with Gage in the shower last night?"

Travis leaned down, licked her nipple as he recalled those sinful few minutes he'd had alone with Gage. "Exactly like that."

"Anyone ever tell you you're spoiled?"

He chuckled, sucking lightly on her nipple, then applying more pressure until she was moaning. His hand joined the party, gliding over smooth, warm skin to cup her other breast, kneading the generous mound.

Travis proceeded to wake her fully with his hands and his mouth, lapping, licking, sucking, until she was whimpering and pulling at him.

"Is this where you want me?" he asked, moving over her, settling his hips in the cradle of her thighs.

Another whimper was her response, Kylie's fingertips digging into his biceps, her knees clasping his hips.

Without preamble, Travis slid into her silky heat, enveloped by the tight velvety clasp of her pussy. He grunted as pleasure consumed him.

He wasn't sure what prompted him to move slowly, to take his time, but it felt like the perfect moment. Brushing Kylie's hair back from her face, Travis smiled down at her as he pumped his hips, pushing in slow and deep, enjoying the way her body locked down on him, those sweet moans coming from her. It wouldn't last long, he knew that much. Kylie was a wildcat in the bedroom, and she preferred fast and dirty to slow and sweet, but he would take this for as long as she would allow it.

When she began rocking beneath him, attempting to quicken the pace, he knew she'd be issuing orders any second, and just thinking about it made him grin to himself.

"Travis," she whispered, her hands moving to his ass, jerking him closer when he sank in deep. "More … please … more."

He punched his hips forward, listening for her satisfied *ahh, yes* before doing it again and again until he had to put a hand on the headboard to hold them in place. He drove into her deeper, faster, watching her the entire time, loving the way her back bowed, her breasts thrust upward, the sleek column of her neck stretched as she twisted and contorted in a desperate effort to find her release. He wasn't giving her nearly enough and he knew it, but Travis wanted to drag it out until she was overwhelmed by the simple pleasure, crazy with the need to come.

It didn't take long until her nails were digging into his flesh, her body vibrating, her pleas coming faster. Only then did Travis shift positions, pushing up to his knees, adjusting so her feet were planted on his shoulders, allowing him to grab her hips and hold her lower half off the bed so he could pound into her hard and deep.

"Yes," she screamed. "God, yes."

With every driving thrust, her breasts bounced, an erotic sight that always got him. In fact, everything about her got him. Thanks to five pregnancies, Kylie's body wasn't the same as it had been before, but the truth was, Travis loved it more now than he had in the beginning. She was curvy and soft in all the right places, and never more beautiful. He knew it had something to do with the fact she was confident in her own skin, having grown into the role as mother and wife with the ease of a woman who knew what she was doing.

And she turned him on like no other woman ever could.

"You ready to come for me?" he growled softly, his fingertips digging gently into her flesh.

"Yes … yes … yes…" she moaned with every thrust of his hips.

Travis shifted again, bringing her feet down his shoulders, slipping his arms beneath her knees and leaning forward, bending her in half as he fucked her, giving her everything he had.

Travis was aware his lovely wife didn't want sweet and gentle. She wanted to fuck, to enjoy the pleasure assaulting every nerve ending. He knew this because she wasn't scared to tell them as much.

It was then Kylie grabbed a pillow, placed it over her head, and screamed his name, muffling the sound so as not to alert the kids.

Unable to resist, Travis followed her right over that precarious edge, slamming into her one final time and draining himself.

When he flopped onto the bed, he pulled her onto her side, holding her close, kissing her forehead, and doing his best to catch his breath.

"Good mornin'," he whispered.

This time, she giggled, nipped his chin, and said, "Yes, I believe it is."

A couple of hours later, after Travis and Kylie had gotten up, showered—separately, much to Travis's dismay—and joined Gage in making breakfast and getting the kids ready for the day, Travis was packing up the last of the snacks Kylie insisted on taking with them to the festival.

Despite their afternoon plans, they'd been doing their best to entertain the kids, but when it became apparent the munchkins were unable to focus on anything except for the upcoming Fantasy Festival being held in downtown Coyote Ridge, Travis decided it was time to get the festivities underway. Or rather, he'd informed the kids they would be leaving at exactly noon, which meant they had to watch the clock so they weren't late.

"Daddy-O! It's time! It's time! Let's go!"

Travis smiled as he tucked his cell phone in his pocket and grabbed the smart key to the Cadillac Escalade.

"I'm comin'," he called back, hefting the duffel bag onto his shoulder.

"Hurry! Hurry!" Kate chanted, echoing her brother's excitement.

For the past five minutes, ever since Kylie told the kids they needed to get their shoes on so they could leave, the house had been filled with whoops and hollers, the munchkins eager to get to their destination.

With key in hand, Travis stepped into the foyer to find the three oldest kids sitting dutifully on the bottom step of the stairs, their little butts wiggling with excitement.

He watched them for a moment, teasing them with his eyes, then laughed. "All right. Let's get on with it."

"Yay!" They were instantly on their feet, stomping toward the door, barely avoiding trampling one another in the process.

"Kylie! Baby, you ready?" Travis called up the stairs.

"We're comin'!"

Kylie and Gage were in charge of getting Haden and Maddox ready, so Travis headed out to get Kate, Avery, and Kade buckled into their car seats.

"I'm gonna play with Derrick today," Kate informed him.

"Is that right?"

"Nuh-uh," Kade argued. "I'm gonna play with Derrick *first*."

Travis tuned out the ensuing argument, a talent he'd acquired from having six brothers, and one he'd perfected after having multiple children. Over the years, he'd gotten pretty good at keeping an ear out for critical moments when he had to intervene. Otherwise, he would leave it to them to figure out.

"Are you gonna play with Derrick, too, sweetness?" Travis asked Avery as he secured her in her seat.

She nodded, smiled.

Avery was his sweet girl, the one who was quiet and shy, rarely instigating, but at the same time, smart enough to know to never back down. And he was pretty sure she'd adopted the same method of dealing with their arguments as Travis had.

Chuckling, he leaned in and kissed her on the forehead.

When he turned and closed the door, he saw Kylie and Gage coming out of the house, locking things up behind them. Gage had a kid on each hip, while Kylie had two more bags, in addition to all the ones Travis had already loaded up.

"Y'all good if I go?" he asked. "I'm gonna swing through and pick up Pop."

He got a nod in response, so he offered a small wave and hopped in the SUV.

Twenty minutes later, with his father riding shotgun and three of his crazy kids raising a ruckus in the backseat, he was pulling into one of the empty spots at his cousin Rex's bed-and-breakfast. He'd checked in with him ahead of time to see if they could secure a few spots for family, knowing the festival would cause everything else to fill up fast.

Gage and Kylie were already there and in the process of getting Maddox and Haden situated in the enormous wagon they used whenever they carted the kids to the park, which was quite often being that it was the only place that seemed to satisfy all of them at the same time.

"You want in, too, sweetness?" Travis asked Avery when he helped her out of her seat.

"Wanna walk," she said in her soft-spoken way.

Travis glanced at Gage, shook his head to relay her answer since they never knew which way she would go. Sometimes she liked to exert her independence, others she wanted to be babied. Looked like she was a big girl today.

Once Kate and Kade were out of the SUV, Travis helped Gage grab the backpacks that contained all their things. They bungeed a couple to the wagon, the others being shouldered by them.

"Hope y'all are ready for this," Curtis told the kids, taking Kate's hand and then Kade's, while Avery latched on to her mom's.

"We are!" Kade confirmed in that boisterous voice of his.

"Good."

"You wanna know a secret?" Kylie asked, falling into step with them.

"What's that, darlin'?" Travis put his arm around her shoulder, pulled her to his side.

"I was hopin' to get a little quiet time today," she said, her cornflower-blue eyes sparkling.

"Quiet time?" Gage snorted a laugh. "Where do you hope to find this at?"

"I told Jess we'd sneak away to do a little shopping, maybe splurge on some coffee and a funnel cake."

Travis ignored the unease that slithered down his spine at the thought of Kylie going off by herself. Although he would've preferred to keep her and the kids locked up in the house, safe and secure and under his protective thumb, he knew he couldn't do that. They deserved to be out enjoying life, not hiding away from the possible horrors this life could bring.

"Well, if it helps, we've got the kids today," Gage told her. "Your only job is to enjoy yourself."

Travis glared at Gage, hating that he could be so lax about it.

When Gage shot a look back his way, Travis refrained from saying anything. After all, he had promised he would stop being so overprotective. It had been almost four months since Kate was kidnapped, and no one had seen or heard a peep from Juliet Prince, the woman responsible, in the time since. While he had his suspicions she was behind the text he received, leading him to JJ's house prior to it blowing up, no one had clued him in one way or the other. He knew his cousin Brantley was working to locate Juliet, and he also knew Brantley was keeping the details close to the vest.

Despite his internal alarm bells, Travis was heeding everyone's advice, backing off the search and doing his best not to look over his shoulder at every turn.

Gage nodded his head toward Kylie, a silent request for Travis to chime in.

"Yeah," Travis agreed, hiding his reluctance. "We've got this. You have fun."

It was her appreciative smile that made him feel both worse and better about encouraging her.

Chapter Three

BY THE TIME AFTERNOON ROLLED AROUND, BRANTLEY was happy for a change of pace. Although he'd claimed to have errands to run, JJ had seen right through him. While she had allowed him to leave the barn, she'd commandeered Reese, insisting his help was necessary. Since Brantley hadn't been in the mood to argue and Reese seemed content to stay, he'd left them to it.

Now, as he drove toward downtown Coyote Ridge and the Fantasy Festival that was underway, he found himself smiling.

"I'm still tryin' to wrap my head around you wantin' to go to this thing," he told Reese.

"Don't pretend you're not excited."

"Excuse me?" Brantley frowned, cutting a quick look at Reese. "Is there somethin' to this event that I don't know about? To hear my mother tell it, they've got games and shit for the kids. What exactly is in it for me?"

Now Reese looked confused. "Your mother told *me* you've been lookin' forward to this."

"She *what*?" He barked a laugh. "She told you that?"

"Yeah. When she called last night."

Well, that explained how they were both willingly going to this shindig that, yes, was an event for kids when they could've easily gone to the gun range to get some downtime. Looked like Reese had been introduced to Iris Caine Walker's manipulative streak.

"Well, the good news is, they've got a carnival," Brantley said, thinking positively.

"Which means what? You're gonna ride the Ferris wheel?"

"No, I was thinkin' more along the lines of the shootin' gallery."

"You wanna win a teddy bear for knockin' down all the tin cans with a BB gun?"

Brantley grinned. "I wanna win *you* one, and I don't care if it shoots Nerf darts. I'm down."

Reese snorted.

There was no denying this wouldn't have been either of their first choice for places to go on a Saturday. Didn't matter that most of the town would be in attendance and the majority of that would be Walkers. His mother had even informed him that his cousins Lynx and Wolfe—his mother's brother's sons—would be there as well. It'd been a while since those two had come around. Probably had something to do with the fact they had all settled down into marital bliss.

While Brantley actually enjoyed spending time with his family, it still wasn't enough of a draw to get him excited, yet here he was because spending the day with Reese, regardless of what they were doing, was the only thing that mattered to him.

And truthfully, they could use some fun. A little time to forget all the shit they'd been dealing with, the cases they'd closed, the ones they hadn't, and the biggest drain on them all: the search for Juliet Prince.

Yep, a few hours to clear the head would be good right about now.

As Brantley neared the park, he wasn't surprised to see that Main Street parking was full. Every angled spot from one end to the other was taken. Even the Double R Bed-and-Breakfast was packed with cars, likely offering up the space for those who needed it.

Brantley avoided the busiest areas and got lucky and found an empty space at the elementary school.

"It's not too bad out here for January," he said as they headed to the park on foot, Tesha leashed and leading the way.

The weather probably couldn't have been any better if it had been planned. A lot of sun, minimal breeze, and the temps hovering in the mid- to upper-fifties. Nothing more than a long-sleeve shirt to make it comfortable.

Brantley did love winter in Texas.

As they got closer, the sounds grew louder, children laughing, machines running, bells jangling, people chatting.

The area had been converted to a fantasy wonderland, complete with hot chocolate stand, bounce houses, and a plethora of carnival rides and games.

But it was the decor that caught his attention, had Brantley taking it all in with a smile.

"I think they managed to find every shade of blue there is," Reese noted when they stepped onto the sidewalk that lined Main Street, where the vendors had set up in front of the shops that were also participating.

In this section, there was cotton candy, funnel cakes, face painting, and you could even get your hair painted with some blue sparkly shit if you were so inclined. Brantley figured he would pass on that.

"Well, look at this!"

Brantley turned at the shout from behind him, smiling when he saw his cousin Sawyer and his wife, Kennedy, walking their way. Their four-year-old son, Matthew, was perched on Sawyer's shoulders while two-year-old Brody was chilling in a stroller, their dog, Buster, trotting along beside him, snagging caramel popcorn as it fell.

"Didn't figure y'all'd get the day off," Sawyer said, gripping Matthew's knees and holding him firmly in place.

"Didn't want to miss the first festival of the year."

Kennedy chuckled. "Well, if you did, you just need to blink and there's another one."

"Don't let her fool you," Sawyer said, bumping his wife's shoulder with his. "She's all about these festivals. In fact, she was on the decoratin' committee for this one."

"Is that right?" Brantley nodded his chin toward the large plastic snowflakes dangling overhead. "Those your idea?"

"As a matter of fact…" Kennedy shook her head and grinned. "Lorrie's."

"Kennedy's contribution was the snow machine," Sawyer told them.

She blushed and elbowed Sawyer's side.

"Well, we're headin' for the horse rides," Sawyer explained, shifting to move around them. "I don't think we'll survive if we somehow miss out."

Horses? But Curtis and Lorrie owned a ranch.

Brantley's forehead creased in confusion. "Don't you have access to horses whenever you want?"

"We do," Sawyer said, nodding dramatically and looking a tad bit deranged. "You'd never guess it."

Laughing, Brantley moved out of the way, allowed them to move through.

That was pretty much how the next hour went. They encountered Brantley's sister Tori and her husband, Killian, along with little Eric, who was begging and pleading for his parents to let him ride the Ferris wheel for the eighth time. Then they passed his cousin Jared and his wife, Hope, with their two little ones, Derrick and Kassidy.

No one stuck around for long, moving kids along, getting them to their destinations. To his shock, the parents were taking it all in stride, most laughing and smiling despite all the screams and shouts coming from the little ones. He figured that wouldn't be the case at the end of the day, but at least for now they could enjoy some time outside.

"Is that Zane?" Reese asked, elbowing Brantley to redirect his attention.

He looked where Reese was gesturing, saw Zane, Beau, and Braydon working to corral probably a dozen kids. Kaden, Keegan, and Ethan were nearby, helping to keep them contained as best they could.

"You wanna go over there?" Brantley dared to ask.

Reese's look was one of … yes, it was possibly fear when he said, "Nah. I'm good if you are."

They quickly turned the other way before getting noticed and asked to help out. While Brantley loved all those kids, there was only so much he could handle at one time.

"Finally," he drawled when he saw the line of games that had been set up. "You ready for this?"

"I don't think *anyone's* ready for this," Reese said with a laugh. "But I'm in if you are."

SITTING AT HER DESK, JJ STARED AT her computer screen, pretending not to hear the conversation taking place downstairs.

As of half an hour ago, the team had dispersed, Trey and Charlie excusing themselves to join the festivities downtown. When Charlie had suggested JJ go with her, she had politely declined. Although it would probably be a decent distraction from the chaos that had become her life, she couldn't bring herself to do it. No sense in bringing everyone else down today.

"Yes, Molly, I heard you," Baz said, his raspy voice drifting up to JJ's ears.

JJ hated that she was eavesdropping, but it wasn't like Baz was looking for privacy. If he had been, he would've stepped outside to take the call like he did the half dozen other times that woman called him.

And boy, did she call. Like every hour on the hour, it seemed.

"I'm not arguing with you," Baz grumbled, clearly frustrated.

JJ glanced at her headphones, considered putting them on. Any other time, she probably would have, but she hesitated now. It had nothing to do with wanting to listen to Baz's conversation. Nope, her trepidation had something to do with having been jumped from behind a week ago, knocked unconscious when that prick hit her over the head.

Try as she might, JJ found herself jumping at every sound. It didn't matter that she was currently living with Baz, staying in his guest room. For the most part, he wasn't home, which should've been the way she preferred it since she was heartbroken that he'd gone and slept with another woman and said woman was claiming to be pregnant with his child. Only, JJ wished he would be there simply so she'd have someone to count on to watch her back.

It was stupid, she knew. The man who'd attacked her was dead. And Dante Greenwood, her ex-boyfriend who had dragged her into his stupid plan, was in rehab for his addiction. The threat had been neutralized, as Brantley would say, so it didn't make sense for her to be so panicked.

If only she could get her brain to process that.

JJ heard footsteps on the stairs. Immediately, she focused on her computer screen.

"Hey," Baz greeted, his soft tone telling her he was aware of her current state of jumpiness.

Turning, she offered a smile. "Hey."

"I was gonna head to the festival. Why don't you come with me?"

JJ's gaze immediately slid to the phone in Baz's hand.

He held it up. "I didn't invite her."

"Why not?" she found herself asking before she could stop the words.

Baz sighed. "I've already told you. It's not like that."

The anger she harbored at Baz threatened to surface, but she swallowed it down, reminding herself it was her fault he'd gotten involved with another woman in the first place. For weeks leading up to that incident, Baz had been making the effort to reconcile with her, but JJ had continued to push him away. Evidently, she'd pushed just hard enough to send him into the arms of another woman. And she was completely to blame.

"Come on," he said, motioning for her to join him. "Let's go hang out with the rest of the town. It's nice outside and we can both use the fresh air."

JJ knew she should say no. It wasn't right to lean on Baz, to use him so she didn't have to be alone. But the truth was, once he left, she would be completely alone until he came back to give her a ride home. Since Reese and Brantley had taken Tesha with them, JJ did not feel comfortable staying in the barn by herself.

"Okay."

Baz's surprise lit up his face and it made JJ relax a bit.

"Really?"

"Yeah. Might as well, right?"

His hesitant "right" said he was still processing her agreement to go. "I'll … uh … wait for you downstairs."

JJ turned back around, undocked her laptop, and slid it into her bag. She cleaned up the clutter on her desk then got to her feet.

Taking a deep breath, she resigned herself to enjoying a few hours outdoors.

Good thing she'd gotten so good at faking it.

BAZ REMAINED SILENT DURING THE DRIVE INTO town. It wasn't much different than their morning drive into work. For the past few days, JJ had been riding with him until she received the insurance settlement for her car, which had been destroyed during the explosion that had leveled JJ's house.

It wasn't that Baz minded driving with her. In fact, he liked it more than he probably should. Unfortunately, he wasn't getting the same vibe from JJ, and he completely understood why. Their relationship had started almost from the first day they met. His attraction to her had led him to asking her out, getting shut down. Being one to never give up, Baz had insinuated himself in her life as her friend. And it probably would've remained a friendship if JJ hadn't been harboring the same attraction for him.

Needless to say, they'd acted on that attraction and their friendship had morphed into more. Or so he'd thought. Unfortunately, they hadn't been on the same page regarding how much *more* it was, and he'd gone and screwed things up by pushing for her to meet his parents. JJ had panicked, and hoping to bring her back around, Baz had backed off for a little while, committed to eventually winning her back.

Only Baz had fucked everything up on New Year's. After JJ had gone off to help her ex-boyfriend, Baz had let the liquor do his thinking for him. That resulted in what should've been a one-night stand, and it would have if he hadn't let his emotions get the best of him. Thanks to his need to block out everything else, he'd done the one thing he'd never done before: had sex without a condom.

Well, technically there had been one, but according to Molly, it had broken and he'd told her it didn't matter. Since the events of that night were still a bit hazy, Baz had no choice but to believe her.

Problem was, Molly had been claiming she was pregnant since the very next morning. As if that wasn't enough, she insisted they talk about it every hour of every day. She called him incessantly. To the point he had to turn his phone off at night from time to time to block her out. Considering his job required him to be available at all times, it was a risk, but at the moment, he didn't really give a shit. The woman was driving him fucking crazy.

"Have you seen the pregnancy test?"

Baz's gaze snapped over to JJ. "What?"

"Molly. Did she show you the pregnancy test?"

Baz turned his attention back to the road. There was no way he could have this conversation with JJ. Hell, he didn't want to talk about it with anyone, but certainly not with the woman he loved more than life. Despite what had happened, despite what he'd done, Baz still wanted things to work between him and JJ, and he was hoping one day she could forgive him.

JJ sighed. "Come on, Baz. We're friends. You can talk to me."

Baz shook his head.

"It's not like you can change what happened," JJ said, her tone soft. "But we can move forward, right? As friends?"

He gripped the steering wheel harder, held his tongue.

His phone buzzed, the screen lighting up with Molly's name, as though the woman knew they were talking about her. Or rather *not* talking about her.

Baz exhaled heavily, hit the button to decline the call.

"Probably be easier to park at the high school or the elementary," JJ said when he began searching for parking spots along Main Street.

He focused on finding a spot, relaxing when he saw someone climbing into their car. A second later, they were pulling out, but before Baz could get close enough, another car pulled in.

"Nice Mustang," JJ said, glancing at the car as they passed. "What is that? Like a '69?"

"'65," Baz corrected, glancing at the car as they passed.

"How can you tell?"

"'69s are bigger."

"I didn't realize you were into old cars."

He was into a lot of things she didn't know about, but Baz kept that comment to himself.

"My brother bought a '69 Mustang when he was in high school," JJ said. "Total piece of shit. He was bound and determined he would restore it to its original glory. He got it runnin' but that was about it."

Baz glanced over. JJ never talked about her family and certainly not about her brother. He knew from Brantley that JJ's brother, Jeremy, had taken his own life, but try as he might, he could never get JJ to open up about it.

"What happened to it?"

JJ glanced out the window. "During one of his dark periods, he sold it. Said it wasn't worth the time and effort." JJ pointed. "There's a spot."

Baz parked the truck, hating that it not only signified they'd made it to their destination but also that it had ended the one and only conversation he'd ever had with JJ where she'd revealed anything about herself.

Chapter Four

REESE WAS SURPRISED BY HOW MUCH HE enjoyed spending the day at the park.

He hadn't been thrilled with the idea when he'd suggested it to Brantley after being encouraged by Iris, but he was glad she'd roped him into it. They'd managed to win probably two dozen stuffed animals, all of which were donated to various kids they encountered, including two of Travis's who'd been catching a nap, snuggled up together in an oversized wagon and draped with blankets.

They'd spent the first half hour greeting people as though they were long-lost friends, when in reality, they'd probably said hello a couple of times during the past week. After all, Coyote Ridge was a small town and people tended to congregate like family.

Several people had asked about their recent case, hearing about it on the news since it had touched so close to home with JJ's house blowing up. They shared what they could, obviously leaving out the part where they had tied it to the woman responsible for kidnapping Travis's daughter back in September.

It wasn't that Reese didn't think people should be aware, or more accurately keep an eye out, but he knew any and all talk would get back to Travis and his family. Today was about enjoying time outside, together, friends and family. No sense ruining a perfectly good day.

"We're still goin' for best outta seven," Brantley reminded him when the game attendant took a step back.

Oh, yeah. There was no way he was going to forget that bet. And since he only needed to win one more round to be the ultimate champion, Reese figured he needed to focus.

"You ready to lose your ass?" Brantley cajoled.

"I'm always rea—" Reese's phone rang, interrupting the game. He would've ignored the call, but he recognized the ringtone as his brother's.

He set the toy gun down and took a step back.

Brantley stood tall, watching him closely.

"Hey, what's up, Z? I thought for sure you'd come down here with RT to enjoy—"

"We've got a problem, Reese," Z said, his voice a bit too high, his words coming way faster than usual.

Reese's body tensed and he could tell Brantley recognized it.

He moved farther from the crowd, lowered the phone, and hit the speaker button. "What's the problem?"

"Remember the software we're runnin'? The one we set to look for Juliet Prince?"

"Yeah." A cold chill slithered down his spine as he held Brantley's gaze.

"We got a hit from one of the toll road cameras down near you. Problem is, the report's delayed."

"By how long?" Brantley asked.

"The time stamp on the photo is eleven seventeen this mornin'."

Brantley looked at his watch. "It's almost fifteen hundred, Z. That's more than three hours."

"I know." Z's tone was filled with apology. "We don't know what caused the delay, but I've spent the past half hour havin' a couple of my guys verify it." Z exhaled heavily. "It's legit. Juliet Prince was just a few miles from where you are now."

"Son of a bitch," Brantley grumbled.

Instinct had Reese scanning the area, as though he might find Juliet Prince lingering nearby.

"Trust me, I know," Z said. "But I had to be sure. I didn't wanna get you all worked up if it wasn't real."

Reese remained where he was, breathing steady, trying to determine what they should do. Did they alert Travis and Gage? Tell Curtis? Bring the sheriff into it?

"How positive are you, Z?" Brantley asked.

"Ninety-eight point seven percent. Which is about as good as it gets. Like I said, we've confirmed. I called RT and Hunter, told them to turn around and head back. The more eyes lookin' out, the better."

"You said it was on the toll road. You show her exiting?" Reese asked.

"The booth camera snapped her pic as she was exiting Highway 79," Z explained. "We've got a call into TXDOT, requesting the make, model, and plate of the vehicle. Our software doesn't look for that. It might take some time."

"Fuck." Brantley brushed his hand over his buzzed hair.

Reese knew what he was thinking: If Juliet Prince took the Highway 79 exit, it wasn't a damn coincidence. It was the exit one would take to get to Coyote Ridge.

"What do you need from us, Reese?" Z offered.

"Unless you can hack all these cams and see if you can find her, there's not much you can do."

Z chuckled. "I'm not a miracle worker, but I'll see what I can do. I'll keep you updated, but I expect you to do the same."

"Will do." Reese disconnected the call. "You think she's here?"

"It's damn sure not a coincidence," Brantley grumbled, turning as he scanned the area around them.

"What's her end goal?" Reese wondered aloud.

"She's a crazy bitch. Who fuckin' knows what she's thinkin'?"

Reese calmed himself, took a deep breath. "How do you wanna handle it?"

Brantley continued to look around, shielding his eyes from the sun. "There're too many people here. We have no idea what she looks like."

"I can get the photo," Reese told him.

"Even if we have that, we have no idea what she looks like *now*. She's a lot of things, but she's not an idiot. If she's brave enough to interact with these people, she'll be wearin' a disguise."

Reese figured that, too, but he was hoping Brantley would talk through this, come up with a plan that would allow them to take the bitch down before something bad happened.

As it was, he knew everyone was getting lax the longer they were out here. Earlier he'd seen Kylie wandering around with her sister. Neither Gage nor Travis had been with her, nor had Jessie's husband, Braydon.

"I'll let the team know," Reese said, pulling up a group text. At the very least, they'd have four additional sets of eyes keeping a look out.

His message read: *Advised Juliet Prince seen exiting toll road nearly four hours ago. BOLO.*

"We need to find Sheriff Endsley," Brantley finally decided. "We need to let him know what's goin' on."

"What about Travis and Gage?"

"They're my first stop. You find the sheriff," Brantley said as he started across the park at a quick jog.

"You heard him, Tesha. Let's go, girl."

Reese didn't waste time, making a beeline to one of the deputy's cars he'd seen parked nearby. Unfortunately, there was no one in or by it, so he had to continue his hunt until he found the sheriff chatting with Curtis on a bench on the corner of Main Street and Park Avenue, just outside the festival's entrance.

He didn't bother apologizing for the interruption, despite the fact it left him feeling awkward.

"Sheriff, there's a potential situation we think you should be aware of," he said, talking fast. "We don't have visual confirmation as of now, but we do have reason to believe Juliet Prince, the woman who kidnapped"—he nodded toward Curtis—"his granddaughter, may be in the vicinity."

Both men were on their feet immediately. The joviality he'd witnessed when he approached disappeared, replaced by what looked to be equal amounts concern and rage.

He went on to explain the conversation he'd had with Z as they walked across the park, heading toward the spot Curtis said he'd last seen Travis and Gage with the kids.

"Unfortunately, we don't have any idea what she looks like, and with so many people, it'd be virtually impossible to spot her if she doesn't want us to."

Sheriff Endsley was on his radio, informing his deputies of the potential threat and putting them on high alert.

Reese's heart was pounding, his blood humming beneath his skin. He hadn't felt this sort of adrenaline rush in quite some time and he welcomed it.

As they walked, Reese continued to scan their surroundings. He tried to put himself in Juliet's shoes, tried to think how she might. He knew she was cunning and evil. She'd had no qualms snatching a six-year-old from a group field trip. And she'd been the brains behind the explosion at JJ's house, luring Travis there shortly before the thing had gone off.

In short, Reese wouldn't put anything past her.

GAGE SAT ON A BENCH, WATCHING THE kids chase one another around the swings, over to the monkey bars, back to the walking beams, then around their little obstacle course again. They'd been at it for an hour, the longest the kids had been focused on one single thing since they got there.

While he hadn't expected this to be an easy feat—taking the kids to the park on a normal day wasn't that—Gage hadn't considered just how much work it would be. Not only had they spent two hours tending to five kids who wanted to do everything there was to do, they were now letting them get out some of the pent-up energy as they took a break from the festivities. Now they were watching their own kids, plus they were keeping an eye on others as Travis's brothers and sisters-in-law stopped by. Their kids would start playing, refusing to leave, and at that point, it was easier to agree to keep an eye on them.

The good thing was, they'd gotten help from Kaden and Keegan, as well as Ethan and Beau, who were attempting to corral their eighteen-month-old triplets with Lorrie's and Arlene's help. Since the ladies were still smiling, Gage figured they had at least another hour in them.

Besides keeping an eye on them while they played, they'd also been dealing with the basic biological functions: hungry, thirsty, needed to go potty, and the occasional "I'm bored." It was a never-ending cycle, and he was starting to wonder how in the world Kylie made it look so easy.

He spotted Travis and Kade returning from the emergency bathroom break. When Kade broke off to join the others, Gage's attention remained on his husband, watching the man move closer with the grace of a jungle cat.

It was true, Gage had never seen a more impressive man in his life. There was something about Travis Walker that, to this day, made his blood heat in his veins. The way he carried himself, the way he spoke, that sparkle he'd get in those steel-blue eyes. Even after all these years, after all the ups and downs, the babies they'd brought into the world, the arguments they'd had over stupid shit, Gage's body still stirred whenever he saw Travis or Kylie. Both of them together ... yeah, that was potential for spontaneous combustion.

His thoughts briefly wandered to last night when Travis had cornered him in the shower. Gage had been finishing up when the sexy man stripped down and joined him where they proceeded to waste a considerable amount of water taking one another to the pinnacle and then over.

Travis had always had an extremely high sex drive, but in the past few weeks, ever since he broke down, admitting he was obsessed with finding the woman responsible for kidnapping their daughter and needed help in moving forward, he'd seemed to replace one need with another. There hadn't been a day since that they hadn't *indulged* at least once, usually twice, and on occasion a few times more than that. Travis was spontaneous about it, too. Whether in the shower, in Travis's office at home, or at the resort, and once or twice they'd even enjoyed some oral indulgence in the SUV.

Not that Gage was complaining. He enjoyed the time he had with Kylie and Travis, especially when they could find some stolen moments, whether it was two of them or all three at the same time. He looked forward to those, but he knew right now he was feeding Travis's need for distraction by giving in when the man gave him that come-hither look.

Good thing was, they were safe from that here at the park.

"You good?" Travis asked, joining him on the bench.

"Yep."

Travis kicked his long legs out in front of him, crossed his ankles, and exhaled. "Nice day."

That it was. Lots of sun, not much wind, and no rain in the forecast. The temperatures were inching closer to sixty than forty, which meant the kids weren't battling cold-weather gear. Couldn't ask for much better than that.

"You think the kids'll sleep all night?" Travis asked, the question drawing Gage's attention to the playground.

"You can bet on it. They might actually—"

Gage's words were cut off when he saw Travis's cousin Brantley running toward them. It wasn't a jog but a full-out sprint, his expression one that had the hair on the back of Gage's neck standing on end.

Brantley slowed upon his approach, his eyes meeting Gage's then shifting to Travis.

"What's wrong?" Travis asked, his voice cold and dark as he got to his feet.

"It's…" Brantley inhaled deeply, exhaled slowly. "We just got a call from Z. At our request, they've been runnin' an algorithm that does some form of advanced facial recognition on any camera with a live feed. As of this mornin', one of the cameras on the toll road caught an image of Juliet Prince."

Gage's heart slammed against his sternum, but he managed to stand. "How do you know for sure it's her?"

"Sniper 1 Security validated it. They've confirmed with ninety-eight point seven percent certainty it is her."

"Where is she now?" Travis demanded, his good mood definitely gone.

Gage gripped Travis's wrist, urging him to relax. The last thing they needed was for Travis to go off the rails before they even understood what they were dealing with.

"She was seen taking the Highway 79 toll exit shortly after eleven hundred this mornin'."

"Eleven o'clock?" Travis snapped. "That was *four hours* ago. Why the fuck are we just hearin' about it now?"

Because that wasn't important, Gage spoke over him. "Have you seen her since? Any cameras catch her?" Gage kept his tone even. No sense getting Travis in a panic when there was no way to prove she was nearby.

"We have not," Brantley stated, his gaze bouncing back and forth between them. "Where's Kylie and the kids?"

Gage motioned to the playground. "The kids're fine. We've got a lot of eyes on them."

"And Kylie?" Brantley repeated.

"She texted me a few minutes ago," he replied, "said she was gonna grab coffee with her sister."

Brantley nodded, his eyes calm, his expression stony. He was the polar opposite of Travis, who was already shifting and moving, looking around.

"Get the kids," Travis commanded Kaden, who happened to be nearby, watching a couple of the rugrats playing in the sandbox. "And don't let 'em outta your sight."

"I got it," Kaden said, meeting Gage's eyes briefly, a silent confirmation that he wouldn't let on that Travis's grip was slipping, something they'd all dealt with over the past few months.

"We need to stay calm," Gage told Travis. "We have no reason to believe she's here today."

Travis's look told Gage he was an idiot.

Before Gage could stop him, Travis pulled out his cell phone and was dialing.

"Who're you callin'?" he asked.

When Travis didn't answer, Gage shot a frustrated look at Brantley. Why did the man insist on doing this? Couldn't he see what this sort of overreaction did to Travis? It turned him into a—

"Where are you?" Travis barked into the phone.

Gage saw Reese, Curtis, and Sheriff Endsley moving their way at a fast clip, and for a moment, he felt the same flare of panic he was sure Travis felt.

Maybe this wasn't an overreaction.

Without stopping to chat, Curtis went to help gather the little ones.

Turning to Travis, Gage tried to get his attention.

"You need—" Travis cut himself off, lowered his voice. "I think it'd be best if you came back to the park," he said into the phone.

Gage could only imagine Kylie's reaction. She'd been just as worried as Gage about Travis's panicked state for the past few months. Like Gage, she had learned to deal with it, had placated Travis by giving in when he insisted they stick close, but he knew she'd grown tired of being bossed around and kept on what she referred to as a short leash.

"It's important," Travis said, his voice a little calmer. "We're with Brantley, Reese, and Sheriff Endsley. No. No, the kids are fine. Everyone's fine." Travis nodded, as though she could see him. "All right. We'll stay here."

When Travis disconnected, he turned back around. "She's on her way back. They're up the block at the bakery."

Reese pulled out his phone, turned the screen toward Gage. "Z sent the image they have."

Gage took the phone, pivoted to block the glare on the screen, and stared at the image of the woman behind the wheel of a car.

As much as he wanted to believe Travis was reacting irrationally, that he'd been expecting the sky to fall for no reason, the picture sent a wave of cold fear over him.

It was her. Despite the grainy image from being magnified, there was no mistaking the woman Gage still saw in his nightmares. He'd looked at her picture far too many times since that horrific day, wondering if they would ever find her, if she'd ever be brought to justice for what she'd done.

But what he didn't understand was why she would come back?

Exhaling and maintaining his composure, Gage handed the phone to Travis, who glared at it.

"Do you know where she is now?" Gage asked, the question directed at Reese and Brantley. "Are we certain she came here?"

Reese was the one to answer. "No, we aren't. That photo was taken at eleven seventeen. My brother didn't get the notification right away, but as soon as he did, he had his team verify it."

Gage glanced at his watch. It was fifteen after three, which meant Juliet Prince could be there now. Hell, she could've been there watching them for most of the afternoon.

Instinct had him turning, scanning everyone around him. His gaze skipped over men, his focus on women. He quickly dismissed any he knew but found it didn't matter. There were too many people. Moms, dads, grandparents, and kids, all gathered to enjoy the first festival of the year.

As it sank in, Gage realized this was the perfect opportunity for that crazy bitch to snatch another kid.

Chapter Five

TRAVIS'S WORST FEARS HAD COME TRUE. THE woman who'd turned his entire world upside down and inside out was coming back to finish what she started.

Worse, his entire family—not just his wife, husband, and kids—was here, all vulnerable. His mother, his father, brothers and cousins, their significant others, nieces, nephews. They were all in the vicinity and they had no idea that this crazy bitch was here.

Despite what anyone told him, Travis knew everyone he cared about was a potential target. Juliet Prince believed Travis to be directly responsible for the dissolution of her marriage. Her ex-husband had met his new wife during one of their visits to Alluring Indulgence Resort. From what Travis had learned, Nicholas Prince had indulged in a swinger lifestyle with Juliet but had traded her in for a newer model—one Nicholas happened to meet during one of those encounters at the resort. The man had also sought sole custody of his and Juliet's daughter, insisting Juliet was unfit to care for her in her current state.

Travis couldn't argue with the latter point, and he was sure that was what had tipped Juliet into crazy land. Now she had a vendetta against Travis, who she claimed was personally responsible for all of it. Which was the very reason she'd kidnapped Kate, hoping to strike a death blow to Travis. It had worked, no doubt about it. Those two days Kate had been missing had nearly leveled him and his family. Having to watch Kylie and Gage suffer had been almost as brutal as not knowing where his little girl was.

Bottom line was, she had to be stopped before she could do any more damage.

"I've put my deputies on alert," Sheriff Endsley told them. "Unfortunately, we don't know what she's drivin', but we're keepin' an eye out for out-of-state plates and rentals. We'll run a cursory check if we come across somethin'."

Travis refrained from telling them it wasn't nearly enough. He could see by the look on the sheriff's face that he already knew. But Jeff was right. They had nothing more than an image of the bitch's face behind the wheel of what was possibly a blue car at some point today. The photo was snapped through the windshield, giving them nothing else to go on. Where she'd gone after that picture was taken was anyone's guess, although Travis's gut was telling him she wasn't far.

"Daddy-O, why do we hafta leave?"

Pulled from his thoughts, Travis peered down to see Kade standing at his side, tugging on his shirt. Those blue-gray eyes so much like his own were pleading and intense.

Travis absolutely detested Juliet for doing this to his family, for targeting them, for making Travis a nervous wreck. And most importantly for making his kids look at him like that.

"We're not leavin' yet," Gage said, drawing Kade's attention. "We just wanted y'all to take a break. Have a drink and a snack."

While Gage and Kaden began distributing snacks to curious munchkins, Travis focused his attention on others. He watched interactions between husbands and wives, moms, dads, kids. Nowhere did he see a lone woman slinking through the throng of people.

Not that he expected it to be easy.

Where was she? He knew she was out here. She had to be. Today was the perfect day and this was the perfect place for her to make a move. The question was, who would she target?

And while he searched for Juliet, Travis scanned the area for Kylie, knowing his heart wouldn't return to its normal beat until he laid eyes on her.

Five minutes passed, then ten, then fifteen.

Didn't Kylie know he was going to have a heart attack? At the very least a panic attack? He hated not knowing where any of them were at any given moment.

"I'm sure she's fine," Gage said quietly. "Probably finishin' up her coffee with Jess, enjoyin' her last bit of peace and quiet before joinin' the fray."

Sure. Probably. But the rationality didn't help to slow the rapid beat of his heart.

Travis reached into his pocket to retrieve his phone but stopped suddenly when the air was rent with a horrific sound. The revving of an engine, the eerie screech of tires, followed by a sickening crash, then a crescendo of screams and shouts.

All eyes shifted to Main Street, instinctively following the sound. The same place the masses were headed, many pulling out cell phones, some making calls, others turning on cameras.

Without thinking, Travis took off running.

He wasn't sure who was behind him, and in that moment, he didn't care. He probably should've thought about his children, ensured someone had remained back to keep an eye on them, but something in his chest was ripping open, and he was merely trying to keep his heart from leaping out of his throat.

"Call 911!" someone yelled.

"Oh, my God! It hit her! The car! It *hit* her!"

It took only a few seconds to make it to the scene, another to navigate through the crowd. He tried to be gentle, nudging people out of the way, desperate to—

"Help! Please! Someone help my sister!"

That statement sent a flash of ice-cold fear through Travis's bloodstream. He recognized the voice.

When he broke through the last of the crowd, he came up short, all the air in his lungs slamming out of him at the sight of his wife's crumpled body on the concrete. Behind her was a small SUV, the backend smashed in, clearly having been hit by another car. And if the scene told him anything, it was that his wife had been pinned between that vehicle and the one responsible for the damage.

"It went that way!" someone was yelling, pointing in the opposite direction.

"Travis!" Jessie sobbed uncontrollably. "Oh, God, Travis! She ... she's..."

Stumbling forward, Travis fell to his knees. She wasn't dead. She couldn't be dead.

"Kylie. Kylie, baby." His voice was so rough, little more than a rasp of sound as he gathered her in his arms, rocking her against him.

He knew he shouldn't move her in the event of a spinal injury, but Travis's brain wasn't processing what he should or shouldn't do. It merely relayed what he *had* to do and that was hold her close, ensure she knew he was there.

"Oh, God," he whispered. "It's gonna be all right. Open your eyes, Kylie. Open 'em for me, darlin'."

There was blood. So much blood. Her face was bruised and bloody, her arm contorted at the wrong angle.

"Oh, shit! No!"

He heard Gage's voice, then felt his presence when he fell down at Travis's side, cradling Kylie's head. Across from them, Jessie was on her knees, sobbing and trembling as she held Kylie's other hand.

"It came outta nowhere," Jessie said, her voice hysterical. She waved her free hand. "Kylie stepped out ... then it was there..." Tears streamed down her face. "Help her," Jessie pleaded. "Please ... please help her."

"The ambulance is on its way," someone called out. "Is there a doctor here? A nurse?"

Travis was unable to move. His entire world felt as though it was caving in and he was at the center, suffocating beneath the weight.

Instinct had Travis cradling Kylie tighter to him, rocking her gently as the rage and the fear coalesced inside him, churning into a storm that would soon erupt, a storm so powerful it would plow down anyone in its path.

"Kylie," he rasped. "Open your eyes, baby."

She didn't move, didn't respond in any way.

A sob tore from his chest. He was absolutely helpless.

Then someone else was there, kneeling down, touching Kylie, urging everyone to move back.

"She's got a pulse, but it's weak."

Who was this guy? And who was he talking to?

"We've got to clear this road for the ambulance. ETA is two minutes."

Two minutes? That was a fucking eternity. Travis huffed in a breath, pushed it out. He didn't move as someone rallied help, got the others to clear the area, giving them room. Gage remained at his side, the two of them holding Kylie, protecting her from everyone around them.

"It's okay, baby," Gage whispered, his voice rough with tears. "Hang on, Kylie. Help's comin'."

It took tremendous effort to swallow past the lump in his throat, but Travis managed even as the tears choked him. His wife looked so battered and broken.

From a few feet away, he could hear the sheriff asking witnesses to tell him what happened. Every so often, he would get bits and pieces.

"The car came from down there…"

"The engine revved…"

"…crossing the street."

"…no time to react."

"I think it was aimin' for her."

"…crashed into that car after it hit her."

"Blue Mustang…"

"A woman behind the wheel."

"Travis, they need you to move back," someone said, gently touching his shoulder.

"They're gonna take her, son," his father said, that familiar voice near his ear. "They need you to let her go."

With gentle movements, he eased her back to the ground, fire burning in his lungs as he released her. He didn't want to let her go. Didn't want to leave her.

"Come on, Trav," Curtis said. "It's all right. They'll take good care of her."

It wasn't all right. None of it was.

He was aware of someone tugging on his arm, pulling him to his feet. He was pushed and pulled out of the way, making room for the EMTs to do their job.

Again there were bits and pieces of conversation that drifted into his ears, barely heard over the pounding of his own heart.

"Pulse thready…"

"Secure her head."

"Call ahead, tell them to have a trauma team ready."

"Fractured … broken … unconscious."

"Only one of you can go," someone said firmly.

Travis managed to focus, saw the EMT was talking to him and Gage.

Because he had no idea what good he would do in the back of that ambulance, Travis nodded to Gage, urging him to go with her. Gage didn't say a word, walking off immediately, as though not to hold things up any longer.

As the sirens split the air, the ambulance taking his wife to the hospital, Travis was consumed by cold.

"Come on, boy," Curtis stated firmly. "I'll drive you."

Travis looked at his father. "Where are…?"

"Iris and Frank are with your mother and Arlene. They've got the kids. They're takin' 'em back to my house."

Iris and Frank. His aunt and uncle. Brantley's parents. They would help. His mom would have help.

Good. That was good. "Someone should…"

Curtis's big, firm hand slid over his shoulder, a gentle, calming touch. "Two deputies are with them, Travis. As are Kaden, Keegan, Jared, and Hope."

Travis found his feet were moving as he let his father lead him to the Escalade still parked at the bed-and-breakfast.

He was vaguely aware of his father speaking every so often, but his mind was already miles ahead of them, in the back of that ambulance.

JULIET'S HEART WAS POUNDING SO HARD SHE thought it would burst right out of her chest. Adrenaline-laced fear made her hyperalert, her foot on the gas as she sought a safe place.

She'd hit her with her car. Kylie.

Everything that had happened was still a blur, but Juliet recalled seeing Travis's wife as she walked down the street, laughing at something the other woman said. Juliet had felt the rage boil up. How could that bitch be so happy? How could they go on with their lives like nothing had ever happened? Like Juliet hadn't lost every damn thing she'd ever had?

And then it hit her. This was her chance. It wasn't coincidence that Kylie had been put directly in her path. It was a sign from God.

The next thing Juliet knew, she was backing her car out of the spot. Once she put it in drive, she slammed her foot on the gas pedal, aiming the car for Kylie just as she stepped out into the street.

Her timing had been impeccable. Another sign, she figured.

It had happened so fast, she hadn't had time to really process it, even after she'd rammed the other car, pinning Kylie between the two. Juliet's fight-or-flight instinct had kicked in and she'd managed to untangle the car from the wreckage and speed away. It surprised her she hadn't taken anyone else down in the process.

Now as she parked her wrecked car behind the cheap motel she'd gotten a room in earlier, Juliet knew she had to make a run for it. Only she couldn't drive that car, which pained her. She had come to love that Mustang. Unfortunately, it was too noticeable. Someone would see it. There had been police at that park. Surely they weren't far behind.

Leaving all her stuff in the room because she kept on her what was crucial, Juliet headed for the little office where she'd paid for the room. She remembered seeing a set of keys hanging in the office.

Luck was on her side because there was no one there when she stepped inside. The bells over the door jingled, and fearing it would alert someone, she darted through the open door, grabbed the key ring from the hook, and turned and headed back out.

"Can I help you?" a woman called from behind her.

Juliet shook her head, not looking back as the glass door closed.

She pressed the button on the key fob, and a horn honked. She smiled. Once more luck was on her side.

A few seconds later, she'd secured a getaway car. The older Chevy Cruze wasn't in the best shape, but she prayed the engine would last long enough to get her someplace safe.

At the very least, it would get her out of the immediate vicinity until the heat died down.

JJ WAS STANDING STILL, WATCHING AS PEOPLE continued to congregate around the scene of the accident.

She was still trying to wrap her head around what had happened, although deep inside she knew.

Baz was currently talking to one of the deputies, informing him they had seen the blue Mustang pulling into the parking space earlier. They'd been watching as Kylie was loaded into the ambulance when someone mentioned what they'd witnessed. In that moment, JJ had looked at Baz, her gut churning.

No one had confirmed that the woman driving the car was Juliet Prince, but she figured it was a safe assumption. After all, like Brantley and Reese, JJ didn't believe in coincidence, and they had just been alerted that the woman was seen exiting the highway only a couple of miles down the road.

"Brantley wants us to come to the hospital," Baz relayed when he joined her.

JJ frowned. "Why?" Realizing she sounded bitchy, she clarified. "I mean, I don't have a problem with it, but won't we be more helpful if we start searchin'?"

"A BOLO's been issued," Baz informed her.

JJ knew that was police speak for a *be on the lookout* notification. It would alert other departments so they could assist in locating the vehicle.

Glancing back at Kylie's sister and the other family members who remained—most had already left for the hospital—JJ recalled the day she'd found her brother. It hadn't been a traumatic incident like this. She'd found him in his bedroom on his bed. She hadn't realized he was dead at the time, rather noticing he looked peaceful in sleep. Of course, she'd yelled at him because that was what she'd done back then. It had been the last time she'd ever spoken to him, but unfortunately, he hadn't heard her.

Swallowing back the emotions she preferred not to dredge up, JJ turned to Baz. "Whatever Brantley needs."

With a hand on her back, he guided her toward his truck just as he'd done so many times. She'd always thought of it as a possessive gesture, one she found oddly intriguing. When he'd done it before, it had made her feel good knowing he wanted her that way. Now it just felt awkward.

Once they were in the truck and on the road, Baz turned something on just beneath his dash.

When radio calls sounded, she looked at him. "Is that a police scanner?"

He nodded, then turned it up.

JJ's eyes widened when she heard what they were saying. Someone had located a '65 blue Mustang with front end damage at a motel just down the road.

"That's half a mile from here," she told Baz. "Turn around."

"JJ…"

"Turn around, Baz," she demanded. "We can't do anything at the hospital that'll benefit anyone. At least this way there's a chance we might find that bitch."

"In case you don't remember, we don't have badges anymore."

"So?" She glared at him. "I've never had a badge before and it hasn't stopped me. Just turn around."

He grunted, but then pulled a U-ey, heading east rather than west toward the hospital.

The radio had gone silent, but JJ held out hope that they'd found Juliet Prince and were taking her into custody.

She fought the urge to push her foot to the floor on the pretend gas pedal that would get them to their destination faster. But as they approached the single-story motel with its rust-stained stucco and threadbare shingles, she leaned toward the windshield, as though that would help her see better. In the parking lot, she noticed a single police car and two officers speaking to a very animated young woman.

JJ wanted to know what the woman was saying.

"Pull in here," she snapped. "By the Coke machine."

Baz swung into a spot and hit the brakes, forcing JJ to put her hand on the dash to avoid a head-on collision. She glared at him as she unbuckled her seat belt and grabbed her wallet. She hopped out and strolled to the machine, listening as best she could to see if she could pick up anything.

"She came right in the office and stole my keys," the woman was complaining. "That's her beat-up piece of crap behind the building."

"Was she staying here?" one of the officers asked.

"Room one-oh-four."

JJ looked over at the door beside her. One-oh-four.

She peered back at Baz, then to the officers. It took a second, but she bought a Coke, then took it to the driver's side of Baz's truck. He was frowning at her as he lowered the window.

"Juliet Prince was stayin' in that room," she muttered, nodding in the direction of the door.

"She's not in there," he said quickly.

"Well, duh." JJ hadn't figured she was. "But what if she left her stuff behind?"

"Why would she do that?"

"I don't know. Maybe she just ran over a woman and was runnin' from the police. She did steal that woman's car."

Baz leaned toward her. "JJ, we don't know that this was Juliet Prince."

Again, she glared at him. "Don't be an idiot, Baz. It doesn't take a rocket scientist to figure this shit out. But I'm startin' to worry about your detective skills. I think they're a little rusty."

That was enough to get a rise out of him.

"What do you want me to do?" he asked, his voice grumbly with his irritation.

"Distract the cops."

His eyebrows shot skyward. "Distract them? And how do you propose I do that?"

"Well, you were a cop once. Figure it out."

He opened the door, stepped out. "And while I do that, what're you gonna do?"

She nodded toward the room. "I'm gonna see if she left anything behind."

Baz shook his head. "No, ma'am, you're gonna get—"

JJ got closer, went up on her toes so they were almost eye to eye. "Distract them," she hissed under her breath.

She didn't wait for him to scold her. JJ pivoted around and headed for room 104. Lucky for her, she'd learned a few things from her mischievous brother when she was a kid. One of those things happened to be how to pick a lock. It had become a game with them, always besting the other, trying to see who could get into a lock faster. They'd mastered a wide variety of locks that way. And it just so happened she had her little set with her. Then again, she almost always had it with her because Jeremy had bought it for her.

Glancing back, she saw Baz approaching the officers. She couldn't hear what he was saying, but she didn't need to. They divided their attention between Baz and the woman whose car was stolen.

Without wasting time, JJ pulled out her tools, stepped in close, and bent down, hoping Baz's truck would hide what she was doing. It took about thirty seconds, which felt like four days, but she managed to get the door unlocked.

She stepped inside, closed it, and flipped on the light.

Sure enough, this was someone's room. There was a towel flung over the wooden desk chair and an empty bag of Fritos on the nightstand. One of the twin beds was unmade and there was an open suitcase on the other.

Knowing she had little time to waste, she hurried to look through the suitcase. She found nothing that would help them figure out what Juliet's next move might be, only a handful of clothes. On to the small bathroom, she glanced at the hygiene products—shampoo, conditioner, toothbrush, toothpaste, and a travel-sized bottle of mouthwash. Aside from some DNA the police could use to identify Juliet, there was nothing of use to JJ.

She hurried back to the door, peeked out the window beside it. Baz was still talking to the officers, but now the woman was no longer out there.

Crap.

JJ turned back around, looked at the entire space, hoping to find something that would help. That was when she saw the computer charger plugged into the wall. There was no computer attached though.

"Fuck."

If Juliet had the sense to take the computer, JJ knew there wouldn't be anything useful left behind. She turned back, peeked through the curtains to confirm she wouldn't be seen, then slipped out of the room and headed right for Baz's truck.

When he returned a few minutes later, JJ tried not to sulk. She'd thought for sure there would be something in that room that would lead them to Juliet. Maybe Brantley was right. Maybe JJ did watch too many crime shows on TV.

"Anything?" she asked when he climbed in and pulled the door shut.

He shook his head. "The woman's the day manager. Evidently, she leaves her car keys hangin' in the front office. She said a woman matching Juliet's description came in, took them off the hook. She didn't realize what had happened until she saw her car leaving the parkin' lot."

"What about the Mustang?"

"They're gonna have it processed, but based on what they said, it's definitely been in an accident recently."

"And it's a '65?"

"It is, yes."

JJ sighed. "So it's true. We had Juliet in our sights earlier?"

Baz didn't say anything, but she didn't need him to. They'd seen the blue Mustang, even waited for it to pull into a parking space. If they'd only…

JJ knew she could insert a ton of *if onlys* in that sentence, any one of which might've prevented Kylie Walker from being run down in the street.

Yet not a single one would change the outcome at this point.

Chapter Six

GAGE WAS AWARE OF SIGHTS, SOUNDS, MOVEMENT, but he was unable to move, barely able to breathe as he sat in the back of the ambulance, Kylie's hand in his. The EMT was working, doing God only knew what as the other drove with obvious intent.

He answered questions when he was asked—What medications was Kylie taking? Any previous surgeries? Medical conditions?—not sure how he even knew the answers. His mind was fogged, his heart breaking as he leaned close to his wife, silently pleading for her to hang on. She hadn't opened her eyes, hadn't moved at all. He wasn't even sure she was breathing on her own, but surely she was, right? They would've said something if she wasn't.

The next thing Gage was aware of was pulling into the hospital, then people filing out, taking over, pushing the gurney while barking orders as the EMTs followed close behind.

Gage managed to keep up, never releasing Kylie's hand. She looked so pale, so fragile, it pained him to think they were going to take her away even for a minute. He needed to be with her, to assure her she wasn't alone.

"Sir, you'll need to stay here," one of the masked people told him. "We'll let you know as soon as we have news."

Gage shook his head, tried to go with her, but the hands pulling at him were strong. Too strong.

"They've got her. She's in good hands."

He knew he needed to hold it together, needed to comprehend what they were saying so he could relay the details to everyone else when they arrived. If he had to guess, Travis was right behind them. He prayed he was because Gage couldn't do this alone. He needed Travis, needed his husband's strength to keep him standing.

"Come on. This way."

It wasn't until Gage was halfway down the hall that he realized Reese was the one guiding him, Brantley right beside him, their dog leading the way.

"I didn't believe you," he whispered.

"What?" Reese guided him into a chair in a brightly lit room with people scattered throughout. "What did you say?"

Gage's legs gave out, the seat coming up to meet his ass. "I didn't believe you."

When he looked up, both Brantley and Reese were frowning.

"I didn't think she was still a threat," he admitted, his voice rough. "I thought Travis was losin' his mind. Overreactin'."

Their expressions went blank immediately.

"It was her. Juliet Prince. She was the one who hit Kylie?"

Brantley's face was full of sympathy. "We believe so, yes."

"Where is she?" His eyes bounced back and forth between them. "Please tell me they caught her."

It was on their faces. Juliet Prince was not in custody. She was not being processed for attempted murder.

"She fled the scene," Reese answered, his tone smooth and low. "But we've got a license plate number, and there's a BOLO out for the car. We'll—"

"Where is she? Where is my wife?"

The voice boomed through the space, drawing the attention of everyone.

Gage was on his feet, moving toward Travis.

The instant Travis saw him, he was marching over, then his arms were around him, holding Gage together. He held on to Travis, inhaling his familiar scent, trying to absorb some of his strength, knowing he would need it.

Travis's hand cradled the back of his head, holding firmly as they leaned on one another. It didn't last long, but it was long enough to assure Gage that Travis was there with him, that he was not in this alone.

When Travis released him, stepping back, Gage gripped Travis's arm, feeling back in control of himself for the first time since leaving the park. "Come on. Let's sit."

"Where is she?" Travis demanded, stopping Gage when he tried to lead them away from the nurses' station.

"They've taken her into surgery," he explained, recalling only briefly what he'd been told.

"Surgery?" Travis frowned. "Why? For what?"

Honestly, Gage had no idea, and he didn't want to lead Travis to believe otherwise.

"Let's take a seat," Curtis suggested, his voice low and commanding as he motioned them to the far side of the room.

"I don't wanna sit," Travis snapped. "I wanna see my wife."

"You will," Brantley said firmly. "Give them time to take care of her."

Gage's first instinct was to placate Travis, to tell him everything was going to be all right, that Kylie would be fine. He didn't say any of those things. Probably because he had so many doubts himself. Fear, even now, threatened to choke him. It was likely exacerbated by the sheer terror he could see on Travis's face. The man who was always strong and stoic looked anything but, and that scared the shit out of Gage.

Someone directed them to an empty corner of the room, offered coffee. They both refused but took their seats. Gage settled for sitting silently, his arm brushing Travis's as they both remained perfectly still, staring at the doors that led to their wife.

Time moved slowly. Too slowly.

"How long has she been back there?" someone eventually asked.

"Not long," someone else answered.

There were a few hushed whispers, maybe even a group praying softly. Gage barely heard them over the steady, painful thump of his heart as he sent up his own silent prayer, begging God to spare the most beautiful, the most vibrant woman he'd ever known.

Suddenly the doors opened and a man stepped out. Older man, pleasant face, serious eyes. Blue scrubs. He pulled off the face mask and the hair covering as he approached. It was in his movements, a sense of regret that had Gage's heart squeezing.

"Walker family?"

No. Please no.

Gage got to his feet, shaking his head. It hadn't been long enough. They hadn't had her back there long enough to fix her broken, battered body.

"Is Kylie gonna be all right?" someone asked.

No.

Gage didn't look away from the doctor. He saw the sorrow and remorse before he heard the words.

No, no, no.

And then the doctor said the words that would irrevocably change the world as they knew it.

"I'm sorry. We did everything we could."

OH, JESUS. FUCK.

Travis tried to take a breath, but someone had replaced the oxygen with shards of glass that rattled around in his lungs, scraping him raw. The pain was unbearable. He could hear the godawful sounds coming out of his throat, but he was helpless to stop them.

God, no. This couldn't be happening.

Travis stepped toward the doctor.

"We got her prepped for surgery," the doctor was explaining, "and that was when we realized one of her ribs had pierced her aorta. There was nothing we could do."

Before he realized what he was doing, Travis fisted the front of the doctor's scrubs. "Go back in there," he growled low in his throat. "Go back and fix her."

A firm but gentle hand was on his. It was the doctor's and he wasn't attempting to push Travis off of him.

"I'm so sorry," the doctor said softly.

Dead.

She couldn't be dead.

No. Fuck, no.

Someone pried his hands off the doctor's shirt, urged him back.

Not Kylie.

Travis stumbled, trying to breathe but it hurt.

It should've been him, not her. Travis would've given his life for hers in a second.

His body was racked with shudders as the sorrow tore through him. This couldn't be happening. It couldn't.

He stumbled back until he hit the wall, then slid to the floor, his legs unable to hold him up anymore. Tears flooded his eyes, made it impossible to see. He was aware of the people around him, moving, whispering, someone still talking to the doctor, others trying to console one another.

Didn't they know it wouldn't work?

Didn't they realize that the light had vanished, that the heat from the sun no longer existed because Kylie was dead? Without her in it, the world would be a cold, dark place.

Travis was vaguely aware of guttural cries. It was enough to draw his attention to where Ethan and Beau were attempting to hold Gage up. Travis could feel his husband's pain, but try as he might, he couldn't muster the energy to console him. Not right now.

"Travis?"

He turned his attention to the man squatting down beside him.

"Reese and I will find her," Brantley declared, his voice low and hard, his eyes glittering with rage. "We won't stop until we do."

Travis wanted to tell him he'd heard that before, that Brantley's promises meant nothing. If they'd found her before now, Kylie wouldn't be dead. If they'd found that bitch and put her in the ground, Travis's world wouldn't be flipped off its axis right now. His kids wouldn't have to live out the rest of their days without their mother.

He didn't say those things, though. He couldn't. Right now, the coldness had frozen his vocal cords, made it impossible to speak, to feel, to move.

It was all he could do just to breathe.

TREY WALKER STOOD ON THE PERIPHERY OF the room, watching, listening.

He could feel the sadness, the heartbreak as it penetrated every person around him. He couldn't remember the last time he'd witnessed something so tragic. They were lucky in that they didn't experience loss often. The Walkers were strong, if not in body then in spirit. There were exceptions to the rule, of course, but most of the deaths he'd dealt with had been after the person had lived a long, fruitful life.

This was not one of those instances.

Kylie Walker hadn't lived nearly long enough. She was far too young, just a few months older than Trey if he recalled correctly. Thirty-six years old. To have been taken like this … stolen from the world without warning, without a chance for anyone to say goodbye … it was heart-wrenching.

As he stood, Trey watched as family members hugged one another. Kaleb was holding his wife, Zoey, against his chest as she cried. Ethan and Beau were holding on to Gage, giving him as much support as they could. Kennedy was sitting in a chair, her head in her hands, a tissue clutched by her face. Sawyer was standing behind her, looking as though he didn't quite believe what was happening. Brendon was on the phone, most likely calling his wife, Cheyenne, since she was currently on tour.

On the other side of the room, Braydon had his arms wrapped around Jessie, Kylie's baby sister. She was hysterical, her sobs echoing as loudly as Gage's. From here, Trey could see that Braydon was sobbing as much as his wife. Not far from them, Curtis was watching over everyone, his eyes sharp and clear, but his breaths were coming far too rapidly. He was on the verge of falling apart, but likely holding it together for everyone else.

And then there was Travis, sitting on the floor, alone, body jerking as he sobbed uncontrollably, head resting on his knees.

To think, there were so many more who hadn't heard the news yet. The pain and sorrow were only beginning.

Trey couldn't help but think this was their fault. If they'd only found Juliet Prince, they wouldn't be here right now. The Walkers wouldn't be suffering such a tragic, unfathomable loss.

Chapter Seven

Thursday, January 14, 2021

DAYS PASSED IN A BLUR.
Sunday.
Monday.
Tuesday.
Wednesday.
They were all the same, time having ceased to mean anything to Travis.

He relied on muscle memory to get him through the daily functions, accomplishing the bare minimum. He was relying on his parents, his brothers. They were all there, consoling one another, pitching in to take care of what needed to be taken care of.

Travis couldn't eat; he couldn't sleep. He didn't want to go into the bedroom they'd shared with Kylie, didn't want to shower in the shower he'd joined her in numerous times, didn't want to eat off dishes she'd eaten off of. It was too painful. He wanted to be blessedly numb, his mind blank. It was his only objective, yet no matter how hard he fought back the memories, they swamped him at the most inopportune time: every second of the hour, every hour of the day.

Like now, when he was sitting at his desk in his home office, staring blankly at the closed doors. He had just processed the payment that would take care of the funeral arrangements. The ones his mother was taking care of for them.

To his absolute horror, he'd found that Kylie had actually had a will drawn up. She had thought of everything, ensuring they were all taken care of in the event of her death. When? When had she done that and why didn't he know about it?

Another tear escaped as he accepted the fact he probably did know. Kylie had likely mentioned it to him at some point, probably even encouraged him to do the same. Whatever it took to ensure the children were taken care of if something bad happened. She had always worried because their relationship was complicated. While Travis and Kylie were legally married, they weren't legally married to Gage. Sure, there was a contract that bound them and covered some legalities, but it didn't cover everything.

He took in a ragged breath, let it out.

How was he supposed to wake up every single day without her? How was he supposed to *want* to live another day without her? He wasn't even sure he could. She was their everything. All of them. They were lost without her.

How in the fuck was he ever going to be able to sleep in their bed knowing she would never be there again? Knowing he would never have the rare moment of watching her sleep? Or waking up and making love to her before the day got started?

Tears dripped unchecked down his face as his chest constricted with every breath.

Who was going to be there to remind him that his socks did not belong on the floor of the bathroom? Or that it was his turn to pick up the kids from daycare? Or suggest he hire someone to mow the lawn because it would simply be easier and the kid down the street was looking to make some money for video games?

And the kids … God, how were they going to get through every single day without seeing their beautiful, loving mother? Who would make Kate chicken-and-stars soup when she didn't feel well? Or add cut-up hot dogs to Avery's macaroni and cheese? Who would cuddle with Kade on the couch and sneak bites of chocolate chip cookie dough right out of the tub while they thought no one was watching? Who would sing Haden those silly lullabies that Kylie made up because it made him laugh? And Maddox … would he even remember that his mother told him every night that she loved him to the moon and back?

She was gone. Kylie was dead and their lives were forever changed. The sun would never be as bright, as warm as it had once been.

And how in the fuck was Gage ever going to be able to look at Travis and not blame him for getting their wife killed?

A knock sounded on the door and Travis brought the room into focus. He didn't bother wiping the tears. It wouldn't matter. More would fall.

The door opened and his dad appeared. "Are you ready?"

Travis shook his head.

Never.

He would *never* be ready to say goodbye to Kylie one last time.

"WE SHOULD GO."

Brantley looked up from his computer screen, saw Reese standing in the doorway to his office. He was wearing a suit, one of a few Brantley hadn't even known the man had. Despite the gloom of the day laid out before them, he couldn't help but think Reese looked handsome when he was all starched and pressed.

Sighing, Brantley glanced at his computer again, then closed the lid. He got to his feet, snagged his tie from where he'd tossed it on his desk.

"What were you workin' on?"

"JJ sent a list of people Juliet's associated with."

"I saw it." Reese started down the stairs. "I skimmed it last night. Sent her a couple more to add."

Brantley followed, settling his tie around his neck. When they reached the bottom, Reese shrugged into his jacket while Brantley looked into the hallway mirror, adjusting the tie beneath his collar. He attempted the knot then grunted when he had to start over.

"Here," Reese said, putting his hand on Brantley's shoulder and turning him.

Brantley stared into Reese's face while the man worked the tie like a pro. Less than a minute later, the damn thing was properly restricting his airway.

"I hate funerals," Brantley admitted, although he wasn't sure what speaking it aloud did.

"I do, too."

With keys in hand, Brantley led the way out to the truck.

For the past few days, Brantley and Reese had divided their time between working with JJ and Baz to find Juliet Prince and assisting Trey and Charlie with family duties. Being that Charlie was dating Autumn Jameson, one of Travis's cousins, she was helping out by babysitting and getting food when it was needed. Trey was filling in where he could, running errands for Curtis and Lorrie while assisting Reese with Walker Demo. Brantley hadn't done much, but he'd made a point to ensure he was around if someone needed anything.

He figured it was beneficial in times like this to have such a large family. Not to mention to live in a small town. Every time you turned around, there was someone willing to help even if those grieving the most barely noticed what was going on around them.

The hardest part for Brantley was feeling as though this was his fault. It was difficult to look Travis or Gage in the eye knowing that if he'd only worked a little harder, searched a little more, it was possible he would've taken Juliet Prince down and this never would've happened. He knew the team was feeling the same, which was the reason JJ and Baz were working nonstop to find her. They'd enlisted the help of Luca Switzer as well as their new counterparts at Sniper 1 Security.

Still no luck and he hated the idea the bitch might go to ground again.

When he got to the truck, he held out his keys to Reese.

"You want me to drive?" The surprise in Reese's tone almost made him smile.

"It seems fitting that it's rainin'," Brantley said as they headed toward town.

The temperature had dropped, too, almost as though Mother Nature was mourning this loss along with them.

"My brother and RT made it down," Reese said. "They're plannin' to stay a while. Help with the investigation."

"We've got a guest room," he said absently, staring out the window.

"I offered it."

They drove in silence the rest of the way, neither of them feeling the need for small talk.

A short time later, Brantley was filing into the church behind his uncle Joseph and aunt Rosalynn. They were greeted by Pastor Bob then by Kylie's father, Joe Prescott, and Joe's wife, Melissa. Curtis and Lorrie were there, as was Travis, who was standing off to the side, alone. Brantley didn't see Gage or the kids yet but knew they were coming.

Everyone was coming today. It wouldn't surprise him if the entire town was there to celebrate the life and mourn the passing of a woman who'd been beloved by all.

GAGE STARED OUT THE WINDOW, WATCHING THE trees pass by in a blur.

From the backseat of the limousine that would take them to the church, then to the gravesite, Gage tried not to think too much, fearful he might throw himself out of a moving vehicle, refusing to do this, refusing to say goodbye to Kylie, to watch as they placed her in her final resting place.

Tears clogged his throat, but he held them at bay. He had to be strong for the kids.

"Where's Daddy-O?"

"He's comin'," Gage assured Avery, planting a half smile on his face. "I promise, you'll see him in a little while."

Gage had spent the past four days feeling as though he was walking through a nightmare without the benefit of knowing he would eventually wake up, that the horror he'd experienced could be put behind him. But this wasn't a nightmare and he wouldn't be waking up. The horror was now his new normal.

Kylie was dead, Travis had retreated from the world, and Gage had been forced to explain to his kids what happened and help them understand that, with time, they would all get through this, even if he didn't necessarily believe it himself.

Thankfully he had help taking care of the details. Lorrie and Curtis were pitching in, cooking meals, helping with the kids, and delegating tasks and chores to Travis's brothers. They were also helping Kylie's parents and her sister, ensuring they had everything they needed so they could focus solely on grieving. Gage knew Jessie was having a difficult time dealing with the loss of her sister. She continued to blame herself, claiming she could've done more, *should've* done more. She was in denial, a stage of grief Gage was all too familiar with.

In all the time Gage had known the Walkers, starting back when he'd first become friends with Kaleb in elementary school, never had he seen them rally together quite like this. And that was saying something considering the Walkers were always there to help those in need. But this ... this sadness was like a wet blanket shrouding everyone. They were doing their best to ensure he didn't feel alone, but even with their kindness, Gage felt as though he had no one to turn to.

He wouldn't deny it helped to stay busy, to have something to take care of, but it would've been easier if he had Travis at his side. Never had Gage thought he would be the stronger of the two when it came to something like this. Then again, Travis wasn't giving him much of an option.

When the car came to a stop in front of the church, the kids turned to him. He could feel all those sad eyes waiting for him to direct them on what to do next. He had already explained to Kate, Kade, Avery, and Haden that today they were going to say goodbye to their mother one last time. Kate was in denial, refusing to believe this was real, retreating from everyone just like Travis. Gage couldn't blame her. If he thought it might bring Kylie back, he would do the same thing. As for the others, he knew they didn't truly understand it, but he thought it was important, as did the rest of the family, that they be here today.

The only person who hadn't chimed in, hadn't offered his opinion had been Travis. Try as he might, Gage could not get Travis to speak to him, and he had a feeling the man believed he was responsible for what happened. Gage understood how he would because he blamed himself, too. If he'd only trusted Travis's gut when he insisted they find Juliet Prince and bring her to justice. If he had only listened, Kylie would still be with them today, not being buried one day after what should've been her thirty-seventh birthday. She hadn't gotten to celebrate her thirty-seventh birthday. Never would.

Gage fought to breathe around the knot in his throat while he helped the kids out of the car, walked with them toward the steps leading into the church. His heart physically ached as he ascended those steps one at a time.

The door was standing open, Pastor Bob waiting inside to greet them.

But it wasn't the pastor Gage saw first. No, his eyes instantly moved to Travis, who was standing there, looking as lost and as gutted as Gage felt.

"Daddy-O!" Kate yelled, racing right into Travis's arms.

Without fail, Travis picked her up, held her tight to him, and kissed her on the forehead as all the other kids, save for Maddox, who simply kicked his feet against Gage's hip, wrapped themselves around Travis's legs.

Their eyes met over the heads of all their kids, and Gage felt a fresh wave of grief. He could see that Travis was doing his best to pull away from them. Not physically but emotionally. Gage knew the man would be there because they needed him, but even if he was there in body, he wouldn't be there in spirit.

Problem was, Gage had already lost Kylie, the woman he loved beyond measure. He didn't think he would survive losing Travis at the same time.

AFTER HAVING EXPERIENCED THE DEVASTATION OF ONE miscarriage, Curtis Walker had been blessed with the birth of seven healthy boys. And from the first moment he laid eyes on each of them, he had prayed they would outlive him, that he would never have to experience the loss of another child, that his beautiful bride would never have to suffer that loss either.

Unfortunately, he hadn't been specific enough with his prayer, because he now knew the loss of another child, felt the gut-wrenching pain of sorrow as it flooded his body.

No, Kylie wasn't his child by birth. He hadn't had the honor of hearing her first word or holding her hand on the first day of school. But he'd had the pleasure of witnessing her grow up. Only he'd seen it through pictures her father proudly showed anyone who wanted to see. Ones of her holding up her lunch box on those first days of school, some when she was proudly wearing her Halloween costume and preparing to take her little sister trick-or-treating. Even one of her standing beside her first car, her smile wide, her joy evident. Joe Prescott had so many pictures—birthdays, Christmases, graduations—so many but not nearly enough, Curtis knew.

Regardless, Kylie Marie Prescott Walker was as much Curtis's child as his own sons were. Without her vibrancy, a piece of his heart was now missing, and he knew the same could be said for Lorrie and every other member of his family.

Curtis had watched his wife these past few days, knew the only reason Lorrie was able to keep moving forward was because she had to. She had to ensure that Kylie's sister had what she needed because Lorrie refused to let Jessie endure another ounce of weight upon her shoulders during this impossible time.

And Lorrie was doing her best to support Joe and Melissa, Kylie's father and stepmother, so they could grieve the loss of their oldest child, something that was painful enough without also dealing with the fact that yesterday would've been Kylie's thirty-seventh birthday.

Thankfully, Lorrie had help. Every single one of them was putting one foot in front of the other, holding each other up, celebrating the beauty that Kylie had brought to this world while also suffering on the inside. Zoey, Kennedy, V, and even Cheyenne, who had put her tour on hold indefinitely, were taking turns watching kids, helping Lorrie cook meals, and sitting with Jessie when they forced Braydon to give his wife and himself a breather.

Ethan, Beau, Sawyer, Kaleb, and Brendon were assisting with chores, helping the women with the kids, trying to keep them entertained as much as possible. They were doing what they could for Travis and Gage; all the while, they were handling the loss as best they could.

As for him … well, Curtis was trying to remain stoic for those who needed him. Especially today, as everyone in the church dealt with the pain of losing one of the most generous and kind women Curtis had ever known.

He'd been sitting here, listening as Pastor Bob reflected on Kylie's life, the fact that she and Travis and Gage had celebrated seven years of marriage last December. He relayed a few details of the day he had performed the unofficial ceremony to unite the three of them.

What Pastor Bob didn't mention was that Kylie and Travis had been married … well, it would've officially been nineteen years in June. The first eleven of those years, no one had known because Travis and Kylie had split up without ever sharing the news. It hadn't been until Kylie sought Travis out to sign divorce papers that they'd rekindled what they'd once had, and Kylie had found herself falling in love with not only Travis but also with Gage. Curtis remembered those days, the way Travis and Gage had been battling it out, until they finally gave in to the love that had developed between the three of them.

And since then, they'd had five beautiful children, whom they cherished and loved. The very children who clung to their fathers now, sobbing because their mother had been taken from them far too soon.

Also here to celebrate her life and grieve her loss was every single member of Curtis and Lorrie's family. Aunts, uncles, cousins. They'd all known Kylie, most having spent a significant amount of time with her over the years, at family gatherings, birthdays, celebrations. But family weren't the only ones gracing the pews of the church on this cold, rainy Thursday. The place was at standing room only because of the love and support that Kylie had garnered over the years. People, most of whom Curtis had been introduced to, had come from far and wide to grieve the loss as well as show their support for Kylie's family.

He was simply glad they were here, grateful that there were those who could help hold up the ones who were suffering the most from this incomprehensible loss. Curtis knew this was only the beginning. They had a long road of healing ahead of them and it wasn't going to be easy, but together, they would learn to cope.

And each day … starting far in the future … it would get a little easier to breathe, to reflect. And the memories that surfaced would be a bit more vibrant without the suffocating haze of such pain.

Chapter Eight

TRAVIS WAS NUMB.

If it wasn't for that fact, he would probably be cold considering he'd been standing at Kylie's gravesite for the past few hours. He had endured the final words, the sobs, the well wishes, and the departure of those who'd gathered. Yet he couldn't bring himself to leave. He intended to be here until her casket was lowered into the earth and covered with dirt, unwilling to leave her side until he absolutely had to.

He couldn't count the number of people who had tried to console him, urging him to go home, get some rest. And he knew exactly how many he'd spoken to. None. He had no words because there was nothing he could say that would make this okay in any way, nor easier to bear, so he'd kept his mouth closed and pretended to listen.

"Travis, they need to lower the casket now."

He managed to drag his gaze over to see his father looking at him with such pain in his eyes. Beyond him, Pastor Bob stood by, his expression solemn. Travis could understand it. He knew everyone was feeling the loss, and while he had nothing to say, he wasn't diminishing their grief in any way. He was simply trying to deal with his own.

"I need a few minutes," Travis managed.

"Of course. We'll wait until you're finished."

Travis didn't care if they waited or if they left. It didn't matter to him. Nothing mattered anymore.

Once he was alone again, Travis stepped forward, placed his hand on the glossy mahogany that entombed his beautiful wife. The casket had been hand selected by Jessie because she claimed Kylie would've loved it. She had mentioned how the royal-blue silk on the inside was Kylie's favorite color. Travis had kept his opinions to himself because he didn't understand the rationale. What Kylie would've loved was to be alive and well and watching her babies grow up, not lying cold and dead on a bed of royal-blue silk.

It was then the tears returned and Travis didn't attempt to stop them.

"It should've been me, baby," he whispered. "It shouldn't be you leavin' us so soon. It shouldn't be you the kids have to live without. It should be me."

He took a deep breath, tucked his hands in his pockets.

"I'm so fuckin' sorry, Kylie. I should've stopped her. Instead, I went off the rails, became obsessed, and lost my focus. I gave her the perfect opportunity to strike at me again." He sobbed. "This is my fault, baby. All my fault."

Travis focused on breathing. His chest constricted so tight he thought he might drop to his knees from the pain of it, but he pushed through because the pain was the least he deserved.

"I will find her," he promised. "I will. Might not be today, or tomorrow, but it will happen. And when I do, I will end her."

As far as Travis was concerned, Juliet Prince didn't deserve a day behind bars with three squares and a cot. The only place she deserved to be was in the cold, hard ground.

"Hopefully," he continued aloud, "once that happens, Gage can forgive me, and the kids won't grow to hate me as much as I hate myself."

And that was his fear now. That Gage wouldn't be able to look him in the eye and the kids wouldn't want to see his face when they realized this was all his fault. And he couldn't blame them.

He heard someone clear their throat, and he peered over his shoulder to see Gage standing there, hands in his pockets, eyes piercing right through Travis.

"Trav," Gage said roughly, taking a step forward.

As much as Travis believed Gage deserved so much better than him, in that moment, Gage was the only person on the planet who could offer him even a modicum of relief.

Rather than warn him off or send him away, Travis turned to face Gage fully, and when his husband moved toward him, Travis took a single step, then another until they were standing there, wrapped tightly in one another's arms as the sobs tore free. Travis cradled Gage's head, while Gage did the same in return. It wasn't a gentle embrace but rather a hard hug that gave them both something to hold on to for those brief seconds.

And when they separated, Travis scrubbed his face with the palms of his hands and took a deep breath.

"Don't make me do this alone, Trav," Gage whispered, his brown eyes glittering with so much pain.

"I would never," he promised, reaching for him again, holding on.

He knew he'd been distant the past few days, and he wouldn't make excuses for it. He'd left the hard parts to Gage and he shouldn't have, but rational thought hadn't been an option. Anyone who knew him knew his emotions ran hot, and when they did, he tended to do the wrong thing. Gage of all people knew that about him.

In fact, it was Gage's acceptance of him that made him love the man all the more.

Several hours later, after Travis had stopped by his parents' house for the reception, listened while people shared stories of how they knew Kylie, how she'd made their life a bit brighter, Travis was glad to be home.

Gage and the kids had come home at his request, and he'd spent the past hour helping Gage get them all settled in. Maddox and Haden had gone right to sleep, the events of the past few days wearing them down. They were safe and warm in the comfort of their own beds, and Travis hoped they would sleep through the night because of it.

Kade, Avery, and Kate weren't giving in quite so easily, but Travis didn't mind. He had settled in his recliner with Avery and her little fuzzy blanket in his lap, while Kade sat on the floor with his video game controller in his hand. Kate was lying on the couch, her head on Gage's thigh as she watched her brother. Every so often, Travis would look over, watch Gage as he lightly brushed Kate's hair with his hand.

Travis focused on breathing, fought the urge to look toward the stairs, to wonder what Kylie was doing. On nights like this, she would often sneak upstairs for some quiet time of her own. She had loved to read, and whenever possible, she would carve out the time to enjoy a bath, a book, and a glass of wine.

Never again.

He felt the emotion bubble in his chest, but he held it back. He did not want the kids to see him fall apart. This was hard enough on them; he did not need to make it worse. But even as he glanced from one kid to the next, he couldn't help but think that this was what Kylie had built. This family … this was all her. And now she wasn't here with them.

Minutes ticked by as they remained where they were. Kate and Avery didn't last long, falling asleep with nothing to keep them preoccupied. It wasn't until Kade reclined on the floor that Travis decided it was time for them all to get up to their beds. They'd had a long, emotional day and they needed to sleep.

With Gage's help, they got the kids tucked in, and when Travis returned downstairs, it was to find Gage in the kitchen. He was leaning back against the counter, a glass of scotch in his hand. When he saw Travis, he picked up another, handed it over.

Travis took it, swallowed a sip, then met Gage's eyes. "I'm sorry about the past few days."

Gage nodded, took a drink.

Travis knew that wasn't forgiveness, because his actions were unforgivable. He'd left Gage alone to deal with the hard parts while he sulked here in this cold, lonely house, acting as though he was the only one affected by Kylie's death.

Before he could offer more apologies or explain so Gage would understand his reasons, his husband finished his drink, set the glass in the sink, and walked past him.

Travis didn't turn around, didn't beg or plead. He deserved the cold shoulder from Gage. Hell, he deserved far worse than that.

The swinging door flapped shut upon Gage's exit, making Travis close his eyes briefly, the sadness of it all filling him once more.

Rather than dwell on it, Travis finished his drink, washed the dirty glasses, and put them back in the cupboard. He checked the contents of the refrigerator, made a note on the grocery list, and planned out the kids' breakfast for the morning. It was important to get them back into a routine and Travis wanted to be ready.

With nothing left to do, Travis forced himself to go to bed, flipping off the lights in the house on the way to the main-floor guest room. Aside from taking the kids to bed earlier, Travis hadn't been upstairs, and for now, he intended to keep it that way. He knew he wasn't strong enough to handle seeing his bedroom or to smell Kylie's lingering perfume.

After pulling off his boots and socks, removing his jeans, he fell back in the bed wearing his boxers and T-shirt. Because he hadn't bothered turning on the lamp, he was forced to lie in the dark room, staring up at the ceiling and the dim lines formed by the porch light shining in through the window.

Sleep didn't come, but Travis didn't expect it to. His brain wouldn't shut off, his thoughts of the day at the park, the horrific scene that had ended the world as he knew it.

He had no idea how long he'd been there when he heard the light squeak of the door opening. When he lifted his head, he thought he would see Kate or maybe Kade needing him to tuck them back in. His kids weren't standing in the doorway though.

"Everything all right?" Travis pushed himself up onto his elbows, watching Gage standing there, backlit from the light in the foyer.

"No," he said simply, stepping into the room and closing the door behind him.

Travis was frozen in place. On one hand, he was grateful Gage had come to him because he needed the comfort even if he didn't deserve it. But at the same time, he was terrified Gage was going to finally lay the blame at Travis's feet, where it belonged.

He held his breath, waiting to see which direction Gage was going with this.

He didn't have to wait long when Gage moved closer, pulling his shirt over his head and tossing it to the floor. The next to go were his sweatpants, and then Gage was crawling over Travis, his hard, warm body a balm to Travis's aching soul.

"I need you," Gage whispered softly, and Travis could hear the tears in his voice.

Travis cupped his face. "I need you, too."

He pulled Gage down to him, their lips seeking and finding the little bit of comfort they could provide. Time became obsolete as their tongues mated, hands roaming. At some point, they managed to remove Travis's clothes, leaving them skin to skin.

It was easy to get caught up in the moment. It was a welcome distraction, something to hang on to for a short time before the world intruded again.

Travis didn't ask for what he wanted, nor did Gage. They'd been together long enough to know what it took to please the other.

When Gage's cool, slick hand gripped his cock, Travis realized his husband had come prepared. With firm strokes, he lubed Travis's cock, drawing long, ragged moans from his throat. And when Travis could take no more, he settled between Gage's thighs and sank into the blessed heat of his body. He growled low in his throat as a sinful pleasure washed over him, a feeling he hadn't expected to ever feel again.

At that point, time stood completely still. Travis stared down at Gage as he slid in deep, retreated. Over and over, again and again. He took his time, getting lost in the man because it was his only safe place. Right here, right now, with Gage he could almost block out everything else.

"Harder," Gage snapped, dragging Travis from his erotic trance.

In all the time he'd been with Gage, never had he heard such a dark command. It shocked him briefly, but Travis damn sure wouldn't hold back if that was what his husband needed. Shifting so he was over Gage, his upper body balanced on his arms, he slammed his hips down, impaling him.

"Is that what you want?" he growled, the emotional turmoil roiling, writhing, turning what had been slow and sweet into an inferno of need and lust.

"Yes," Gage hissed, his head falling back. "More."

Travis slammed into him again, enjoying Gage's hard, eager grunts.

Again and again, he didn't hold back, driving in rough and deep, delivering that erotic bite of pain that would allow Gage to escape everything else for a while. It was what Gage needed. Hell, it was what Travis needed more than anything.

"Faster… Fuck me." Gage exhaled harshly. "God, just fuck me."

Realizing Gage was still attempting to escape it all, including their connection, Travis stopped, pulling out of Gage's body long enough for them to shift positions, Gage rolling onto his stomach. For whatever reason, this was a position that worked so much better for them, with Travis lying atop him, arms sliding under, fingers curling over Gage's shoulders. They were touching from chest to knee while Travis rocked, fucking him from behind. And this way, Gage couldn't escape. He would be overwhelmed by Travis, feel him everywhere.

Gage's hands gripped Travis's wrists as they were lost in the sensations together, this time the emotions were a tidal wave that took them both under. When Gage cried out, his orgasm triggered Travis's, dragging another ragged moan from him.

And when it was over, the only thing Travis could do was roll to his side, holding the man he loved as the tears broke free once again.

It would never be the same. They both knew it. What they had … without Kylie … even that was different. And they would have to figure out how to make it work for them.

Travis considered mentioning it to Gage, but he didn't get the chance. A few minutes later, Gage pulled away, then got out of the bed. Without a word, he picked up his discarded clothes, pulled them on, then slipped out of the room, leaving Travis staring after him.

Travis hadn't thought the hole in his chest could get any bigger, but right then it did. With Gage pulling away, the chasm widened, making him feel empty and cold.

As he lay there, he prayed that Gage would find a way to forgive him, because Travis wasn't sure he could go on without him. He knew one thing for sure: he damn sure didn't want to find out.

BRANTLEY STOOD ON THE UPPER DECK THAT extended off the back of his house, hands in his pockets as he observed his surroundings. To his left, above the barn, he could see the lights of downtown Austin in the far distance. To the right, his cousins' house. A few months back, Kaden and Keegan had bought the ranch and had been working to fix it up.

He found he enjoyed coming out here, listening to the wind rustle through the trees. Every now and then, a donkey would make his presence known. Sometimes a cow. But tonight he didn't hear any of that. Tonight, his thoughts were far too loud for him to enjoy the solitude.

"You okay out here?"

Brantley glanced back briefly, silently acknowledging Reese. "I'm not sure I'll ever be okay again."

He exhaled when Reese came to stand behind him, those strong arms sliding around, his palms flattening on his chest. In return, Brantley pressed his hands to the backs of Reese's, relishing the warmth and the strength.

"I know I'm not responsible for Kylie's death," he told Reese. "Rationally, I'm well aware that Juliet is to blame. She was the one behind the wheel. She's the one who made a conscious effort to hurt an innocent woman."

Reese's arms tightened.

"Doesn't mean I don't feel like I could've done somethin' to stop it."

Reese's chin rested on his shoulder as he leaned in. "Maybe we could've," he said softly. "In hindsight, it's always easy to see a better way of doin' things."

True.

"But if that's the case," Reese continued, "how did she manage to vanish? If we could've done something differently before, surely we could've done something after this tragedy. Yet she's completely off the grid."

She was. Gone.

Although the sheriff's department hadn't been able to track her from the scene, they had managed to trace her steps afterward. Thanks to the BOLO on the car, they'd been able to recover the blue Mustang at a motel right down the road. And because the manager of the motel had reported her car stolen, they knew Juliet had gotten away in it.

Unfortunately, they weren't sure what she'd done after that. Based on traffic camera footage that Sniper 1 Security had combed through, Juliet Prince had not left the area, and she had abandoned the Chevy Cruze in a Target parking lot. Which meant she could be anywhere. If she'd stolen another car, they didn't know what they were looking for. And if she was hiding out, they didn't know where.

And that was something Brantley hadn't yet told Travis or Gage. As much as he wanted to keep them updated on the hunt, they had all agreed they would refrain until absolutely necessary. Preferably until they had Juliet Prince in a cage where she belonged, because they weren't giving up until they found her.

Brantley shifted, forcing Reese to drop his arms. When he turned around, he drew Reese back to him.

"I am gonna find her," he stated, allowing Reese to hear his conviction. "I won't stop until I do."

Reese nodded. "That's exactly what I told RT when I talked to him earlier."

"Is that what y'all were chattin' about after the funeral?"

"Among other things."

Brantley cocked an eyebrow, waited for Reese to explain.

"RT has given us the full backing of Sniper 1's resources. They will do whatever's necessary to help us find her. Even dedicate people to come down here for the search."

"For how long?"

Reese shrugged one shoulder. "Until we find her. He wants us to hand select a team to assist with her apprehension."

Although his pride told him to reject the offer, to do this on his own and prove himself capable of completing what he'd set out to do, Brantley didn't care how they took Juliet Prince down. She'd caused more damage than anyone thought possible, and the only thing that mattered was ensuring she was stopped.

One way or the other.

"When do we start?"

"Whenever you're ready." Reese stepped back, canted his head to the side.

"I'm not doin' anything tonight," he said with a solemn sigh. "I don't think my head's in it."

Reese nodded his understanding, then took Brantley's hand, tugged. "No. Tonight's not good for me either."

"No?"

Reese shook his head as he led the way into the house. "No. Right now, I think we need a little alone time."

Yeah. Brantley couldn't argue with that. After having witnessed so much sadness, so much loss, Brantley wanted nothing more than to remember the good things he had. A reminder to never take anything for granted.

After all, it could so quickly be gone tomorrow.

Chapter Nine

Friday, January 15, 2021

THE DAY AFTER THE FUNERAL, BRANTLEY FOUND himself up early, brimming with restless energy. Even the ten-mile run he took with Reese and Tesha did little to settle him. The eggs and bacon Reese made refueled him, and the coffee left him edgy.

And the phone call from the governor was not doing a damn thing to help his nerves.

"I understand, sir. I will," he said politely before disconnecting the call.

Taking a deep breath, he walked back into the barn.

What had recently been dubbed HQ now appeared to have been transformed into a conference room for Sniper 1 Security. He skimmed the faces as he kept to the perimeter, heading directly for the kitchen. Before he could sit in on another one of these brainstorming sessions, he needed more coffee. Edginess be damned.

He had no idea what they could have left to discuss since they'd been at it since early this morning when a handful of Sniper 1 Security personnel arrived at Brantley and Reese's doorstep to join RT and Z, who'd taken over not only their guest room but also their offices and their barn.

Sure, it was one thing to gather for a sitrep—an update on a current military situation—but Brantley was learning that in the private sector, they gathered for damn near everything. Initially he'd been opposed to the idea, urging Reese to understand they'd serve more purpose if they were out in the field. Unfortunately, Reese seemed to agree with RT, Z, Hunter, Trace, and the rest of the S1S crew.

In other words, Brantley had lost the battle and he was man enough to admit it.

However, he was also man enough to know he would ultimately win the war.

With coffee in hand, Brantley stepped back into the main room.

The entire space had been rearranged—again—only this time, the desks had been shifted to form a … well, he believed they were aiming for a circle but had formed more of a distorted oval so that everyone could be facing one another in order to openly discuss options for next steps.

From what Brantley gathered, they had yet to actually talk about what those options were because they were still gathering facts.

RT was sitting on the far side of the room talking to Trace Kogan, one of Hunter's brothers, who happened to be an executive with the company. A few chairs down, Hunter was talking to Kye Sterling, one of his spouses. Their wife, Dani, was in Dallas holding down the fort. Back near the door, Trey, Luca, and JJ were going over something on her laptop. Near the whiteboard wall, Charlie was pacing back and forth on her phone, while Baz, Reese, and Z were skimming through a stack of papers someone had printed out.

"Ah, there he is," Hunter said when he looked up to see Brantley.

Brantley offered a nod. "Sorry about that," he said, apologizing for being called away briefly. "That was Governor Greenwood. He was askin' for an update."

When RT's gaze shifted to him, Brantley shook his head, immediately answering his silent question.

"It was personal, not business. He's close with the Walker family, wanted to see if we had anything yet. Or if we needed anything."

RT nodded, then addressed the others. "Why don't we resume now that everyone's back."

Figuring he would get more details if he planted his ass, Brantley took a seat across from RT. Reese came to sit at his side.

"We're already aware Brantley's opposed to these forums, as he refers to them," RT said, grinning, "but I figure this is necessary to get everyone on the same page."

All eyes remained on RT.

"As you're aware, we're dedicating a number of our resources to locatin' Juliet Prince. As of now, we have every reason to believe she's still in the area. We haven't uncovered anything to contradict that theory, anyway."

"I've been monitorin' all the stolen vehicle calls in the area since she seems adept at that," JJ announced. "We've researched all of them so far, and there's nothin' that looks to be Juliet, but I will stay on it."

Brantley sat back, letting the others take the lead on updating the team.

Trey motioned to JJ. "And we were able to pinpoint a route we believe Juliet took since she left Mississippi back in September and arrived here last Sunday."

They'd been tracking that for months now. As far as Brantley knew, it'd never been fully confirmed, more hearsay than fact, but it was a decent timeline.

"Looks sporadic," Trace noted, reviewing the image on the television screen. "Do we know if she's got family or friends who might've been helping her along that route?"

JJ was shaking her head. "The only family we're aware of is her parents. Unless they've acquired a burner and are communicatin' with her on a phone other than the one she used to talk to Marcus, then she hasn't been in touch with them. I'm still monitorin' their calls, as well as her mother's email account." She held up a hand, as though someone might want to argue with her. "And before you give me shit, yes, it's a violation of their privacy. Considerin' the circumstances, I don't really give a shit."

No one said anything, but there were a couple of smirks. Ever since Trace had made a comment about intrusive methods of investigation, JJ'd been on the defensive. Brantley was pretty sure Trace had done it to see if he could get a rise out of her, but he didn't bother to share that with JJ.

"Any word on her social media accounts?" RT prompted.

Luca was the one to speak up. "As far as I can tell, she stopped usin' her previous accounts prior to abductin' Kate Walker back in September. Her last communication via Facebook Messenger was three days before, in fact."

Brantley shifted to face Luca more fully. "Who'd she talk to?"

Luca was quick to respond, clearly having anticipated someone asking. "A woman by the name of Amy Gregson. I did a little diggin' and she's a friend of Juliet's ex-husband's new wife."

For a second, everyone seemed to be connecting the dots in their head.

"Figurin' why the hell not, I reached out to Amy. Accordin' to her, the only communication she's ever had with Juliet was that particular message, which she said was basically a bunch of"— Luca looked down at his screen—"'hate-filled babble from the mouth of a bitter bitch.' She reported it as spam and blocked Juliet's account."

Bitter was certainly an apt description of Juliet Prince.

"It doesn't give us much," Brantley acknowledged, "but it's more than we had before." He glanced at JJ then back to Luca. "Nice find."

One of these days, something very similar to that would lead them right to Juliet's doorstep. It didn't unearth anything important this time, but at some point, she would fuck up and they'd have her. It meant they simply had to keep digging.

"And we know she dumped the burner and the motel manager's car," JJ explained. "All her accounts are frozen, which means she's either stayin' in a shelter or she's still got some runnin' money."

"I figure it's the latter," Reese noted. "We know she cleared out a couple of accounts before Nicholas cut her off."

"But how much are we talkin'?" Hunter asked.

"One had a balance of two-fifty, the other five."

"I don't suppose we'd get lucky and that'd be under a thousand total?" Kye asked.

"Seven hundred fifty thousand," Reese clarified. "We do not know how much of that she's runnin' with. She has to keep movin', and in order to do that, she's payin' cash for everything, includin' a couple of cars she's had." He glanced from face to face. "If the Mustang she was drivin' is anything to go by, she's not bein' frugal in her selection, either."

"Nor is she buyin' from dealerships. Cash transactions only," Baz elaborated. "I was able to track down the previous owner of the '65 Mustang. Bill Warren, address in Homer Glen, Illinois. I spoke to him briefly, and he confirmed he sold Juliet the vehicle, only she was going by the name Joan Anderson. Said she was pleasant but twitchy."

Trace spoke up. "From the profile I had done on her, Juliet's not lookin' to go lean. She feels she deserves the finer things in life, and in her mind, Travis had no right to take that away from her. Doesn't mean she's not bein' smart." Trace motioned toward the screen. "We can see she's stayin' in cheap motels, but it's not to keep costs down, more so to stay off the grid."

Brantley agreed with that assessment. "He's right. She's stayin' in those motels to avoid scrutiny on an identity. If she doesn't have one already, I figure she'll be lookin' for a fake one soon enough, but only the best'll do. Until then, she'll stay where they'll take cash with no questions."

"And we know she's still spendin' money because she bailed on all her personal items at the last motel," JJ noted. "Her stash included high-end beauty products, new clothes. She's shoppin' and not at Walmart. But she is keepin' her computer with her. I found a charger still connected to the wall, but the laptop was MIA."

"Did they find any cash?" Hunter asked.

"Not anything significant. About two grand in an envelope under the mattress," Reese relayed. "So that means she's keepin' it hidden or she's burned through it already. It has been eight months since she took the money."

Trey spoke up when the conversation lulled. "I have a question."

All eyes shifted to him.

"Any chance we can lure her out?"

Brantley liked his brother's line of thinking. "How?"

Trey shrugged a shoulder. "I haven't thought that far ahead."

"What if we leveraged the daughter?" Luca questioned.

"Doubt it'd help," Reese answered. "From what we can tell, she's made no attempt to see her daughter."

"I've confirmed that with Nicholas Prince," JJ said. "I called him the day after…" She cleared her throat. "After the festival. I wanted to see if he'd heard from her. He was firm in sayin' he has not spoken to her. And accordin' to him, he doesn't expect to. I got him to open up a little about their former relationship and her relationship with the kid. It sounds to me like Juliet never had an interest in bein' a mom. Her reason behind wantin' to keep her daughter after the divorce had been for financial gain."

"That could be what he wants you to think," Trace said. "Makes him look like a stand-up guy since he filed for sole custody and was granted it."

"Could be," JJ agreed. "But I don't think so. He sounded sincere. When I explained what she'd done—bombin' my house and runnin' down Kylie—he was horrified but not surprised. He said Juliet's always been unstable."

"Why wouldn't he open up before now?" RT asked, his gaze swinging from JJ to Brantley.

"He's been out of the country for a while," Brantley told him. "We've made numerous attempts but he was initially hidin' behind his lawyer."

"He thought someone was gonna come after him for damages," JJ mentioned. "He told me himself. Plus, he's scared of her."

"He said that?" Brantley asked, surprised.

"Not in so many words, but I could tell. Evidently, Juliet's been siccing people on him. Her hatred runs deep and it runs hot, and from the sound of it, she's spreadin' it around to anyone who's wronged her in the past."

Brantley knew that to be true. Juliet Prince had graduated from sending nasty messages to kidnapping, and now to murder. The woman had unraveled, and if they didn't find her soon, there was no telling what she might do next.

"Well, I think we should start scoutin' the homeless shelters in the area. Churches, too," RT said. "Anywhere she might find refuge, even if for only one night. She can't stay completely hidden."

"Don't bet on that," Luca said. "This ain't the big city. There's a number of abandoned houses and buildings in the area. If she's determined, she could hide for quite some time."

"Maybe," Brantley acknowledged. "But I think RT's right. Juliet's not gonna stay hidden because she's got an ax to grind. I don't think she set out to kill Kylie that day. I think it was a spur-of-the-moment decision to run her down. She's been on the run and her need for revenge against Travis didn't fade away. I think it's safe to say she's harborin' more. Which means she's not stayin' in the area because she can't get out."

"She's stayin' 'cause she's not done," Reese finished for him.

"Exactly."

AFTER THEIR BRAINSTORMING SESSION, REESE CONTINUED TO review the information they'd compiled, wishing something would jump out at him. Anything to help them find where Juliet was currently hiding. They'd dug up some useful details, but he wasn't seeing anything that led to a pattern of behavior. From what he could tell, Juliet was winging it. And he fully agreed with Brantley. Reese did not believe Juliet had set out to kill Kylie, but when the opportunity to cause harm presented itself, she acted on her rage and the result was deadly.

"Any update on Travis?" Baz asked, drawing Reese's attention.

Reese leaned into the desk behind him, where he'd been staring at the map on the television screen while waiting for Brantley to return from a quick conversation with Hunter and RT.

Everyone had been asking about Travis and Gage, checking to see how they were doing several times a day. Like most of those who knew them, they were worried. Reese included.

"I've talked to Curtis," Reese answered. "He's processin'. They all are."

"They need anything? Help at the resort?"

"Sawyer and Kaleb have agreed to manage it for the time bein'." Reese crossed his arms over his chest.

"What about Walker Demo?"

"Autumn's back at the helm, plus their cousin Jaxson is helpin' out. They promised to reach out if they need help."

"Well, let 'em know I'll do whatever I can. Whatever they need."

Reese nodded. "I'm sure they'll appreciate the gesture." He motioned toward the map on the screen. "The best way we can help any of them is to find Juliet," he said, keeping his voice low. "No matter what it takes."

They both turned when Trey approached, the other man's gaze swinging back and forth between them as though gauging whether it was appropriate to interrupt.

"What's up?" Reese prompted.

"I've got an idea. Thought I'd run it by you."

Reese raised an eyebrow, urging Trey to spit it out.

"I know it might be a stretch, but Tesha's trainer … he runs a search-and-rescue operation, doesn't he?"

Reese found it interesting that Trey didn't refer to Magnus by name, but he answered anyway. "Yeah. Why?"

"Well, we've got some of Juliet's belongings, which means we've got a decent scent. If we can get a bead on where she might be…"

Reese knew where Trey was going with this. Yes, Baz had called in a favor, and they'd gotten their hands on a couple of her personal effects, but he wasn't sure they were at the point where search dogs would do them any good. Not yet, anyway. Didn't meant it wouldn't come in handy in the future.

Definitely wouldn't hurt to get Magnus on board, and since they were currently at a standstill, it'd give Trey something to do, as well.

"I like the idea," he told him. "Why don't you take point on that? Head over to Magnus's place. Get his thoughts on what our options might be. If we can narrow down a search grid, it'd definitely be worth a shot."

Trey's gaze shot to Baz then back to Reese. "I wasn't suggestin' I be the one—"

Reese had no idea what had happened between the two men, nor was he going to ask, but he knew they had to work it out eventually. Maybe this would move things along.

"I'll get you his address," he said, not giving Trey a chance to back out.

Chapter Ten

TREY COULD'VE KICKED HIMSELF IN HIS OWN ass.

What the hell was he thinking suggesting they utilize Magnus's skills to assist in their investigation?

"Damn it," he grumbled, steering his truck along the long, narrow dirt drive that led to Camp K-9, the facility owned and operated by the one man Trey had no business talking to right now.

In his defense, it had been an innocent request, one he'd thought might move them forward in their search. At the very least, it was a logical ask. Magnus trained canines as search and rescue, and since they were searching…

"Idiot," he muttered.

He pulled the truck to a stop, put it in park, and stared up at the metal building with the sign announcing they were open for business.

Inside those walls was the man Trey hadn't seen since New Year's, when he'd accepted Magnus's offer of a single night together. He still remembered the moment he'd given in. Standing outside of Moonshiners, the man so close Trey could smell Magnus's cologne, see the challenge in those hazel eyes.

"*You know there's only one thing I want from you,*" *Trey told him, moving in close, keeping his voice low.*

"*Then you should take it.*"

Magnus was so fucking cocky, so sure of himself, and damn it if that didn't turn Trey on.

"*I will shred you,*" *Trey promised. "It's inevitable.*"

"*Maybe. Or maybe I'll shred you.*"

Unfortunately, Trey knew that was the more logical outcome, because he tended to get in over his head where men were concerned, but he was doing his best to warn Magnus off. It would save them both a hell of a lot of time and save Trey another round of heartache.

"*Only one thing, Magnus,*" *he repeated*

"*I'm not expectin' roses and wine here, cowboy." Magnus leaned in, voice low and gruff. "I'm expectin' you to* fuck. Me.*"

Even now, the memory of that moment when Magnus had all but given himself to Trey made his dick hard. Never mind the beyond-satisfying events that had happened after that.

Despite tremendous effort, Trey's thoughts drifted to that night when he'd gone and done something completely out of character for him. And it'd taken place only fifteen minutes after he'd told Magnus to follow him back to his place, a few minutes after he'd tried to talk himself out of it and failed miserably. He remembered walking into his house…

Trey could hear Magnus's SUV pulling into the short driveway, knew the man would be walking in any minute. He could easily shut the door, lock it, ignore him. Not like Magnus could do a damn thing about it.

But he wouldn't because he was selfish like that, and this man … Magnus had already pushed him to the point of no return. Trey couldn't remember a time he'd been turned on like this. With a heat that bordered on violence, a need that was all-consuming.

A soft rap on the door had him turning around, seeing the sexy man standing in his open doorway.

He wasn't sure what it was about Magnus, but just looking at him made Trey want to sin.

"*Shut the door,*" *he instructed.*

Magnus stepped inside the house, shut the door behind him.

Trey didn't let him take a single step beyond that. He was on him, slamming him into the door, their lips crashing together. He devoured him even as he yanked at his clothes, tugging his shirt up and over his head, tossing it to the floor. When Magnus tried to do the same, Trey gripped his wrists, held firm.

"No promises," Trey told him. "No strings."

"None," Magnus agreed, hazel eyes glittering with heat.

Trey believed Magnus meant it. Then again, he meant it, too. No way was Trey opening himself up to anyone else. He'd had enough of that in his life. He'd never been the sort to fuck for the sake of it, but that was going to change. He didn't have a long line of men he'd burned or a stockpile he kept for a later date. He tended to go all in.

Until now.

"Fuck me, Trey," Magnus moaned against his mouth. "I know you want to."

"I'll get there," he assured him. "In time."

Gripping Magnus's face, Trey owned the kiss, slowing things significantly but not cooling them off in the least.

The heat he'd felt back at the bar ... it'd morphed into a conflagration that burned hotter, brighter with every swipe of that eager tongue. Made him want to do dirty, raunchy things to this man again and again. He wanted to know what sounds Magnus made when he had Trey's cock lodged in his throat, how deep his groans were when he came.

Eager hands tugged at his jeans while Trey's hands roamed over the smooth, sleek skin of Magnus's back. Desperate to maintain control, Trey gripped Magnus's wandering hands, stilling them for a moment as he pulled his lips free and stared down at him.

"If I didn't know better, I'd think you were in a hurry," he said, letting his eyes graze Magnus's deliciously muscled form. His chest was broad, with just the right amount of dark hair, his nipples small and dark, his pecs flexing as Trey's eyes lingered. The narrow trail of fine, dark hair that bisected his abs and disappeared into his waistband beckoned to Trey, had him eager to start the exploration with his tongue.

"Trey…"

When Magnus leaned forward, reached for Trey's cock, Trey gripped his wrist again. "You're too fucking impatient."

There was something about seeing such a sexy man like that: chest heaving, muscles bunching, lips swollen from his kiss. Eager, anxious.

"I don't have time for games, Trey."

Pinning him with a hard stare, Trey smirked. "If I wanna play games, we'll play games."

Stepping forward, he brought his hands up and cupped Magnus's neck, firmly, roughly, his thumb sliding along the hard line of his jaw. Damn, but the man was hot.

"Unbutton my shirt," he whispered, curious as to whether Magnus would comply since Trey had stopped him once already.

He didn't. Not immediately, anyway. But when Trey tilted his head to the side, then leaned in and fused their lips once more, he drew in a raspy breath when Magnus's fingers began deftly freeing the small discs. By the time cool air caressed his overheated skin, the kiss had ramped up a few degrees. He hated to do it, but he released Magnus's face so he could shrug out of his shirt, letting it fall to the floor, forgotten.

With Magnus still backed against the wall, Trey leaned into him, rested his forehead to Magnus's, hissing in a sharp breath when those hands made contact, sliding over his shoulders, down his back. When those wandering hands returned to his chest, Trey focused on breathing while he covered Magnus's hands with his own, holding them tightly against him, gliding them higher, lower, over and over. He groaned low in his throat, desperate for his touch.

How the fuck had he gotten here? He had no business taking what this man was offering. Perhaps Magnus wasn't a kid at twenty-four, but he was still far too young for Trey. Twelve years younger, in fact, which should've meant he was off-limits.

But there was something about him. Something Trey couldn't quite pinpoint. Perhaps it was because it was wrong on so many levels, and at this very moment, wrong felt so fucking right.

"You think too much," Magnus whispered, his hand sliding up behind his neck again, kneading the tense muscles.

"You're right. I do." Trey gripped his hips, pulled him closer. "That stops now."

Then he was leading the way, urging Magnus backward, through the sparsely furnished living room, down the long, narrow hall. He turned to the left, into the darkened guest room, then over to the queen-sized bed. Not that he was opposed to taking a man in his own bed, but Trey had stopped sleeping in there as of late. It reminded him too much of the past, of the mistakes he'd made, of the men who had hurt him.

He followed Magnus down, careful not to crush him but maintaining the kiss.

As he covered Magnus's body fully, Trey dropped his hips, grinding his aching cock against the hard ridge tenting those damn jeans Magnus still wore. His breath lodged in his throat when Magnus moaned, a sinfully rough rasp against his senses.

"Once won't be enough," he warned, his lips never leaving Magnus's.

There was a soft chuckle, followed by an amused, "Maybe. Maybe not."

"Is that a dare?" he taunted, lifting his head and meeting those intense hazel eyes. "Because I'm game if you are."

The smile he earned was unexpected.

And most definitely a dare.

A knock on his window drew Trey out of the memory, brought him back to the present. That was when he realized Magnus was standing outside the truck, watching him intently with a satisfied smirk on his face.

No way could Magnus know what Trey had been thinking.

No fucking way.

Because he couldn't very well drive off and pretend he hadn't shown up at his damn doorstep, Trey opened the door, got out of the truck. It was slow going as he attempted to hide the hard-on he was sporting. His shirt was untucked, which helped. Not that it was doing a damn bit of good if the gleam in Magnus's eyes was anything to go by

"Shut up," Trey grumbled irritably.

Magnus chuckled softly. "I didn't say nothin'."

"You were thinkin' it."

"Oh, I was thinkin' somethin', all right."

Trey's gaze shot back to Magnus, and he wondered briefly if Magnus had relived that night, too. Based on the heat he saw in those hazel eyes, he figured the answer was yes.

Question was: had he relived it every fucking day the way Trey had?

WHEN MAGNUS REALIZED WHO WAS BEHIND THE wheel of the truck that had pulled down his driveway, he wouldn't say he'd been disappointed.

In fact, the opposite.

As for why Trey Walker was gracing him with his presence, he had yet to find out, but based on the frown on Trey's handsome face, the man wasn't happy to be there. Which meant he hadn't stopped by for a repeat of the night they'd spent together two weeks ago.

Not that Magnus thought he had. Sure, he'd wished the man would make a move, but Magnus was fully aware of the tragedy that had rocked the Coyote Ridge community as well as the Walker family. It was the main reason he hadn't reached out to Trey, sought a repeat of that incredible night.

"What brings you by?" he finally asked, motioning for Trey to come inside.

"Business."

Of course it was. "Reese send you?"

"I wouldn't be here if he hadn't," Trey grumbled.

Magnus found it impossible not to smile. He happened to find Trey's ornery side rather appealing. And the banter they shared between them was a unique form of foreplay that, honestly, Magnus wished he had more of in his life.

Opening the door to the building, Magnus led the way inside. He partly expected Trey to stay outside, to refuse to be in a confined space with him. It sure as hell wouldn't have surprised him if he had.

But he was happy to see Trey had stepped inside, let the door close behind him.

"What can I help you with?" Magnus turned around to see Trey's tense form near the door, his eyes fixed on the dogs currently watching him with curiosity. "They won't hurt you, I promise."

"I wasn't worried about that," he muttered.

"Sarge, Aurora, meet Trey. These two belong to me." Magnus looked at the black Labrador retrievers currently relaxing as they'd been instructed to do. "Heel."

Instantly both were on their feet. A second later, they were heeling at Magnus's feet, one on each side. He took one step forward. They did, too, remaining right at his side, eagerly watching him for another command, just as they'd been trained.

"Did you have a reason for bein' here?" he asked Trey. "Or did you come to ogle me and my dogs?"

That doom-and-gloom look was back on Trey's face as he glowered.

"You've heard about what's goin' on?"

Magnus sobered. "I did, yes. I'm sorry for your loss."

Trey's gaze cut to the floor as he nodded. "Thanks."

"I take it your team's lookin' for the woman responsible? The one who kidnapped the little girl and murdered that girl's mother."

Trey nodded, eyes lifting. "We've got an active team tryin' to determine where she is. We know she's in the area, just don't have an exact location."

"By *in the area*, you mean what? Central Texas? Coyote Ridge? Taylor? Embers Ridge? What?"

Trey's expression remained neutral when he said, "Yes."

Magnus chuckled. "Not exactly helpful. And unfortunately, unless I have a vicinity in which to work, I can't be of much help." He canted his head. "I assume that's why you're here? My services?"

He watched as heat flashed in Trey's eyes, and Magnus fought back a grin. Yeah, it was safe to say Trey hadn't forgotten that night they'd shared.

"Yeah. Your ... uh"—Trey cleared his throat, motioned toward the long counter with the Camp K-9 sign behind it— "services. I..." More throat clearing. "*We* thought you might be able to... I just ... I wanted to ask."

Magnus opted for serious for a moment. "If you're askin' whether or not I'll help with the search when and if it comes to that, absolutely. I'm there in a second, just say the word. I've got enough dogs and handlers, we can work a decent-size area. I just prefer to know we're in the right spot before we go that route."

"Understood."

Magnus watched Trey. He could see the uncertainty in the man's eyes. He suspected it didn't have much to do with his case and more to do with being near Magnus.

What they'd shared that night ... it'd been by far the best sex of Magnus's entire life. It had surprised him, actually, being that he'd had some pretty phenomenal sex with no shortage of partners.

But it was more than that. There was something about Trey that he connected with. A similar vulnerability, maybe. Whatever it was, Magnus had thought about it numerous times over the past couple of weeks, ever since that one fantastic night.

Realizing he was about to venture down a road he'd promised Trey he wouldn't, Magnus reined in his thoughts. "What else can I help you with, Trey?"

Those steel-blue eyes pierced him, and for a brief second, he saw the same heat he'd seen on New Year's.

Yeah, it was safe to say Trey was thinking about that night, too.

"Just say the word," he teased. "That's all you've got to do."

Trey frowned as though he didn't understand. Magnus knew better, so he kept his mouth shut.

"I'll … uh … let Reese know you're willin'," Trey said, clearing his throat and turning toward the door.

Magnus chuckled at the double entendre he knew Trey hadn't intended.

And then he was staring at the man as he walked out the door.

Peering down at Aurora and Sarge, Magnus grinned. "That's not the last we'll see of him, I promise."

Chapter Eleven

Monday, January 18, 2021

ON MONDAY MORNING, JUST FOUR DAYS AFTER Kylie's funeral, Travis woke up with a new determination.

He'd spent the weekend with Gage and the kids, a dark cloud hanging over them all as they went through the motions just to get through the day. His mother and father had stopped by on Saturday morning, then later, Sawyer and Kennedy brought Matthew and Brody by. The kids had enjoyed the visits because it gave them the distraction they needed, but Travis found himself growing irritable with the attention.

Because his mood hadn't improved by Sunday, he'd skipped the weekly dinner at his folks' place. Gage had insisted on going, and Travis saw no reason for them not to. It was while they were gone that an idea had come to him.

"Hey, Trav. Didn't think we'd see you here for a while," Kaleb said, his eyebrows dipped down in concern.

Travis gave his brother a single shoulder shrug. Kaleb and Sawyer had informed him they would gladly handle the management of Alluring Indulgence Resort until the time Travis felt he could return. Although he had graciously accepted their offer, Travis had known he wouldn't be able to stay away. Not because he preferred to be taking care of the resort rather than his family, but because Travis knew he would need something to do. He was here because he wanted to be here. As far as he was concerned, there was no reason to ignore his responsibilities. It wasn't like it would change the outcome of anything if he did.

He got similar comments from others on his trek to his office, and he offered the same response: nothing. He had more important things to deal with than making others feel better because they weren't sure how to deal with him.

Once in his office, he closed the door. Figured there was no reason to invite more sympathetic looks from those who meant well.

No sooner did his ass meet his chair than he picked up his phone and dialed.

"Mornin'," came a gruff, uncertain response.

"I want to offer a reward for any information leadin' to the capture of Juliet Prince," he said, rocking back in his executive chair and staring at the door.

"Well…"

"Brantley, I'm not askin' for permission. I want it done. I figured I'd give you an opportunity to head it up since you claim you're handlin' the investigation. But if it's too much for you…"

His cousin sighed. "Where are you?"

"At the resort."

"Okay. Give me half an hour. Reese and I'll stop by to chat. And before you get all up in arms, I think a reward's a good idea. I just want to talk it out. Is Gage there with you?"

"No."

"Should he be?" Brantley asked.

Travis wasn't sure it was his place to decide that. And since Gage seemed to be content keeping his distance, he figured he could return the favor. "No."

Another sigh. "All right. Half an hour."

"See you then."

After disconnecting, Travis found himself typing up a text to Gage. He kept it short and sweet: *Meeting with Brantley and Reese. Offering reward. If you want to be part of the convo, meet in my office, half an hour.*

Travis never did get a response.

As promised, Brantley arrived thirty minutes later with Reese in tow. They took their sweet time getting up to his office, probably stopping to chat with his brothers along the way. He half expected to see a line of people behind them when they finally knocked on his door, but there were no stragglers.

And there was no Gage.

"Come in." Travis leaned back, trying to appear relaxed and not letting on that his stomach was twisted in knots. He'd thought coming to work would allow him to stop thinking about Kylie for a little while. That didn't seem to be the case.

Both men walked in, their eyes scanning the room as though they were expecting someone else.

"Have a seat," he said politely, although he didn't expect them to be there long.

They sat, neither of them saying anything.

Travis wasn't sure why they'd gone mute, but he didn't really need their input, and he certainly didn't need small talk.

"Like I told you on the phone, I want to offer a reward for any information that leads to the capture and arrest of Juliet Prince in relation to my wife's murder."

He probably shouldn't have tacked on the last part so harshly, but it was all he could do to spit the words out.

"I know I mentioned to you that the governor discussed disbandin' the task force," Brantley said. "I just want to make sure you understood that happened. We no longer have jurisdiction over anything. In fact, we've gone private. The task force is under the umbrella of Sniper 1 Security."

Travis wasn't sure what that had to do with anything, but he nodded.

"We've got a large team of their agents down here assistin' with the search. Includin' RT and Hunter."

For some damn reason, that loosened the knot in his chest.

Yes, Travis had been holed up in his house, and his warped and twisted thoughts had led him to think that no one was out there doing anything to find the bitch. Despite the fact he'd blamed them more than once—at least in his head—he should've known Brantley and Reese wouldn't stop looking.

"We are pursuin' several leads. I just want you to understand, we're actively workin' this. In fact, it's the *only* thing we're workin' on."

Travis swallowed a hot ball of emotion and nodded.

Brantley glanced at Reese, then back to Travis. Silence hung between them as though Brantley thought Travis might have something to say. If he thought he could get words out, perhaps he would, but it was taking everything in him to sit there.

Brantley nodded. "You mentioned a reward. How much are you thinkin'?"

Travis reached for his water, took a drink. "Whatever's appropriate. Money's no object."

Brantley and Reese shared a look and then Reese spoke up. "We need to make you aware of what'll happen once that reward is posted. Once it's made public, we'll be inundated with leads. Unfortunately, the majority of them will be bogus. And while it only takes one actual lead to get the result we're lookin' for, it'll require additional resources to handle the influx. That means those who're currently in the field will be called back in to answer the phones."

"I'll have the calls come here," he offered.

Brantley shook his head. "Not a good idea. Then we're dealin' with secondhand information. If you want to do this, I'd rather we take the calls directly." He sat up, leaned forward, his eyes hard. "I just need you to know that we will stop at nothin' to find her, so whatever you think'll help make that happen, we'll gladly adjust our strategy."

Travis considered it, then said, "Five hundred thousand dollars."

Brantley exhaled heavily. "I know you said money's no object and there's no amount you won't pay. We get that. Really. But I suggest we start out with fifty or a hundred. Something reasonable. Like I said, we'll be inundated with bullshit that we have to sift through. The more you offer, the more crazy you invite."

"One hundred, then."

Brantley nodded. "Okay. Now the next issue we need to deal with is the press is gonna want a statement. I talked to RT before we came over here, and he suggested we have Sniper 1 represent you and your family. They'll take the lead. They'll make the public announcement regardin' the reward and they'll field any questions."

Travis immediately shook his head. "I should be the one. That way Juliet sees that I'm not takin' this sittin' down."

"Actually, we were hopin' to do the opposite." Reese's stare was intense. "We believe Juliet has remained in the area because she's not finished with you yet. Based on the profile that was done, it's believed she has developed an obsession with you. By givin' her access to you on live television, it'll play into what she needs."

"I don't see a problem with that," he told Reese.

"If we can keep you out of reach, unavailable to her, we're hopin' it'll draw her out. At this point, that's our best option."

"Before you ask," Brantley added quickly, "we've got agents placed throughout Coyote Ridge. They're keepin' a close eye on your parents, your brothers, their SOs, kids. We've even got a pair stayin' across the street from you. Like I said, RT pulled out all the stops for this." His voice lowered and Travis heard the pain in it when he added, "She won't get another opportunity to hurt anyone else."

He could tell they expected him to say that she never should've had the chance in the first place. Yes, it was the first thing he thought about every fucking day. And while he had laid the blame right at their feet during the first couple of days, Travis knew it was not their fault. Brantley and Reese had saved his daughter; they'd done something no one else was able to do at the time. He would not allow his anger and his hatred to get the best of him. They didn't deserve to be accused of something they had no control over. And ultimately, placing blame wouldn't make Travis feel better.

"We'll do things your way," he conceded. "Under one condition."

Based on Brantley's expression, he'd been expecting a stipulation.

"When you get the lead that zeroes in on her … I'll be right there with you when you go after her."

Neither of them said anything.

"Otherwise, I'll do this on my own."

And he didn't have to tell them what that meant, because as far as Travis was concerned, Juliet Prince was as good as dead already.

BRANTLEY HAD KNOWN FROM THE MOMENT TRAVIS said he wanted to offer a reward that he was inserting himself back into the investigation.

Granted, he'd always expected Travis would be there for the takedown. Problem was, Brantley remembered Travis's comment about needing an alibi. His cousin hadn't been bluffing. Not the day JJ's house blew up and not today. They could either include him when it came to it or he would go rogue. And anyone who knew Travis understood the repercussions of letting the man go off on his own.

Brantley needed to ensure that didn't happen.

"Once we have valid intel that leads us to her, you'll be the first to know," he promised, getting to his feet.

"You need to talk to Gage," Reese said as he slowly stood. "Don't leave him out of this, Travis. He deserves to be included."

Brantley was surprised by Reese's statement. More so by Travis's reaction. At one point in his life, Travis would've told Reese to mind his own business, probably with a couple of f-bombs in there for good measure. Would've told anyone that, in fact. Instead, Travis was staring at Reese as though the advice was warranted.

"We'll keep you in the loop," Brantley said, nodding for Reese to lead the way.

They headed back through the resort and out to the parking lot. It had started to rain, just a light drizzle for the moment, and it seemed to fit the mood. As though the gloomy weather had found the spot over the resort and settled in. It was still hard to grasp the fact that Kylie was dead, that the Walkers had lost someone so special to them.

Because his career had kept him away from Coyote Ridge for so long, Brantley wasn't particularly close to most of his cousins. Sure, he'd interacted during family functions when he was able to get home for them. But in the past few years, many of his cousins had settled down, gotten married, had kids, and Brantley hadn't been around. Even in the six months since he'd been back, he hadn't spent much time with most of them.

The same could not be said for those who'd remained in Coyote Ridge. His mother and father, brothers and sisters… they were all close to the rest of the family. They spent time with each other, at family gatherings, in town, at church, and whatnot. They'd all had a personal connection with Kylie, and he knew it was as much for them that he was determined to find Kylie's killer as it was for Travis.

But that didn't mean Brantley wasn't aware of what was going on. Nor did it mean he hadn't developed friendships since. He'd spoken to Kylie a few times at Curtis and Lorrie's. She was kind and funny, with a positive outlook that had been refreshing. Her loss was felt by all.

"You're worried about him."

Brantley glanced at Reese as he climbed in the truck. "I am, sure. I think everyone is."

"He's strong."

Yeah, Brantley knew that, too. Didn't mean the man could go it alone. "You think we should give Gage a heads up?"

Reese shook his head. "We have to trust Travis to do that."

Fair point.

Three hours later, Brantley was standing shoulder to shoulder with Reese, alongside Baz, JJ, Charlie, and Trey. They had invited Luca and Holly to join them, but Luca had insisted on being available to take calls once they started coming in, and his sister had wanted to help out.

The task force was joined by other members of the Sniper 1 Security team, as well as Mayor Bianca Stewart and Sheriff Jeff Endsley, all backing RT, who was standing behind a microphone in front of a handful of reporters.

When Brantley had first mentioned Travis's desire to offer a reward for Juliet Prince, he'd had his concerns. Even now he knew it was a risk, but in all fairness, it was the best option they had for finding the woman. There were only so many of them, but a reward would increase their numbers tenfold by bringing the public into the investigation.

After a lengthy discussion, RT and the team had agreed it was the best avenue to pursue, so he'd gotten some people in place to man the hotline that was being set up and started the process of gathering the press.

Brantley was grateful RT had agreed to speak. The man had a way of articulating that brought people together, had them rallying for the common goal. He listened as RT outlined the events that had taken place, the tragedy that had impacted the Walker family and the community as a whole. He spoke of the kidnapping of Kate Walker, then outlined the devastating loss of Kylie.

While he spoke, Brantley watched the cameramen, the media correspondents, and the few onlookers who'd gathered. He had to wonder if Juliet was watching this live, if she was stalking the town the way she had been for months. He hoped so. Brantley wanted her to see they were stopping at nothing to find her. And he wanted her to see that Travis wasn't giving her the time of day.

"With that said," RT continued, "the Walker family is offering a one-hundred-thousand-dollar reward for information that directly leads to the arrest of Juliet Prince."

That announcement set the press in motion. Questions were lobbed at RT, who handled them brilliantly. He seemed to have an appropriate response prepared and Brantley admired him for it. The guy was definitely good at what he did.

Now it was time for Brantley's team to prove they were good at what they did, too.

JULIET GLARED AT THE TELEVISION SCREEN.

At all of them, in fact, since she was currently standing in the electronics section of a Walmart watching what was evidently the biggest news story in five counties.

With her sunglasses and ball cap on, no one was going to recognize her, even if there'd been more than three people in the store at the moment. This small hick town didn't have many people to begin with, and at one o'clock on a Monday afternoon, they apparently had better things to do.

One hundred thousand dollars.

She snorted, taking her cart and pushing it toward the beauty department. She'd come into this godforsaken store to pick up a few extra pairs of clothes, although she felt sick at the idea of having to wear such crap. She'd been stupid to leave the clothes behind at the motel. She'd spent good money on that stuff and hadn't been able to wear half of it. Now she was stuck in this shithole of a town, and the Walmart was the only store they had, so she had to make do. Temporarily, of course.

Now that she'd scrounged a few pieces that were relatively decent, she needed something that'd help alter her appearance a little more.

The thought of putting cheap hair dye on her hair had her stomach cramping, but Juliet knew the days of salon highlights and coloring were out. At least until she figured out a way to start over, to change her identity for good. One day, she would get back to the glam life, of that she was certain. She had even started her list of potential husbands. There were several she knew who had bank accounts worthy of her. It was just a matter of getting through this debacle and reinventing herself. At that point, she could marry money one more time and live happily ever after.

As she skimmed the rows of boxed hair color, she couldn't help but wonder where Travis Walker was. He hadn't been part of the group backing the guy who'd stepped up to the microphone and made the big announcement. Juliet had expected Travis to be the speaker, but at the very least, she thought he would be standing in the background.

No. It looked as though Travis Walker couldn't be bothered to show up.

So where was he? At home, cuddled up to his husband, maybe? Juliet wouldn't doubt it. The guy was disgusting. A wife *and* a husband? Who did that? Was he too good to settle down with just one person so he grabbed one of each?

It sickened her to think about. Maybe Travis Walker had already moved on. Maybe the reward was his family's way of avenging the woman's death.

Now that she thought about it, most of what she'd ever read was about Travis and the husband. Rarely was the wife even mentioned. Could be he hadn't wanted the wife in the first place.

Had she done him a favor by offing that bitch?

Juliet felt her face heat with her anger. Had she killed the wrong person? Was that woman of so little importance to Travis that he couldn't be bothered to offer a reward himself?

She grabbed a box of red hair color, threw it in the cart, and stomped toward the register.

If Travis Walker couldn't be bothered for Kylie, then Juliet would find someone else to eliminate. Someone whose death would bring that asshole to his knees once and for all.

But first, she would have to find a place to go for a little while. Somewhere to hide until the heat died down. The reward would have people actively looking at her. It raised the chances of her being caught.

As much as it pained her, she knew she would have to leave the area for a little bit. Not too far though. Juliet liked knowing Travis Walker was close.

Mexico wasn't ideal but it would take little effort to get there. Only a few hours from here.

Then again, crossing the border on her own would likely result in her being caught. She would have to get creative, which meant a little more time.

Nope. Not Mexico. Not yet.

A touristy spot might work. Somewhere along the coast. South Padre? It was close to Mexico. That way, if it came down to it, maybe she could make a run for it.

As she scanned her items through the self-checkout lane, Juliet came up with a new plan.

Chapter Twelve

Three weeks later
Thursday, February 11, 2021

REESE HAD KNOWN THAT OFFERING A REWARD to the public would result in an overabundance of crap sightings of Juliet Prince.

What he hadn't expected was to have spent the past three weeks chasing one lead after another only to come up with absolutely nothing. Every single time they had what sounded like a legit sighting, they investigated. And so far, they'd done nothing more than harass innocent people.

The calls had died down significantly in the past couple of days. They'd been prepared for that, too, realizing there would be a heightened sense of awareness in the beginning, when the story was hot, but eventually the buzz would wear off. With each passing day, people were forgetting about the reward, moving on with their lives. Eventually they would stop looking for the woman whose picture had been flashed on the television and social media for several days, asking for any information leading to her whereabouts.

If he was being honest, it pissed him off.

Now as he stood in the shower, his head down, the heat of the water beating over his tired muscles, Reese tried to relax. He needed to regroup, to come up with a new plan. Juliet Prince was out there. It was just a matter of pinpointing where. No one could hide forever, regardless of how determined they were.

He must've been so lost in his own head that he hadn't heard Brantley come into the bathroom, because it wasn't until he felt the man press up against his back that he even realized he had company.

"You've been in here a long time," Brantley said, his arms banding around him, palms flattening on his chest and pulling him back.

Reese leaned into the hard body, letting Brantley keep him upright.

"You're thinkin' too much." Brantley's voice was low, guttural. "I can help with that."

"Can you?"

The hands pressed to his chest slid lower, gliding over his stomach, down, down.

Reese groaned softly when Brantley teased and tormented before finally fisting his cock. His touch was featherlight but more than enough to awaken every nerve ending in Reese's body.

Tilting his head to the side, he gave Brantley access to his neck as warm lips caressed his skin.

He let himself be touched, enjoyed the attention, admired the confidence he felt in Brantley's movements. The man could bring him pleasure unlike anything he'd ever known. He found it interesting how the rest of the world could fade away, even if only for the briefest of moments. Nothing else existed except for the two of them. Right here. Right now.

Reese turned in Brantley's arms, needing to solidify the connection. He palmed Brantley's head, pulled him closer until their lips fused. Leaning into the tiled wall, he let that kiss take him to new heights, enjoying the way Brantley explored his mouth. Always seeking, always searching, as though there was something new to find.

Reese's hands wandered, gliding over slick skin. He was content just like this, although his body was prepping for more, his cock throbbing incessantly, the need for release igniting.

Brantley never pushed, his hand continuing to stroke Reese's cock. Up, down. Slow, steady. It was enough for Reese's heart to beat harder, faster, his breaths rasping in and out of his lungs.

Then the kiss broke and Brantley's forehead rested against his, but his exquisite touch never disappeared.

"Come for me," Brantley whispered as they both watched what Brantley was doing to him.

Reese groaned, his fingertips digging into Brantley's hip as he held on, fought the insurmountable pleasure for as long as he could until…

"Fuck," he groaned low in his throat, knees turning to jelly as his release barreled through him.

And then Brantley's lips were back, his tongue leisurely sliding into his mouth as he came down from that incredible high.

"I love you," Reese whispered, needing Brantley to hear the words, to know he meant them.

Brantley pulled back, their eyes met, and what he saw sated Reese on a different level.

"I love you, too," Brantley whispered. "More and more every single day."

Those words … they were his anchor, even when he didn't realize he needed one.

NOT WANTING TO GO HOME TO AN empty house, Trey decided to go to Moonshiners. It wasn't that he necessarily cared for a beer, but it seemed a better option than going to the diner alone. It sucked to eat dinner by himself, whether at a restaurant or at home.

He'd spent the better part of the day with the task force, listening as they berated themselves for not being able to find one woman despite all the information they'd received in the past few weeks. He felt their frustration, mirrored it even, but for the life of him, Trey didn't know how to fix this. He didn't know how to get them what they needed so they could end this once and for all.

Then Brantley had suggested everyone go home and sleep on it. To get some rest so they could come back tomorrow with renewed purpose.

Trey knew sleep wasn't going to happen because it had eluded him for weeks now. He was running on adrenaline and fucking hope, neither of which was sustaining him.

So this was the only option.

When he walked in, he saw Mack was behind the bar, and the familiar face relaxed something inside him. It seemed Mack was working less and less these days, shifting responsibilities to Rafe Sharpe. Sure, Trey liked Rafe, but he wasn't the man they'd come to expect to be there, the one who would listen to their bitches and moans because that was his role as the small town's bartender.

"How's it goin'?" Mack greeted, his eyes both friendly and concerned.

Being that Mack was married to the sheriff, Trey figured he was up to speed on the case.

"Slow," he said truthfully.

"Beer?"

He nodded as he took a seat, gave the room a cursory glance.

There weren't many people in tonight, just a couple of old-timers sitting around shooting the shit, a guy and a girl back at the pool tables laughing and making eyes at one another.

Okay, so it turned out this wasn't much better than sitting alone at a table for dinner. For whatever reason, he'd thought there would be a few more people than this out tonight. What with Valentine's Day coming up and all, surely he wasn't the only sad, lonely soul seeking a little bit of company.

"Thanks," he said when Mack passed over his beer.

Before Trey could strike up a conversation with the bartender, the door opened.

He looked up as he took a sip, and instantly the brew went down a little harder.

There, strolling in and cutting a path right to the bar, was Magnus Storme. He greeted Mack with a smile and a nod, then motioned toward the end of the bar where Trey was seated.

Surely he wasn't—

Yes. Yes, he was coming to sit down right next to Trey.

"Hey."

Trey took another drink, not bothering to offer any pleasantries.

The smirk that formed on Magnus's too-handsome face said he was amused by Trey's obstinance.

"Why're you here?" Trey finally blurted after the silence began suffocating him.

Magnus glanced at him sideways. "Didn't realize it was an invitation-only place."

"Are you stalkin' me now?"

"Yes," Magnus said matter-of-factly. "Yes, Trey, that is exactly what I'm doin'. I've been hangin' outside local watering holes waitin' for you to make an appearance so I could pounce."

"You're an ass."

"I am, sure," Magnus agreed.

So fucking agreeable.

"Why're you really here?" Trey demanded.

Magnus glanced around as though checking to see who might be listening. The only other person within earshot was Mack, and he was currently typing something on his phone.

"I've decided I'd like a rematch."

Trey snorted. "Yeah? And what makes you think I'm interested?"

"Are you sayin' you're not?"

Trey wasn't prepared for that comeback, and the moment of silence was enough to give the impression that, yes, he was interested, which meant he had to lay it on thick.

"Not a chance. I told you. One night." He gave a light shrug of his shoulder. "Wasn't good enough the first go-round to warrant another."

Damn it if that didn't seem to amuse Magnus. The fucker chuckled softly.

"Keep tellin' yourself that." Magnus leaned in. "But we both know it was the best fuck either of us has ever had."

Trey took a long swallow and stared at the back wall of the bar. He was not going to comment, nor would he give away any facial expression that might confirm that statement.

As far as he was concerned, it didn't matter how fucking good that night was or how many times Trey had relived it in his dreams or used it as fuel for taking the edge off with his own fucking hand. He was not interested in a relationship, and as far as he was concerned, more than one night constituted something more.

Nope, he had every intention of remaining celibate. Even if it killed him.

Which, based on the tightness of his jeans at the moment, it very likely could.

MAGNUS COULD PRACTICALLY FEEL THE TENSION COMING off Trey, and he didn't have to be a genius to know exactly what he was thinking about.

Same thing Magnus had been thinking about for the past month and a half. Ever since that night when he'd followed Trey home from the bar, then ended up half-naked, on the bed, both of them too hot to think of anything but the next kiss, the next touch.

Honestly, that night he'd figured Trey would back out, back down before they ever got that far. He'd seen it in the man's eyes during their initial encounter when Magnus had interrupted what had appeared to be an argument between Trey and Cyrus. Something in Trey's eyes had warned him he should proceed with caution. He'd felt Trey's desire, knew he couldn't deny there was something between them, but at the same time, Trey had a desperate need to be defiant, to go against his own desires. Someone—Cyrus, maybe—had hurt him and he'd been licking his wounds, protecting himself.

Magnus had proceeded with caution, telling himself he could help. After all, he wasn't looking for anything and he certainly wasn't looking to hurt him.

Didn't mean he would love Trey or want more than a brief fling. He wasn't that man, didn't look to the future. At the same time, he didn't pretend not to want what he wanted. Magnus lived in the moment and never, *ever* took anything for granted. There was nothing to say it wouldn't be ripped right out of your hands with your next breath. He'd learned that lesson early.

But that night… He still remembered every kiss, every touch, but most often, he relived it so he could enjoy Trey's dominance one more time. And he wasn't lying when he said it'd been the best sex he'd ever had.

He took a long pull on his beer, stared at the wall as the memory flashed once again.

Magnus focused on the weight of Trey's body grinding against him in all the right places, the warmth of his skin beneath his palms.

"Christ, you taste good," Trey rumbled, his lips trailing down Magnus's jaw, his neck.

"Fuck." He palmed Trey's head, holding him close so that wicked mouth moved over him, so skillful, so determined.

Unfortunately, Trey slipped away, getting to his feet, ending the moment abruptly.

Magnus shifted on the bed, angling for more space while he watched Trey in the dim light provided from the hallway. A soft click was followed by a warm yellow glow highlighting the sexy man so that Magnus no longer had to squint to admire.

"Better," Trey said, his eyes still on Magnus.

Oh, yeah. "Definitely better," he agreed, smiling.

He watched as Trey toed off his boots, stripped off his jeans and socks, leaving him in only the ass-hugging black boxer briefs that did little to hide the thick shaft tucked beneath.

"So much better," he said on a long exhale.

One thing Magnus knew for sure, Trey might consider himself old, but his body was still in prime condition. Lean and defined with a set of rock-hard abs that made Magnus's mouth water. Every move was a perfectly choreographed shift of sleek muscle and sinew beneath smooth, taut skin.

He made sure Trey saw the heat in his gaze as he eyed every delicious inch the man revealed.

Magnus jerked his chin toward Trey's hips. "Might as well lose those, too."

Trey's eyes glittered, a smile forming as he teased him, lowering his underwear and revealing his rock-hard cock. Magnus admired the way he fisted his erection, stroking slowly, eyes never leaving Magnus's face.

Magnus didn't have to pretend to be appreciative. The man's cock was glorious. Long, thick, with a slight curve and a wide head currently glistening with pre-cum, proof he was as excited for what was about to happen as Magnus was.

Although it would've behooved him to stay where he was, to wait to see what Trey had in store for him, Magnus wasn't the sort to wait for things to come to him, not even sinfully delicious men whose eyes gleamed with passion.

Without haste, he sat up on the bed, scooted to the edge, then quickly eased to his knees on the floor in front of Trey. He heard the hitch in Trey's breath when he slowly wrapped his fingers around his shaft while he stared up at him. Opening his mouth, he stuck out his tongue, then dragged the wide, glistening head over it, earning a hiss from Trey.

Magnus maintained eye contact as he teased with his tongue, outlining every ridge, learning the shape of him before taking him into his mouth. Trey's beautiful cock was soft as silk and hard as steel. So. Fucking. Hard. Trey's cock pulsed against his tongue, as strong and steady as the man himself.

This was going to be so damn good.

Trey's hand shot to his head, palming it firmly. "Fuck."

And when Trey took control, holding him in place, pumping his hips, Magnus gave himself over to the pleasure of it. He relished the velvety flesh that slid over his tongue, sucking and licking just to hear the sounds Trey made.

Trey inhaled sharply, held tight to Magnus's head, hips pumping rhythmically as he fucked Magnus's mouth. All the while, Magnus watched him, his goal to give Trey all that he needed, all that he wanted in this moment. And seeing him like this … uninhibited, wrapped up in the pleasure … it made him ache for things he hadn't ached for in a long damn time.

"Christ Almighty … that mouth … fuck." There was strain in Trey's voice when he added, "Not yet, Magnus. Not yet."

A little disappointed when Trey stopped him, Magnus sat back on his haunches, stared up at the man, waited.

He didn't have to wait long before Trey was gripping his arm, manhandling him to his feet, then shoving him back on the bed. He landed with a bounce, laughing as the breath shot out of him even as Trey began to unbutton Magnus's jeans, yanking them down his hips.

He had never had such a forceful lover and he couldn't deny he liked it. A lot.

The laughter died the instant Trey's mouth circled his cock.

Magnus's back arched, a bellowing groan slipping out as pleasure unlike anything he'd felt in a long damn time consumed him. And then it slowed, morphing into something that kept his skin prickling, his spine tingling as Trey worshipped his cock. Magnus shifted, eager to watch as those succulent lips glided up and down his shaft.

"Fuck, you look good like that." He slid his hand over Trey's hair but didn't attempt to hold him. He simply wanted to touch, because the sensations were so powerful he feared, if he gave himself over to them, he'd come before he was ready.

While he continued to suck, Trey worked Magnus's jeans down his legs. He tried to help, but it was futile. He was trapped, overwhelmed by the pleasure, so he left the chore of stripping him to Trey.

When he was finally naked, Trey joined him on the bed, his hand replacing his mouth as he stroked firmly, keeping the tension coiled tightly within.

"Definitely taste good," Trey said, leaning in until their lips collided again.

Magnus rolled so that he was on top of Trey, tongues thrashing, bodies grinding together. To his surprise, Trey didn't buck him off. No, those big, rough hands gripped the backs of Magnus's thighs and held him there, cock gliding against cock. The air raced out of his lungs as the friction sent shards of exquisite pleasure darting down his spine.

He was dangerously close to the pinnacle when Trey rolled them again, this time knees settling between his thighs, shoving his legs wide, cool air gliding over his skin when their chests parted.

"Trey…"

"Is that a warning?" Trey chuckled, nipping his lower lip.

"Fuck. Me."

"I plan to."

"Now." Magnus sucked in a rush of air when Trey's cock grazed his taint.

Had they not needed protection, Magnus would've welcomed Trey inside him right then and there. Screw the lube, screw all common sense, he would've taken the man inside his body. He was that fucking desperate to be used by him. It was rare for Magnus to get so caught up in someone, especially during sex, so it took him by surprise just how willing he was.

Luckily Trey was still sane, because he was off the bed in an instant, padding naked out of the bedroom. When he returned, he was carrying a strip of condoms and a bottle of lube.

Magnus had enough time to ease his heart out of the dangerously-close-to-exploding range, watching as Trey ripped open a condom, rolled it on, then crawled back onto the bed, lube in his hand.

"You sure you're up for this?" Trey asked, kneeling beside him.

"Do your worst," he goaded.

Trey's eyes were dark in the dimly lit room, but Magnus could see the glint in them as he pumped the lubricant into his palm, stroked himself with one hand.

Christ. This was going to fucking hurt. He knew it, and part of him hesitated. It had been too damn long since he'd bottomed for anyone.

"Turn over," Trey said, smacking his thigh.

Magnus tried to hide his hesitation as he slowly rolled onto his stomach. He didn't have much time to be reluctant, because Trey gripped his hips, jerked him back so he was on all fours. Fully expecting Trey to ram inside him, he braced himself, locking his elbows, gritting his teeth. That was the very reason he cried out when Trey didn't thrust into him with his cock but rather his tongue.

"Oh, fuck," he hissed, his chest crashing to the bed as the pleasure made his limbs weak.

When was the last time he'd been rimmed? Hell, he couldn't remember, but fucking hell, it felt good. Too good. He moaned in earnest, cock throbbing as pleasure assaulted him.

It went on and on, but not nearly long enough before Trey's mouth slowed.

"You ready for me?" Trey asked, his words darkly erotic as his lips trailed over Magnus's ass cheek.

Magnus found he was rocking, forward, back, desperate for more as cool liquid ran down the crack of his ass. The chill on his overheated skin made goose bumps appear but he welcomed them. He was a riot of sensation, dangerously close to sensory overload.

When Trey pushed a finger inside him, Magnus's cock swelled, his balls tightening as sparks ignited along his spine. It had been so long since…

Trey wasn't rough, but he wasn't gentle. He fingered Magnus with skill and attention. It was heaven and hell at the same time, too much but not enough, exquisite yet terrifying.

And Magnus never wanted it to stop.

"Oh, fuck … Trey … oh, fuck."

That finger remained inside him, pumping slowly, but Magnus was aware of Trey shifting behind him. Another finger pressed inside, scissored, causing a bite of pain that was quickly overridden by pleasure.

"More," he pleaded, knowing he was too damn close to the edge.

Trey's fingers disappeared, then the pressure of his cock against his hole became his only focus. Time seemed to slow as the tension mounted again, fear of more pain took over, had his muscles locking. He didn't even realize he was doing it until he felt Trey's breath against his ear.

"Relax. Let it feel good."

If only.

Trey's lips glided over his shoulders as the weight of him covered Magnus, forcing his upper body flat to the mattress. The reprieve gave him time to breathe, time to pull himself back from the brink even as he anxiously awaited Trey's next move.

"You wanna feel my cock inside you?"

Magnus nodded.

"Tell me."

"Yes. God, yes." He relaxed as Trey shifted and moved, his cock aligning once more, but this time he was pushing in slowly, gently, stretching him wide as he filled him.

"So tight," Trey groaned. "You feel so fuckin' good, Magnus. Too fuckin' good."

The pain … it was there, but it was manageable. To the point Magnus focused solely on the pleasure, the feel of Trey on top of him, the choppy breaths he was taking as he sank in deeper.

Trey retreated, pushed in. Shallow strokes meant to torment, Magnus knew. He did that until Magnus was breathing hard once more, panting and eager. When Magnus groaned Trey's name, the man thrust his hips forward and drove in as deep as he could.

A guttural groan escaped him, followed by another as Trey began rocking his hips, burying himself impossibly deep. Only when Magnus was begging for more did Trey comply. Next thing Magnus knew, he was on all fours, Trey pounding into him from behind, again and again, his fingers curling over Magnus's shoulders as he held him firmly in place.

Trey grunted, groaned, and continued to plow into him. Magnus's muscles locked as the pleasure—so intense it was damn near painful—had him shouting Trey's name as that mounting tension came dangerously close to shattering.

"Fuck," Trey hissed. "Come for me, Magnus."

He did. A storm of sensation overwhelmed his body and mind, had him groaning low in his throat as his orgasm ripped right through him.

Before the electrical storm waging war inside him could settle, Trey slammed into him one final time and growled his name in a way that had Magnus praying there would be a round two.

Back in the present, Magnus downed the rest of his beer. His entire body was hard, aching and desperate for the release he'd found that night. He hadn't found it since, despite numerous attempts.

Glancing over at Trey, he saw the man was watching him. And if he had to guess, Trey was reliving that night right along with him.

Magnus knew there was only one way to handle a man like Trey Walker.

"Take me home with you, Trey," he said, his voice low, eyes serious. "What do you have to lose?"

Chapter Thirteen

TREY RAISED A HAND, ORDERED ANOTHER BEER.

It was the only thing he could think to do to stall.

What he should've been doing was telling Magnus he was out of his fucking mind. That there was no way he was taking him home.

No.

Fucking.

Way.

Dammit.

He was going to take Magnus home.

It was inevitable and Trey knew it as well as he knew his own fucking name. He'd spent far too much time thinking about that night. His memories were so powerful, there were times Trey wondered if it had really happened at all. Surely his imagination had taken a decent fuck and turned it into an epic moment. No way had those sensations been real.

There was one way for him to be sure though. He could take Magnus up on his offer. They could go for round two, see if it lived up to the hype. When it didn't, Trey would know with certainty, and he could move on with his life.

Son of a bitch.

"Never mind, Mack," he said quickly, standing up and pulling out his wallet. He slapped down a twenty to cover both his and Magnus's beers.

The bartender lifted an eyebrow, watching him closely.

Trey started for the door. "You comin' or what?" he called back to Magnus without turning around.

When he stepped outside, the cool wind hit him in the face. Too bad it wasn't cold enough to knock some sense into him.

Because Magnus knew the way, Trey didn't bother waiting. He hopped in his truck and headed out. The man would follow or he wouldn't. Either way, it was out of Trey's hands now.

Fifteen minutes later, he was standing in his doorway watching Magnus's SUV park in his driveway.

This felt much too familiar. Just like the first time.

And like that night, Trey felt the surge of adrenaline the instant Magnus stepped through the doorway.

"God help me," he muttered seconds before he slammed Magnus against the wall and kissed him.

Magnus didn't hold back, yanking Trey in close, hard hands roaming, desperate.

"For the record, this was your idea," Trey said, moving back, bringing Magnus with him as he headed for the bedroom. "I was content with one night."

"Shut up," Magnus growled, crushing their lips together.

Trey couldn't take his mouth off the man. He tasted good, like beer and man. And maybe a little like mistakes and broken promises, but Trey pretended not to notice. He didn't care. He wasn't thinking about tomorrow or the next day. They were in the moment. Right here. Only here.

When he made it to the bedroom, he pushed Magnus against the door again, pulled back enough so they could both shrug out of their coats, letting them fall to the floor. Trey ripped his shirt over his head, flung it behind him, then took the liberty of doing the same to Magnus.

"Trey…"

Oh, yeah. He loved the way Magnus said his name. He shouldn't, of course, but he did.

Next to come off were boots and jeans, and finally they were naked, falling into one another.

Unlike last time, he wasted no time with foreplay. There'd be time for it later.

"Where're you goin'?" Magnus growled, reaching for Trey when he leaned over to grab the condoms from the nightstand.

He snagged them as he fell back into Magnus. Their lips crushed together once more as he performed a magic trick, ripping open a condom with only one hand.

It pained him to do so, but he pulled back long enough to roll on the condom. He took another moment for lube before he leaned over Magnus once more.

Then there they were, face-to-face as he positioned himself against Magnus's tight hole. He held the man's gaze in the dimly lit room, trying to rein in the sparse remnants of his control as he guided himself home. He gritted his teeth, locked his muscles. Although he wanted this man more than his next breath, he didn't want to cause undue pain, so he forced himself to slow down.

"Don't you dare hold back," Magnus whispered, his hands cupping Trey's neck, those intense hazel eyes pinned on his face.

"You sure about that?"

Magnus lifted his head, his breath fanning Trey's mouth. "I've thought of this every single fucking day." He nipped Trey's lower lip. "Fuck me."

Ah, hell.

Without preamble, he pushed inside the man, the blistering heat of Magnus's body consuming him as it chased the air from his lungs. Trey closed his eyes for a moment and succumbed to the pleasure.

When he opened his eyes, it was to find Magnus still staring at him, his mouth partially open.

"Fuck me, Trey," he whispered, a gravel-laced plea that triggered something deep inside him.

Trey shifted so they were as close as they could be, then he pulled his hips back, slid out slowly, then drove his hips forward.

Magnus's deep grunt spurred him on.

Trey retreated, slammed in again.

And then all thought fled as he fucked Magnus with all the pent-up lust that had been coursing through his veins since their first and only time together.

Trey drove into Magnus over and over, staring down at him. For a brief moment, he allowed himself to get lost in the sensations.

"Oh, fuck," Magnus moaned, his hands tightening behind Trey's head.

No words followed, but they weren't necessary. When Magnus threw his head back and came with a low groan, Trey was quick to follow.

Oddly enough, he had needed that. It had taken the edge off. Albeit only temporarily.

Trey was still hard five minutes after he'd fallen off of Magnus, allowing the man to breathe while he fought to drag air into his own lungs.

That was … he wanted to say unexpected, but he knew that was a lie. It was exactly as he'd thought it would be. He hadn't been imagining their chemistry, and round two proved it.

From the beginning, Trey had figured sex with Magnus would be mind-blowing because there was just something about him, something erotic, something that made Trey want to do dirty, dirty things. And he'd been right, although mind-blowing did seem like a slight understatement.

Forcing himself up, Trey headed for the bathroom, took care of disposing of the condom. He splashed water on his face and purposely avoided his reflection. He did not need to see the satisfaction he knew he'd find there. Whatever that was … it had been perfect. No strings, no expectations. Fucking for the sake of fucking and a man who could give as good as he got.

Yeah, Trey liked fucking Magnus. He liked it a lot.

Needing more time, he turned on the shower and climbed in, not bothering to wait until it was hot. Lukewarm would have to do, because going back to that bed, to Magnus … it wasn't an option right now. The only thing he wanted was to continue what they'd started. He wanted to spend the next few hours lost in the pleasure of it, lost in the man, and he wasn't sure that was a wise idea.

Sighing, he grabbed for the three-in-one soap, lathered his hair and his face before turning into the spray. It was while he was letting the water wash it all away that he heard Magnus come in. The shower curtain pulled back with a slight screech of metal rings on a metal bar, closed again, and then there were hands on him. Calloused hands. Steady hands.

"Tryin' to run already?" Magnus's raspy voice was followed by warm lips across Trey's shoulders. His nipples tightened from the sensation, skin prickling because it felt so fucking good.

Trey was one who needed to be touched. He enjoyed it immensely, something he found wasn't for everyone. His ex-husband, for example. Unless sex was involved, Paul hadn't been interested.

Magnus's arms came around him, pulling him back. Trey didn't resist, leaning into him, letting those hands roam over him while the water continued to heat, steaming up the bathroom. Reaching back, he placed his hands on Magnus's thighs, moaned when Magnus began flicking Trey's nipples with his thumbnails.

"You like that."

Since it wasn't a question, Trey didn't confirm or deny. It was obvious he did and Magnus knew it.

Gentle hands turned him, urged him back. Trey leaned against the wall, watched as Magnus leaned in and used his tongue and teeth to torment his nipples, making them harden more. When he bit down, Trey dropped his head back and groaned. Bliss. Pure, unadulterated bliss. That little bite of pain was what he needed, what he craved.

Magnus didn't stop. His hands continued to roam while his mouth followed suit, trailing over Trey's chest, his shoulders, arms. He could hardly breathe for how good it felt. More than he bargained for. More than he deserved.

As though his goal was to be thorough, Magnus had him turn again, his ministrations moving over Trey's back, lower. Completely blissed out, he had no choice but to let Magnus maneuver him this way and that until Trey ended up with his palms flat on the tiled wall, his hips back, and a talented tongue working him into a frenzy.

This hadn't been the agreement, he knew. Trey had intended to fuck Magnus, not the other way around. It was easier that way. Trey could keep his distance that way.

But at some point, he'd lost his determination, given in, and now he was eager to feel Magnus inside him.

When Magnus's lips trailed up his spine once more, Trey didn't move. He remained where he was when he said, "Fuck me. Fuck me now."

A deep groan echoed in the small space, and he could feel the air being displaced as Magnus moved around. He heard the ripping of foil, sent up a silent thank you for a man who was always prepared. Then the sound of a cap opening told Trey Magnus had found the lube he kept there for those times when his palms were just too damn rough to do any good.

"Oh, fuck, yes," he groaned, pushing back against the finger that slid inside him. He twitched and jerked as Magnus skillfully teased his prostate, drawing ragged breaths through his lungs as he fought to maintain his composure.

Trey let it overwhelm him, the way Magnus fingered him, adding another, then another until Trey was breathing hard from the stimulation and the bite of pain.

And when Magnus withdrew, replacing his fingers with his cock, Trey braced his hands firmly on the wall and accepted the brutal thrusts that shook him to his very core. The slap of their bodies, the rush of the water, their grunts, their groans, it all coalesced into sensory overload. And when Magnus came, Trey was quick to follow with Magnus's name on his lips and a violent shudder that nearly swept him off his feet.

After washing up, rinsing off, then shutting off the water, they returned to the queen-sized bed, bodies colliding all over again. This time, Trey took his time, used Magnus's body in an effort to give and take pleasure in equal measure until they were both too tired, too wrung out to do anything but drift off.

When Trey woke a few hours later, it was to find that regret had set in. Not because he was alone in the bed, Magnus having slipped out like a thief in the night for the second time. No, he was grateful for that. The regret came from knowing he'd allowed himself to feel too much once again. He'd promised himself he would stop this, stop letting himself be used, stop succumbing to his desire to not be alone.

He feared he was exactly what his ex-husband had accused him of being: fucking needy.

As he lay there in the darkened room, his thoughts drifting to Magnus, to what they'd done and how fucking good it had felt, Trey knew this wasn't going to work. Not for him. Inevitably, he would push Magnus away. No, better yet, he would *chase* Magnus away, and Trey was sick and fucking tired of being the one left behind because of his absurd need to be wanted.

Which meant the celibacy thing really was a good idea.

Abstinence was his only real option.

For real this time.

And for the foreseeable future.

Chapter Fourteen

Tuesday, February 16, 2021

TRAVIS SAT IN HIS OFFICE LISTENING TO the meteorologist go on about the epic winter storm that was blowing through Texas. Admittedly, it was the first major storm Travis had seen like this. At least that he could remember. They'd actually gotten snow already, big, fluffy flakes, something that was rare for central Texas.

But it wasn't the four to six inches that the weatherman predicted that had everyone worried. No, that was the ice and the record low temps that were taking a significant toll on the power grid. As of now, they hadn't lost power, but Brendon and Cheyenne had, which meant they probably would at some point. As for the water, well, it was spotty at best. The emails from the utility companies said the water treatment plants had lost power, affecting the water, so they were to expect to be without for some time.

Oddly enough, it wasn't Mother Nature or her wrath that had Travis so preoccupied. Everyone was settled in place, getting regular updates from family on the group text, so he was sure they would reach out if there was a problem. And if worse came to worst, they had the ability to move and shift people around to accommodate. For now they were hunkering down, hoping it wouldn't last long.

Which meant Travis was left to focus on the sealed envelope sitting on his desk. Nothing nefarious, just your standard number-ten white envelope. On the front was his and Gage's names, scrawled in Kylie's lovely cursive. Beside it, the gold-plated letter opener Kylie had bought him when she'd been updating his home office.

The lawyer Kylie had hired to handle her will had delivered it a week ago, and Travis couldn't bring himself to open it, much less read what it had to say.

"Daddy-O! Daddy-O! Let's make a snowman!"

Like a kid caught with his hand in the cookie jar, Travis snatched the envelope, sliding it into his top drawer just as Kade was storming into his office. The little boy was bundled up in a coat, mittens, scarf, and earmuffs, only his little nose and eyes visible on his face. It was a wonder he could see.

And the sight of him made Travis smile.

"A snowman?"

Kade nodded enthusiastically. "Daddy said we could."

"Well, you better get to it."

"With you, too. Daddy wants you to help."

Travis swallowed hard, a ray of hope igniting in his chest even as he wondered if Gage had actually said that. Things weren't exactly kosher between him and Gage these days. In fact, they rarely spent any time together, and when they were under the same roof, it was usually without conversation.

Oh, but their interactions weren't completely hindered. Every night Gage would come into the guest room Travis had moved into. And every single night they would fuck like two men who hated each other but secretly craved what the other could offer. It was only during those hours that Travis felt any sense of calm, though he wasn't sure he was supposed to.

"Come on," Kade whined.

Knowing it would only disappoint his kids if he didn't join them, Travis pushed up from his chair.

"All right, all right. Let's do this."

"Yay!" Kade took off, waddling back the way he'd come.

Travis pulled on his wool-lined Carhartt, also something Kylie had bought for him, and walked out onto the back porch. Gage was holding Maddox in his arms while Kate, Avery, and Haden were smacking their hands on what appeared to be a snowball. It wasn't much of one, certainly not what most people expected would turn into a man of any sort, but it was a start.

Kade raced over to them, squealing with excitement.

"You better scoop more snow," Gage told them, his gaze swinging around to Travis.

For a moment, they stood there staring at one another.

Like every time their eyes met these days, something clenched deep inside Travis. It was true—whenever he looked at his husband, it reminded him of what they'd lost. He would immediately think of Kylie, wishing she was there with them.

At the same time, he was reminded of what he had to lose if they couldn't keep it together. Although he still couldn't sleep and he'd lost nearly ten pounds from not eating because he missed Kylie, he also missed Gage. The man had been his rock for so long, and not having him there ... well, it was killing him slowly.

"I want a giant snowman," Kade yelled, swinging a purple shovel—one they'd bought to make sandcastles at the beach—around. "The biggest one ever. Bigger than a *building*," he exclaimed, hopping to reach as high as he could.

"Me, too," Avery said, her voice not as loud but equally enthusiastic. "Bigger than a *tree*."

"Buildings are bigger than trees," Kade argued.

"No, they're not."

"Uh-huh."

"What about you, Kate?" Gage asked, politely breaking them up.

Travis's attention shifted to Kate, who was slowly gathering up snow into a little yellow bucket. She didn't answer, so Travis walked down the steps to join them.

"Kate?"

She turned her head, clearly not having realized Travis was there. Her brown eyes glistened with what he knew were tears.

"What's the matter?"

Kate looked at him, then looked at Gage. "I wanna make a snowmommy."

Travis's chest tightened and he had to swallow the knot that formed in his throat. He looked at Gage, saw his eyes were glassy, too.

"Then let's do that. Let's make a snowmommy," Travis told her. "What does she look like?"

There was a hitch in her voice when Kate said, "Like Mommy."

For a second, he thought he might be having a heart attack, his chest constricted so tight, and it was painful to breathe. But Travis pushed through, wanting to support Kate. The therapist she was still seeing had told them the best thing they could do right now was to be supportive, to show her they were there for her.

"What should I do?" Travis offered, hoping to distract her.

"We need more snow," she decided.

"Here!" Kade hopped over to him, passing off his purple shovel. "You can use mine."

"You can use mine, too, Daddy-O!" Avery said, giving him her blue shovel.

With one in each hand, Travis squatted down, scooped snow into a pile. Kade and Avery transferred it over, forming it into a ball.

It took some time, but they managed to scrape enough snow from the grass to build a decent-sized snowmommy. And by decent, it topped out at maybe two feet, not quite the building or the tree they'd been going for. When they were finishing up, Kate took off inside, leaving Travis and Gage to stare after her.

"You think she's all right?" Gage whispered.

"I hope so." He looked at Gage. "You want to talk to her? Or me?"

Gage passed Maddox over to Travis. "I'll do—"

Just then, Kate came racing back outside carrying a handful of things. She stopped at Travis's feet and stared up at them.

"Can we use these?"

Travis smiled through the tears that formed as he saw the sunglasses Kate was holding. They were Kylie's favorite pair, the ones they'd bought her for her birthday a few years ago. She was also holding a rainbow-colored scarf. Or what was supposed to be a scarf. It had been Kylie's attempt at knitting, one she'd done with Kate and Avery. Aside from being long and slender, it didn't much resemble a scarf, more like a scraggly, skinny attempt at a blanket, but he knew Kylie had worn it on occasion because it made the girls happy.

"Perfect," Gage said. "You wanna put 'em on?"

The kids worked together to get the glasses and scarf situated. Travis focused on breathing as he held Maddox.

"She needs arms," Kade decided, wading over to the row of bushes along the back porch.

After a couple of minutes of deciding, and after snapping off a dozen or so twigs, he returned holding two, one twice as long as the other. He passed one to Avery before stabbing his into one side of the snow.

"We need to take a picture," Kate informed him.

"Definitely pictures," Gage agreed before snapping a few dozen as the kids posed with their attempt at a snowman … or rather, snow*mommy*, as Kate was referring to it.

Travis didn't think this was a turning point—not by a long shot—but it was baby steps. And he had to think that one day they might be able to move forward.

As much as it still hurt, Travis knew that they needed this.

"IT'S GETTIN' WORSE," GAGE TOLD TRAVIS WHEN he joined him in the living room a few hours later.

After their outdoor excursion, they had gathered the kids back inside, warmed them up with hot chocolate and vanilla wafers. Now the kids were doing their own thing, Maddox and Haden having gone down for a nap, Kate, Avery, and Kade working on bead jewelry at the little art table they'd set up in the corner.

"We're lucky to still have power," Travis said, motioning to the television.

On the screen, a reporter was talking about thousands being without power and water, urging people to stay home if at all possible. Austin had all but shut down in its attempt to accommodate. The schools that had shifted to virtual learning to keep kids home were now shutting down completely due to the power outages. Businesses were doing the same in an attempt to keep their employees safe.

They'd been lucky that they only had a few guests remaining at the resort, and they'd been able to cancel anyone coming in this week, but because flights had been cancelled in and out of the area, those remaining few were stuck. However, from the updates Gage was getting as they all rotated to manage the place, no one seemed to mind. As long as they maintained power, he figured. If that went out and the generators failed, he doubted the guests would be all that pleasant.

"I moved the buckets of snow into the kitchen," Gage said. "Figured it might melt that way on its own."

They had decided they would start melting snow to use for flushing the toilets since the water had gone out completely an hour ago. No one seemed to know when it would come back on.

"I could've helped," Travis said, glancing over at him.

Gage shrugged, as though it was no big deal.

They sat quietly for a few minutes, something that had become the norm for them. The past month had proven painful for everyone as they attempted to come to terms with Kylie being gone. It wasn't easy, that was for sure. The kids had nightmares, waking up crying for their mother often. Gage wasn't getting much sleep either, lying in their bed by himself. Part of him understood why Travis couldn't go in their bedroom. It certainly wasn't easy, but Gage needed it. Being in there allowed him to remember that connection.

During daylight hours, it was a little easier. The kids had their good days and bad. Taking cues from the therapist, Gage and Travis were suggesting little projects for the kids. Drawing pictures of their favorite memories with their mom, hanging them on the refrigerator. Making craft projects—paper flowers, beaded bracelets—they planned to put on Kylie's headstone the next time they went to visit.

They were dealing in their own ways.

It was still hard to believe it had been a month since the funeral. It felt like just yesterday. The only difference was it was getting easier to breathe, to make it a few hours without feeling the unbearable pain. Time would heal them, of that he was certain, but he doubted they would ever be whole again.

When it was clear Travis was going to remain glued to the television so he didn't have to interact, Gage got to his feet.

"I'm gonna make SpaghettiOs for lunch. And I'll scrounge up some candles just in case."

Travis nodded. "I was thinkin' I'd start a fire."

And that was the extent of their conversation for most of the day. They spent the afternoon coloring with the kids, watching movies, and playing video games. From the outside looking in, it would appear they were a highly functioning family, but Gage knew it was all to keep from thinking about Kylie.

As usual, Travis was dealing with work, taking phone calls, checking in to ensure everything was being handled at the resort. Gage left him to it, figuring it was what Travis wanted and needed. He was keeping himself separate as much as possible, more so from Gage than the kids, and Gage was attempting to respect that.

But when Travis had disappeared after dinner, not coming back even after the kids were situated in front of the television and their iPads, Gage went to look for him.

He wasn't surprised to see him sitting at his desk, staring blankly at the desk.

No. Not the desk. He was looking at a white envelope that sat neatly on top of his leather blotter.

Gage stepped into the room. "What is that?"

Travis's eyes shot up to him as though he'd been caught doing something wrong. His hand immediately went to the envelope, covering it.

"Travis?" Gage watched his husband closely, saw the guilt on his face. "What's goin' on?"

"It's a letter," Travis finally said as Gage approached.

"From?"

Travis pulled his hand back, revealing the cursive writing on the front. "Kylie."

Gage stopped, his legs locking. "What?"

Travis turned the envelope so Gage could read it. "Evidently, she wrote us a letter and left it with the attorney. Said we were to get it in the event of her death."

Although he wasn't sure he wanted to know, he asked anyway. "What does it say?"

Travis shrugged. "I haven't opened it. Can't."

Gage's attention was locked on the standard white envelope and the familiar handwriting. He knew Travis didn't mean it was physically impossible to open the letter, but rather he couldn't bring himself to do it. Gage understood fully because, looking at it now, his first instinct was to back away from it.

Although he was a far cry from getting over what had happened, he felt stronger than he had in the beginning. That first week ... he'd been a mess. And it had taken days for him to be able to breathe without tears clogging his throat. But suddenly all the progress he'd thought he'd made faded away, leaving him breathless and sad.

"Should we read it?" Travis asked, his voice scratchy and raw.

Gage looked at him, looked at the letter.

If he read a letter from Kylie ... especially one from the grave...

Gage shook his head. He couldn't do it.

"I was gonna tell you," Travis said softly. "I've only had it for a couple of days. Wasn't gonna open it without you."

That wasn't what Gage was worried about. Strangely, he believed Travis, knew the man wouldn't keep something like that from him. Not unless it was to protect him.

"Do you want to open it now?" Travis repeated, the letter still sitting there between them.

"No," he blurted, backing up. "No, I don't."

He felt Travis's eyes on him as he left the room, leaving the letter and Travis behind him. Now he had to deal with a fresh wave of grief.

Chapter Fifteen

Saturday, February 20, 2021

BRANTLEY WOKE ON SATURDAY MORNING WITH A migraine hangover.

While he hated the feeling, he would take it over the actual headache any day. And last night's had been brutal. It had hit him midafternoon and lasted well into the night.

Although he rarely tried to tie the headache back to a trigger since they seemed random and indiscriminate in their assault, he wanted to believe this one was brought on by the stress of the past week. The winter storm that had all but leveled central Texas had been brutal, leaving a mess in its wake.

There were still large portions of the area without power and water, and while they'd lost both for a short time, it appeared they were up and running despite the boil notice in effect.

Of course, the storm had completely derailed their investigation, mainly because it had shut down the town and the neighboring cities. Having been forced to lock down, they hadn't been able to actively search for Juliet. The Sniper 1 Security team had been impacted, the storm taking a bite out of the Dallas area as well.

Now that it was over, he hoped they could get back on track, because while they hadn't found her, Brantley had thought they were making progress. Thanks to JJ and Luca's combined efforts, they'd made a connection between Juliet and a computer programmer by the name of Samuel Aldering. It wasn't a huge breakthrough, but they were able to track him down and learned Juliet had had an affair with the man, something good ol' Sammy wasn't proud of, obviously. And thanks to some blackmail on Juliet's part, Sam had helped her to hack into a few camera feeds and a phone.

The information wouldn't necessarily lead to them finding her now, but it did fill in some of the holes and answered a few questions.

"You awake?"

Brantley rolled over toward the sound of Reese's voice. He offered a small smile as an answer.

"How're you feelin'?"

"Like I was run over by a truck. The headache's gone, at least." But that meant he would be moving slowly, his body's natural response as it tried to avoid doing something that might bring the pain back.

Reese took a seat on the edge of the bed on the opposite side.

"And everything else? Texas no longer at a standstill?" Brantley prompted.

"They're openin' most everything. Said the roads are clearin' but it'll take a couple of days over freezing to get rid of all the ice."

At least there was an end in sight.

"You up for some breakfast?"

Brantley grinned. "I thought you'd never ask. Eggs, bacon, pancakes?" he asked hopefully.

Reese chuckled. "The works, huh?"

"Yep."

"All right." Reese stood. "Why don't you grab a shower now that the water's back on. I'll start cookin'."

Twenty minutes later, Brantley joined Reese in the kitchen. The bacon was in the oven, scrambled eggs piled high on a plate, and Reese was flipping a pancake at the stove.

"Coffee's made."

"Have I mentioned how much I love you?" he said as he grabbed a mug and headed for the coffee maker.

"You can love me all day long, but you're still doin' the dishes," Reese retorted.

"My pleasure," he said at the same time his phone rang. He took a sip of his coffee and hit the button to answer the call, immediately changing it to speaker. "Walker."

"I don't wanna get your hopes up, but there's a good chance we know where she is," Z said, his tone a bit urgent although it was obvious he was attempting to hold back.

Setting the mug on the counter, Brantley stared down at the phone. "Where?"

"It's not one-hundred-percent vetted, but it's the second tip we've received in a few hours, so I think there's reason to be optimistic."

"Where, Z?" he demanded.

"I'll tell you under one condition."

Brantley could feel his face heat, his frustration growing.

"You and Reese have to stay put until RT gives you the go-ahead."

"That's not the deal," he argued, realizing too late that he wasn't going to get the information.

"Look. I get that you and my brother are renegades and you're ready to beat feet if there's even a remote possibility you'll find this woman, but we have to be careful in how we handle this."

"I know you mean well," he said, his voice low, anger palpable, "but I don't need anyone tellin' me how to do my job, Z. I've been on missions far more sensitive than this."

"And what'd you do before you went on those missions?" Z countered, his irritation evident.

Brantley's anger cooled almost instantly. "Touché."

"It's all in the planning and recon. You know that." Z exhaled slowly. "The objective is to capture her, is it not?"

Capture or kill. Brantley didn't really give a shit what happened to her. Rather than tell Z he was having homicidal thoughts, he said, "Of course."

"Then our best bet is to chill until we can get eyes on her. RT's sendin' a couple of agents down for some recon. And no, before you try to nail me to the wall, he's not takin' over. He's doin' his due diligence. When the time comes, he's agreed to let you go in and get her."

Brantley didn't bother to tell him the same agreement had already been made between him and Travis. Some things were better left unspoken.

"Where's she at, Z?" he asked again.

"I've changed my mind. I think it's best I sit on this for the time being. Like I said, if it's vetted, you'll be the first to know."

Before Brantley could lose his shit, Z disconnected the call. It took effort not to throw the damn thing through the plate-glass window. Instead, he planted his hands on the counter and focused on breathing.

"If it's valid, he'll give us the information," Reese said, sounding far too reasonable.

Brantley bit back the retort. It wouldn't do any good to pick a fight with Reese.

"I'm just glad there's a good chance we'll end this soon," Reese added.

"You think we should tell Travis?" Brantley picked up his coffee, forced his shoulders to unknot.

Reese turned around, holding the plate of pancakes. "No. He knows we're lookin'. Once we have a definite, we'll loop him in."

Christ Almighty. Why did he have to be so fucking rational?

"Keep it up and your headache'll come back."

Brantley glared at Reese but walked around to the other side of the island. He took another sip, sat on a stool, and shifted his head side to side.

"You're right. We'll sit on it until we know for sure."

Reese placed the pancakes beside the plate of eggs then retrieved the bacon from the oven. Once it was all set out, he handed Brantley an empty plate, took one for himself.

"There's somethin' else you should probably know about," Reese said, his tone hesitant.

Brantley lifted his head. Slowly.

Reese was looking down at the counter, rather than meeting his gaze.

Tension knotted Brantley's shoulders. He already knew he was not going to like whatever it was.

"Spit it out, Tavoularis."

"Travis has been in touch with Max Adorite."

Brantley schooled his expression. "About?"

Reese looked up, cocked his head, and gave him the look that said, *Think about it, dummy.*

Brantley knew plenty about Maximillian Adorite, infamous for his role as the head of the Southern Boy Mafia. He'd done a significant amount of research on the man and his organization, learning everything he could. Admittedly, his initial interest hadn't been because of the organized crime family's business dealings. No, Brantley had been curious about Madison Adorite, the woman Reese had been *almost* engaged to. He'd actually learned very little about the woman but more than he cared to about the family.

"Max has done some favors for Travis in the past," Reese said.

"I'm sure I don't want to know what those favors are."

"Probably not. Nor do I."

"Bein' that he's a mob boss, I'm sure Max Adorite calls in favors, too, does he not?"

"Of course. And I'm sure Travis has paid out a few of his own over the years. But they're close. Closer than most people probably realize."

As close as you and Madison were? Brantley didn't voice the question, but he knew it would ping around in his head for a while after this conversation was over.

"I guess what I'm tryin' to say is that there's a good chance Juliet Prince'll never be found."

Brantley narrowed his eyes on Reese. "Are you tellin' me she's dead?"

Reese quickly shook his head. "No. I think we'll get eyes on her at some point. I just don't think there'll be anything left when we move in."

"So what you're tellin' me is Travis *is* gonna need that alibi he mentioned? To keep him in the clear."

Reese's expression turned serious. "I think there's a good chance we all will."

Later that afternoon, Brantley slipped out, using the excuse that he was stopping by his parents' house to check in.

Granted, he did that because he couldn't bear to lie to Reese, but once that was done, he headed for Alluring Indulgence Resort. As had been the case the last couple of times he'd stopped by there, Brantley was greeted with friendly waves and greetings. He figured they were getting used to seeing him, which got him thinking about how many times he'd been there, but never once had it been by invitation.

Rather than go straight to Travis's office, which was his ultimate destination, he made a couple of stops, talking with Kaleb and Sawyer, checking to see how they'd fared through the storm. He considered chatting with Gage, but when he stopped by the small office the man had commandeered as his own, he found it empty.

That left him with no more excuses to put off seeing the man of the hour.

When he knocked on Travis's door, he was met with a less-than-friendly, "What do you want?"

Opening the door, he stepped inside. It would've been easy to ask Travis if he had a minute, but Brantley didn't care whether he did or not. As far as he was concerned, Travis was going to make time to talk, because this particular topic couldn't be put off.

Instantly he felt shitty for not giving Travis advance notice of his arrival. The pure hope that radiated from the man made his stomach hurt.

"No news yet," he prefaced. "I just came to talk about somethin' I heard this mornin'."

Travis's face fell as he leaned back in his chair and regarded Brantley with what looked a lot like disappointment.

When his cousin didn't suggest he sit, Brantley did so anyway.

"Rumor has it you're talkin' to Max Adorite."

Travis's expression remained passive. "Max and I are friends. Why?"

Brantley chose his words carefully. "You and I both know what Max does for a livin'."

There was no comment.

"And I figure it's safe to assume one of his specialties might come in handy at a time like this."

Still nothing.

"Travis…" Brantley exhaled. "I'll be straight with you. I know you'd like to see that bitch in the ground—"

"That's where she belongs," Travis snapped, leaning forward and slamming his palms on the desk.

"I don't disagree with you." He kept his eyes locked with Travis's. "Keep in mind, there are a lot of eyes on this right now. Not only local law enforcement but also the feds. Not to mention the media."

"What do you want from me, Brantley?" Travis's eyes narrowed. "It's been forty-two days since my wife was murdered. Forty-two days that you and your team have been searchin' for the woman responsible. That's forty-two days longer than I care for."

Brantley knew there was nothing he could say to that. It was true. They'd been working day and night—for far longer than forty-two days—utilizing all the tools they had to find the woman. As much as he would've preferred Juliet Prince be an idiot, she was proving to have some skills. At the very least, a very strong survival instinct.

"It's time we finish this," Travis continued. "Once and for all."

It was obvious Travis wasn't referring to having the woman arrested and spending God only knows how long waiting for her to be found guilty by a jury of her peers. And because it was hanging in the tension-filled air, Brantley decided to broach it as straightforward as he knew how.

"I get it," he said softly. "I really do. No, I haven't lost a spouse, but I have lost people I was close to. The rage, once it kicks in, it burns hot. And trust me when I tell you, I'd be thinkin' the same thing if I lost Reese."

Travis's eyes narrowed slightly, almost imperceptibly. As though he'd been gearing up to argue but changed his mind.

"I haven't been with him for seven years or even seven months, but I love him. Hell, I'd give my life for his. So we're on the same page there. What we're not on the same page with is how you go about this."

To his surprise, Travis didn't speak.

"You mentioned needin' an alibi before. You and I both know you weren't blowin' smoke up my ass. What I need is for you to remember you have a husband and five kids at home, Travis. Five. They're already sufferin' enough. Don't make it worse."

"Then I suggest you find her."

"I intend to," he bit out, getting to his feet. "And when I do, you'll be able to tell your children she got what she deserved. Just stay out of it. Take care of the ones who need you most right now. Let us deal with this."

Brantley didn't wait for a retort, knowing he wouldn't like whatever Travis had to say. He'd said his piece.

Now it was time he did something to prove to Travis he could be trusted to take care of shit.

AFTER BRANTLEY LEFT, TRAVIS COULD HEAR CONVERSATIONS taking place in the hall outside his office. He wasn't sure if it was his cousin chatting with others or if it was merely business taking place. It didn't matter to him either way, so he didn't bother to get up to see if they needed his help. Rather, he remained in his chair, staring out the window overlooking the outdoor space still glittering with ice as he tried to figure out what he'd ever found appealing about this place.

Alluring Indulgence Resort had been his baby. He could still remember back in the planning phase, before the enormous structure ever got off the ground. He remembered conversations with the city council, the mayor, and the residents whose land was adjacent to where he wanted to build. It had been exciting back then, an endeavor unlike anything he'd ever done before.

He honestly expected he would always be in love with it, find comfort within the walls. Over the years, he'd opened it up for family gatherings, utilizing the space to accommodate all who wanted to come. And yes, he'd made a lot of money from the idea and had invested just as much.

For what?

What the fuck had he accomplished by creating a fetish resort? Hell, if he had to guess, he'd ruined more lives than not. All those people who'd come here seeking an experience they couldn't find anywhere else. Did they go home satisfied? If so, how long had it lasted? Was there a long list of disgruntled spouses who wished Travis and his family dead?

He swallowed down the emotion that still lodged in his throat when he thought about his beautiful Kylie.

Turning in his chair, he stared at the picture of her on his desk.

"I miss you, baby," he whispered, the same as he did every single day. He prayed to a God he wasn't on good terms with, willing him to take care of her now. Everyone knew Travis had failed in doing so.

A knock on his door dragged his attention from the photograph. "Yeah. Come in."

The door opened and Gage strolled in.

Travis immediately sat up straight, surprised to see him.

"Kaleb needs those forms signed."

No greeting, no smile, just right to the point. Exactly as things had been for the past month, more so since he'd revealed that letter Kylie had left for them.

Travis pushed the pile of papers in Gage's direction. "Anything else?"

There was fire in Gage's brown eyes when he met Travis's gaze. "No."

Nodding because he knew it wouldn't do a damn bit of good to pick a fight, Travis leaned back and waited for Gage to leave. If the past few weeks were anything to go by, he wouldn't be sticking around to strike up a conversation. Hell, they hadn't said more than ten words at a time to one another since they buried their wife. Unless, of course, it pertained to the kids, but even those conversations were light on words.

Oh, but they'd done some silent communicating. Sex had become Gage's go-to topic. Every time Travis turned around, there his husband was, eager and ready for some down and dirty, angry sex. Of course, Travis hadn't bothered to tell Gage he didn't appreciate being used. Hell no. Why would he go and do something stupid like that? And risk Gage turning his back on him for good?

No, these days, Travis found himself waiting around, almost desperate for that little bit of physical contact because it was the only time he felt even remotely human. The rest of the time, he was simply going through the motions, feeling empty, bitter, and cold.

Just as he predicted, Gage turned and strolled back to the door, those fucking forms in hand. When he reached it, he paused for a second, glancing back over his shoulder. "You need to go by your parents' after work. Pick up Maddox."

"Will do," he replied, just as he did every other time Gage issued an order.

Gage nodded, then disappeared.

When he was alone once again, Travis glanced at Kylie's photograph, and not for the first time, he wished she was here to take care of Gage and the kids. They deserved that. They deserved her.

Instead, they were stuck with him and he was doing a shitty job.

Two hours later, Travis was pulling into his parents' driveway. All the lights were on in their two-story farmhouse with its wraparound porch, but there were no extra vehicles parked nearby. Being that it was Saturday, he had expected at least one of his brothers to be there, probably with a kid or two in tow.

Instead, he found his father sitting in his rocking chair on the front porch, coat and boots on, an insulated travel mug on the little square table beside him, steam coming out of the lid.

"Hey, Pop. You come outside for some peace and quiet? Or just to freeze your ass off?"

Curtis smiled, continuing to rock in his chair. "Your mama kicked me out. She insisted I was the reason Mad won't eat his peas. Said every time he looked at me, he'd spit 'em out."

"That true?"

His father chuckled. "Maybe." Another laugh followed, this one a bit louder. "He thinks it's a game."

Of course he did. Travis knew his father enjoyed getting the munchkins riled up from time to time. He claimed it was a grandfather's right.

"Have a seat," Curtis instructed.

"I can't stay."

His father looked up, met his gaze. "Have a seat," he said more firmly.

Travis found it interesting that he was forty-two years old—a grown man for quite some time—yet when his father told him to do something, it was like he was ten all over again.

With a resigned sigh, he lowered himself into the other chair and relaxed almost instantly. Not because he was comfortable but because he knew he had a slight reprieve. Although he loved his kids more than life itself, he dreaded going home these days. He didn't want to be anywhere else, but he hated the tension that seemed to follow him. It was affecting everyone.

"How're things at work?"

"Fine."

His father continued to rock in his chair and Travis waited patiently for him to get to what he wanted to chat about. Clearly something was on his mind.

"How're things at home?"

That question wasn't so easy to answer. "As good as can be expected."

"I saw the pictures of the snowman."

Travis nodded, stared out into the twilight. "Snowmommy."

Curtis peered over at him. "What now?"

"Kate called it a snowmommy. She dressed it up in Kylie's things."

He could feel his father's eyes on him, but Travis didn't look over. It wasn't like he could explain her reasoning for wanting it.

Silence descended for a minute or two as Travis stared out at the yard, the big oak tree. Nothing was nearly as vibrant as it had once been, even if it still looked the same. Well, mostly. The snow that remained beneath the tree wasn't something he was used to seeing, but he'd gotten an eyeful this past week. Enough to last him another four decades if he was lucky.

"I talked to Reese again today," Curtis finally relayed.

He looked over, his chest suddenly devoid of air. "I'm sorry, what? What do you mean *again?*"

"He's been keepin' me updated on the investigation."

Travis leaned forward, prepared to get to his feet, but stopped when his father barked for him to sit his ass down.

"Pop, I don't have time for this. I don't wanna hear about Reese or Brantley or whatever—"

"They think they've received a valid tip."

Clearly he'd been wrong about not having air in his lungs, because that statement sent it out of him in a mad rush. Considering Brantley had been in his fucking office just a few hours ago and hadn't said a damn thing about it…

"Where is she?" he asked when his head stopped spinning.

"They haven't been told yet. His brother's apparently keepin' it close to the vest until they've vetted it." Curtis peered over. "My guess is they don't trust Brantley not to go after her."

They didn't trust Brantley? Or they didn't trust Travis?

"Why'd Reese share this with you and not me?"

"He calls me every coupla days, fills me in. Most of the time it's nothin', but he seems upbeat about this one. Said it's worth pursuin'."

Travis had more questions—like when were they going to get confirmation?—but he couldn't force words past the lump in his throat.

"I think he uses it as an excuse to check up on you and Gage, see how y'all are doin'."

Reese could've called him if he really wanted to know. Then again, Brantley and Reese weren't high on Travis's list of people he cared to talk to these days. The conversations they did have were necessary, nothing more.

His father looked at him, those blue-gray eyes wary. "I know you wanna blame those boys for what happened, but we both know it ain't their fault."

Rationally Travis knew that, sure. But he wasn't doing a lot of rational thinking as of late. And it was just easier to lay blame than it was to figure out what his next move should be. He had honestly thought offering a reward would work. He'd thought for sure someone knew exactly where Juliet Prince was and the enticement of money would have them reporting it. That hadn't been the case.

"Does Gage know about this new lead?"

He watched his father, seeing the answer long before the words came out.

"You kept him in the loop but not me?"

Curtis started rocking in the chair again, his gaze sliding out over the yard. "He asked me about it. I didn't offer."

"But he's known what's been goin' on?"

Clearly his father thought that rhetorical because he didn't respond.

Travis stared out into the yard, the sky already dimming as night descended.

"They won't stop until they find her," Curtis finally told him.

He didn't reply immediately, choosing his words carefully. When he did, he kept his voice low, even. "I don't want her in prison, Pop. I want her in the fuckin' ground. I don't even care if she's breathin' when she goes in, I'll shovel the dirt myself."

Based on Curtis's expression, that wasn't as much of a shock to his father as he'd thought it would be.

"You and me both, son."

Chapter Sixteen

B AZ FINISHED TYPING UP HIS NOTES AND pushed back from his desk. He stretched his neck, moving his head side to side in an attempt to alleviate the tension building. It had been a long day. Hell, a long week, and while he'd spent most of the past few days sitting in his apartment with no water and the electricity flashing intermittently, it hadn't felt like a vacation. Partly because he'd been stranded with JJ and they weren't exactly on good terms.

Or rather, they weren't on the good terms he preferred them to be on. They were getting along just fine. Friends, even. They could talk and joke, but there was still a tremendous gap between where they were now and where they had once been.

As he pushed to his feet, Baz's stomach growled, reminding him he hadn't had lunch. He'd spent the majority of the day catching up on a few of the stragglers coming into the tip line. Nothing worth noting, but it had required a follow-up to make that assessment.

He ventured up to the loft, following the sound of busy fingers on a keyboard. When he reached the top of the staircase, he found JJ furiously typing away.

Baz cleared his throat, wanting to alert her to his presence. He wasn't sure if it was just his imagination or not, but these days JJ seemed jumpier than usual. Ever since New Year's.

When she turned her head slightly, he asked, "How long you think you've got left?"

Since JJ had yet to buy another vehicle, partly delayed because of the weather, Baz was still driving her to and from the office, which meant he stayed until she was ready to go.

JJ glanced over her shoulder, frowning. "What time is it?"

"Six thirty."

"Holy shit." She pushed back from her desk. "Seriously?"

"Seriously."

His stomach grumbled again, this time loud enough for JJ to hear. It pulled a smile from her.

"Thought maybe we could grab some dinner before we head back to the apartment?"

"You're speakin' my language, Detective."

Yes, he was sure he was. For the past couple of weeks, JJ's attitude toward him had changed. She'd shifted into friendship mode, and he could almost believe she was sincere in it. And while he appreciated the effort, even enjoyed talking to her, Baz couldn't get past the feelings he had for her. He wanted something he knew she didn't, and since he wasn't willing to lose her, he'd adopted the same outlook: they would be friends.

"I can finish this up at home," she said, undocking her computer.

"The diner?" he suggested while she tucked her laptop into her bag.

"God, yes. I heard they brought chicken livers back on the menu."

Baz stopped, his nose instinctively scrunching up. "Nasty."

"Oh, but they're not," she insisted. "You'll have to try them."

He was shaking his head as they walked down the stairs.

She rambled on about chicken livers, French fries, and cream gravy all the way to his truck. Once inside, she moved on to dessert while Baz listened with half an ear.

He had to admit, he had grown fond of this new development in their relationship. It was nice to not have JJ looking at him like she wanted to singe him with laser beams coming out of her eyes. But at the same time, he got the feeling there was more to this than she was letting on. More than them merely moving past his indiscretion.

Ever since the night she was attacked in her house, JJ hadn't been the same. She found one excuse after another not to be alone, and he was beginning to think she was scared.

Not that he necessarily blamed her. She had been through a serious ordeal, one she had pretended at the time was nothing. Being bashed over the head and knocked unconscious, then drugged and doused with blood was not nothing. It was major but she still wouldn't discuss it, keeping it all inside. He figured that was the main reason she was focusing so much on him.

His cell phone buzzed on the center console, the screen lighting up.

JJ looked over at it at the same time he did, but she quickly looked away. Baz tapped the button to send the call to voicemail.

"You're not gonna talk to her?"

"Not right now."

JJ was silent for a minute, maybe two, but then the questions began.

"She doin' all right after the storm?"

"Seems to be."

Truth was, Baz hadn't gone to see Molly in a couple of weeks. He didn't care to see her, didn't want to spend time with her. The only reason he was doing it at all was the fact that Molly was pregnant. And according to her, the baby was his.

In fact, she was exactly seven weeks pregnant, a fact he knew because Molly had sent him a meme noting it. Every week she sent them with hearts and flowers and *Molly + Sebastian = baby* as the heading.

The only problem he had was that she wasn't interested in proving it with hard facts. And since he felt like a shithead for even insinuating she might be lying, Baz had decided to embrace it. No, he didn't want a life with Molly, but he had every intention of taking care of his child. He had even told Molly he would share the news with his parents after the first trimester.

"I'm gonna start lookin' for a place soon," JJ said as he was pulling his truck into the parking lot of the diner.

It was the same thing she said every couple of days, as though she thought he needed to hear it. Usually Baz would nod and offer to help if she wanted him to. This time, he decided to go with the truth.

"I really wish you wouldn't," he told her, focusing on the parking lot. "I like havin' you around."

And yes, he said it because he knew JJ needed to hear it.

Plus ... well, it *was* the truth.

OF ALL THE THINGS THEY COULD'VE TALKED about, JJ hated talking about Baz's relationship with Molly, but she didn't know what else there was. It was different when they were at work or out and about. When they were at the apartment, they could talk about television shows and movies they liked or hated. They could have lengthy debates over them, even.

Sometimes JJ would get so caught up in the moment, it was as though they were still a couple, still enjoying the getting-to-know-you phase of their relationship. Only that damn phone would ring and Molly's name would appear and JJ would be reminded all over again that they weren't. Never would be.

Once they were seated at a table and had ordered drinks, JJ pretended to mull over the menu while giving Baz ample time to do the same. When the waitress returned, she rattled off her choice, then listened as Baz once again ordered a double bacon cheeseburger with a side of fries. That was his go-to meal and he ordered it every time, without fail.

"I'm gonna get you to try somethin' else one of these days," she promised, hoping to get his mind off the phone call he had avoided a few minutes ago.

"Not if it has liver in the name, you're not."

She smiled, took a sip of her tea. "How's your dad doin'? I heard you talkin' to him earlier? They make it through the storm okay?"

"They did. Weathered it in Cancun, actually."

"Cancun?" JJ's eyes widened. "Well. How about *that?*"

She recalled the days of no water and wondering when the electricity would go back off after coming on for a couple of hours at a time. She'd gotten pretty good at predicting it, her electronics plugged in and ready for when it did. The worst part for her had been the spotty cell service since she'd been utilizing her phone's hot spot to continue researching while she toughed it out.

"They travel a lot," Baz said. "A trip every few months. He says it keeps them young."

It kept them something, JJ figured.

"And your mom? You talk to her?"

"Every day through the storm. She's good. Had to work from home, which damn near killed her."

JJ watched his eyes light up when he talked about his mother. She envied the relationship Baz had with his parents. It was a far cry from the one she had with her own. Hell, she'd texted them during the storm but hadn't gotten a message back for a couple of days. From either. Which was saying something considering they hated one another as much as they hated her.

His phone buzzed again, the screen lighting up with Molly's name.

"You should answer it," she said, reaching for her own phone as though that might give him enough privacy to have the conversation.

Baz sighed. "If I don't, she'll just keep callin'."

Oh, JJ was well aware of that. The woman called a few dozen times a day. And if he didn't answer, it was usually once every twenty minutes or so. The only reason she didn't show up was because Molly didn't know where he lived or worked. A wise choice on Baz's part.

"Hello," Baz answered, head down, eyes on the table. "Yep. I know you called."

JJ pretended to be skimming her text messages, but there was nothing new aside from some great buys on bedroom furniture at Wayfair.

"And I told you I'd call you later." He sighed. "I doubt it, Molly. I've been workin' all day and I just want to go home and sleep."

JJ couldn't make out what was being said, but she could hear Molly's voice. Not for the first time, she wondered what the woman looked like. What type was Baz drawn to normally?

"No, I'm out right now." His head lifted, eyes meeting hers. "Yes. I'm with … a friend."

She met his stare, held it, hating herself for wondering what he was thinking. Did it make her a bad person to be grateful he didn't seem to be infatuated with this woman? Hell, he didn't seem to like her much at all.

The petty side of her wanted to grab the phone from Baz's hand and tell Molly to leave him alone. That side didn't care that the woman was pregnant with Baz's baby, she just wanted to banish her from Baz's life.

But the rational side said this was how things were going to be. The most she would ever have with Baz was friendship, and she had to be happy with that. Sometimes JJ wished she could be a bigger person, that she could consider having a relationship with a man with a child. Perhaps she could if the man already had children when they met. But Baz … no, she knew her heart would never be capable of sharing him with Molly and her baby.

"I'll call you later," he said firmly, then disconnected.

"If you need to go see her, I can call an Uber."

Baz's teal-blue eyes darkened. "I've told you, it's not like that with her."

Yes, he'd explained a couple of times that the only reason he was talking to Molly at all was for the baby.

And yes, it did probably make her a bad person that every time she thought of Baz having a baby with another woman, her insides churned. It was a nervous anxiety, one she wasn't fond of.

"Any updates on the baby?" she asked, hoping to lighten his mood even though the question left a bad taste in her mouth.

"Seven weeks along," he said, his tone bland.

"When does she get to find out the sex?"

"I have no idea. She's not very forthcomin' with the details."

No, she didn't seem to be. From what she'd heard, Molly wouldn't provide a positive pregnancy test, and she had declined his requests to go to the doctor with her. Which honestly JJ found a bit odd considering how obsessed Molly was with Baz. You would think she'd want him to be a part of it. If for no other reason than it might bring them closer.

Before she could ask another question, Baz spoke up. "If it's all the same to you, I'd prefer we don't talk about her."

Yeah. JJ preferred that, too.

More than she was ever willing to admit.

Chapter Seventeen

GAGE HAD JUST CONVINCED KATE TO TAKE a bath when Travis came home with Maddox.

No sooner was he in the door than Gage realized something was wrong. Or rather, something was *really* wrong since everything between them was wrong these days.

"When they go to bed, we're gonna talk," Travis said under his breath, his tone leaving no room for argument.

He didn't even get a chance to reply when Travis pivoted and stormed out of the room.

Gage sighed. Looked like just another Saturday night.

Two hours later, after they'd sat with the kids until they'd all but fallen asleep, Gage was about to come out of his skin. For weeks now, he'd been the one to instigate any and all conversation with Travis, and now that Travis had shown even a modicum of effort, he wanted to know what was on the man's mind.

After putting Avery to bed and checking on Kade, Gage went back downstairs. He'd expected to find Travis in the living room, where he'd left him, but he wasn't there. He started toward the guest room where Travis had moved his things shortly after Kylie died, but he came up short when he heard his voice coming from Travis's office.

Gage stepped into the room to find Travis pacing the floor, his phone to his ear.

"I understand, but when you know for sure, I expect to be your first call. Not my father, not Gage. Me. Do you understand what I'm sayin'?"

That was all it took for Gage to realize who Travis was talking to. Rather than wait so they could have a knock-down-drag-out, Gage turned and walked right back out of the room. He went for the stairs, took them two at a time, and headed for his bedroom. He shut the door behind him, knowing Travis wouldn't come in.

Taking a deep breath, he paced the room a couple of times to calm down, then decided a shower was in order. After all, this was his routine. Every morning, he woke up, then with Travis's help, he got the kids up and moving. If it was the weekend, he tried to come up with something to entertain them with, and during the week, he would get them ready for daycare. After what had become a daily battle regarding who didn't want to go, he would finally get them dropped off, then he would go to the resort to put in his eight hours. Most of those were spent working with one of Travis's brothers because he sensed Travis didn't want to be in the same room as him.

Which had made this past week, when they'd been stuck in the house, a complete hell. For both of them.

And then, when the day was over, Gage would reverse course, pick up the kids, bring them home. Dinner was generally whatever he could scrounge together in a few minutes with five kids underfoot. With each passing day, as their new normal set in, they were finding a routine that worked for them. Generally Travis would come home in time to help with baths, then they would get the kids to bed before going their separate ways.

And every night, without fail, Gage would go to Travis because he couldn't stand to go a single day without that connection. He knew it was painful for them both, being without Kylie, but he wasn't willing to let go of what they'd worked so hard for. Gage wasn't ready to lose everything, although at times, he felt like he already had.

After stripping off his clothes, Gage got in the shower. As was the case every time he took a minute to breathe, the tears would come. Fortunately, he reserved that emotional unloading for when he was alone, so as not to let the kids see the pain that still consumed him. It was hard enough to get through the minutes of the day. It would be even harder if the kids had to shoulder the weight of everyone else's emotions.

Once he'd let the hot water beat out some of the tension in his shoulders, Gage focused on his frustration rather than his grief, avoiding the tears as he hurried through the shower, got out. He pulled on sweatpants and a T-shirt—always clothed in case the kids needed him—then fell into bed, not bothering to pull back the covers.

It wasn't until he was lying there, in the dark room, when he heard movement on the other side of the bedroom door.

He waited, expecting to see Kade or Avery peek inside as they had done a few times in recent weeks, seeking comfort.

But no one opened the door.

Was it…?

"Travis?"

The throat that cleared from the hallway was definitely that of a full-grown man.

Gage hated that his chest inflated, hope filling him. He knew the only reason Travis would come to their room would be to hash out whatever was on his mind. And clearly he felt it was important, otherwise he would wait until morning.

He remained silent, waiting to see what Travis would do. After several minutes passed, he sighed, disappointed. He'd hoped that Travis would've made the effort, would've—

The doorknob turned and Travis appeared, backlit by the butter-yellow glow from the light in the hallway.

Neither of them said a word when Travis stepped into the room, closed the door behind him.

Neither of them said a word when Travis walked toward him only to stop, turn back around.

Gage wasn't sure he was breathing as he waited, watching Travis as he gripped the doorknob as though leaving the room. Several heartbeats passed and still Travis was there.

"You should've told me."

"Told you what?" Gage asked, playing dumb.

Travis let go of the knob, turned around. "You've been talkin' to Reese."

"And?"

"You've been up to speed on the case. Probably before I was."

Yes, Gage had gotten some updates. But he didn't figure it had been relevant to what was going on. Until Brantley and Reese actually found Juliet Prince, it was all moot. Or until the FBI tracked her down, it didn't matter. Everyone knew she was out there somewhere. He didn't see the point in discussing it.

"You should've told me," Travis repeated, his voice harsher than before.

"What good would it've done?" he countered. "How the fuck would it help? Tell me that, Travis. Tell me how knowin' what they're doin' would help any of us get through another day."

As he expected, Travis didn't answer.

And yet, Gage still waited for a response.

Travis had never hyperventilated a day in his life. Until now.

Until this moment when he was standing in their bedroom, the room they had shared with Kylie for seven amazing years. He couldn't seem to get enough air in his lungs despite his efforts to do so. The walls felt like they were closing in around him, making his vision go gray at the edges.

"Travis."

He could hear Gage's voice, even comprehended the concern in it, but he couldn't move, couldn't react, couldn't *anything*.

Why had he come in here? Why? What was the purpose of subjecting himself to this?

Hard hands were turning him around, then suddenly cupping his neck, thumbs brushing along his jaw, Gage's face filling his line of sight.

"Trav, relax," his husband whispered, his tone so gentle it caused another ache in his chest. "Breathe."

Travis shook his head. He couldn't. No matter how hard he tried, he couldn't fill his lungs. His airway was getting smaller by the second, his chest constricting.

Those strong hands grew firmer as Gage leaned in. And then Gage's breath fanned his lips.

"I'm here, Trav. I'm right here. I want you to breathe. In and out. Slow. It's all right. I swear to you."

"I … I can't… Oh, fuck…" He sucked in air, the panic attack beating down on him. He felt his legs weaken. He was going to pass out.

"Breathe." Gage leaned in closer, pressed his lips to Travis's. Just a gentle brushing, but it gave Travis something to focus on. The imaginary band on his chest loosened slightly.

It was then he realized he was crying, tears streaming down his cheeks.

"I miss her so fuckin' much," he forced out. "So much, Gage. I. Miss. Her."

Gage's arms banded around him, jerking him close, tightening in a hold that should've been constricting, but it wasn't. It was comfort. It was … home and hope and love all right there. This man … despite their issues, despite the distance they'd put between them, he was there when Travis needed him. Always there.

"We're gonna get through this," Gage said, his voice so low, if he hadn't been right at Travis's ear, he wouldn't have heard him. "We will. All of us. It'll never be easy, but we'll get through it."

"I love you," Travis blurted, holding him, clutching his T-shirt in his fists, scared to let go. He just needed Gage to know that, to understand. Yes, he was fucked up. Yes, he was doing this all wrong. But that didn't change the fact that Gage meant everything. "I do," he added. "I love you so goddamn much."

"I know."

They remained like that for several minutes, holding one another up, tears falling, the fear and anger they'd built up finding a small but effective outlet.

"I hate this, Gage. I hate her not bein' here. I don't want to get outta bed anymore. Without her ... without you..."

"You've got me," Gage snapped, pulling back and gripping Travis's neck again. "You understand me. You've got me. Always. No matter what."

Travis's eyes searched his face, praying he meant that, but he wasn't sure what was real anymore. He'd never felt so much pain before. Never had anything hurt as much, cause such a brutal agony in his chest as losing Kylie. And the past several weeks ... they were hell on earth as Travis navigated this new path, tried to figure out how he fit in his own life now. *If* he fit in it.

"I can't be in this room. I can't sleep in that bed." Travis glanced over at the spot Kylie used to occupy, and his chest constricted again, but this time there was anger boiling in the pain. "I can't." He looked back at Gage. "I made love to her that mornin'. Right there. Right there in that fuckin' bed. I can't be in here without thinkin' about that. About her. Missin' what we were supposed to have for an eternity. That was it. My last moment with her."

He saw something flash in Gage's eyes. Pain? Misery?

"At least you had that," Gage whispered.

Oh, that was far more than misery. That was agony and despair.

"At least you have that to remember, Trav. Those precious minutes you had with her that mornin'." A tear streaked down his face. "I didn't even get that."

It wouldn't have hurt more if Gage had punched him in the stomach.

"I..." Travis didn't know what to say. Words were not going to help, of that he was certain.

"It's not your fault, Trav. It's not." Gage took a deep breath, his hands relaxing as he leaned in, forehead to forehead. "I was mad at you initially. Sure. For about a minute. You got that and I didn't. I couldn't understand why *I* didn't get that. Why I couldn't've had just five more minutes with her."

Travis fisted Gage's shirt tighter, feeling the sorrow as it poured off of his husband. He hadn't seen that last precious moment he'd had with Kylie as a blessing. But Gage was right. He'd had *that*.

"Every minute without her is agony, Trav. That's to be expected. We've lost somethin' important. Somethin' crucial. But we have to keep puttin' one foot in front of the other. We can't keep dwellin' on what we don't have. It's not good for us; it's not good for the kids."

He knew Gage was right. Of course he did, but that didn't make it any easier.

"How do we fix it?" Travis honestly wanted to know. He *needed* to know because going on like this wasn't sustainable.

They stared at one another for a moment.

"The letter," Gage finally said.

Travis didn't speak.

"Tomorrow, we'll read the letter. Together."

Travis managed a nod.

"But tonight we'll start by sleepin' in here. Both of us." There was so much pain in Gage's eyes. "I don't wanna be alone, Trav. You said you wouldn't make me do this alone."

Travis knew Gage wasn't referring to taking care of the house, the kids, the responsibilities. Travis was putting in his time as promised. Yet he was ignoring their relationship, their bond. He'd all but written it off because he didn't believe he deserved Gage. In doing so, he was hurting the man he loved.

"We'll start with one night," Gage continued. "See how it goes."

Travis wasn't sure he'd survive it, but at the same time, he knew he wouldn't survive leaving Gage alone tonight. Hell, he couldn't survive much more of this rift they were creating between them. It was tearing him to shreds with each passing day.

"Okay."

Gage must've known he was having a difficult time processing even with his agreement because he didn't go far, leading the way to their bed.

Every step Travis took felt heavy. His heart picked up a new rhythm, a drumbeat of both pain and need, loss and love.

"Be with me tonight, Trav. Just me. Just *us*. For a little while."

Travis focused only on Gage, on the man he had fallen in love with, the man who'd been his lifeline and his anchor over the years.

"I love you," Travis whispered, sliding his palms over Gage's whiskered cheeks.

"I know."

Travis realized that was the second time Gage had responded that way. He hadn't returned the sentiment, merely acknowledged it.

"Tell me you love me, Gage," Travis insisted, pulling back enough that he could see Gage's face clearly, so he could look in his eyes. "Tell me."

"I do, Travis. Of course I do."

He cupped Gage's face firmly. "Tell. Me."

Gage's eyes flashed with pain once again.

Travis stepped in, holding Gage roughly. "Tell me you love me, damnit."

"I love you," Gage blurted, a sob tearing free. "Goddammit, Travis. I love you."

"Why's it so hard for you to say it?"

Gage's brown eyes shined with unshed tears. "It's not."

He wouldn't say that was a lie, but it damn sure wasn't the truth.

"Tell me again," he demanded, sliding his hands into Gage's hair, gripping firmly as he looked down into his eyes.

"I love you," Gage rasped, as though the words were torn from his chest. "I love you so fuckin' much, Travis. So much, but it hurts. I know you loved Kylie more, I know—"

Travis staggered back, dropping his arms. "What? Why the fuck would you think that?"

Gage's eyes scanned his face. "How can I not? You can't even look at me. I'm the one who has to pin you down just to get a few minutes of your time. I'm the one who comes to you every fuckin' night because I don't want you to forget me."

Travis stared, mouth agape.

"Without her, what's left, Travis?" Gage asked, eyes pleading. "Tell me that. You've always said you couldn't have one without the other. That was your reasoning, was it not? The reason you and Kylie went your separate ways in the very beginning? Because you needed both."

Travis had no idea what to say. Not because there was any truth in what Gage was saying. Well, not anymore. He had said that. Yes. A long fucking time ago. Long before he'd fallen in love with both Kylie and Gage individually.

"I don't want you to forget me, Travis," Gage said, his tone defeated. "I don't—"

Travis cut him off by slamming his mouth down on Gage's. He kissed him, taking them both down to the bed. He was rough, but he was angry, so it made sense. How could this man think so little of him? How could he believe that he would ever not want him?

"I don't love her more," he growled, settling over Gage.

"It's all right if you do, Trav. I understand."

Travis lifted his head, stared down at the man beneath him. "You don't." He shook his head to emphasize his words. "You don't fuckin' understand."

Gage stared, his eyes imploring him to explain.

"For fuck's sake, Gage. I love you equally. The kids … you … Kylie…" Travis was unable to hide his frustration as he tried to spell it out. "All of you make up my whole heart. All the pieces." He shifted, sliding over Gage so that he covered him fully. "But you … you're my best friend, my lover, the man I want to have my back for the rest of my life. You, Gage."

He could feel the emotions churning between them, knew Gage was listening.

"I can't lose you, too," Travis whispered, pressing his lips to Gage's. "I won't survive it."

Gage's hand caressed the side of his face as their lips melded together. "I'm not goin' anywhere, Trav."

It wasn't the hard, furious kisses they'd indulged in recently. This was slow and sweet and more than a little sad.

And exactly what Travis needed. This was what they both needed. A minute together to share their pain, to know someone else was there, someone would hold them up when the weight of the world became too much. They'd avoided this for weeks now, avoided opening themselves up because the emotional turmoil was already more than they could bear.

"Love me, Gage," Travis mumbled.

"Always," he whispered.

Gage's hands moved first, lifting Travis's shirt, forcing him to rise. They moved together, rolling and shifting but never releasing one another. It wasn't long before they were skin to skin, limbs tangled as their lips remained locked, tongues searching, seeking. On their sides, legs twined, neither of them made a move to pull apart, in tune with one another on a deeper level.

When Gage slid his hand between them, fisting Travis's cock, he hissed in a breath, pressed his forehead to Gage's as his hips automatically pumped to increase the friction. And when Travis did the same in return, fisting Gage's cock, stroking, teasing, they lost themselves.

Travis hadn't been looking for this when he came in the room. He hadn't been seeking Gage out for this type of comfort but it happened. There, in one another's arms, they touched and claimed, stroking one another to a climax that wasn't just physical. It was the release they both sought, solidifying the bond they'd had all along, strengthening it.

When Gage grunted, Travis gripped him more firmly, stroked harder, drawing him closer and closer until it was inevitable. Only then did he nip Gage's lower lip, as they both came.

Afterward, Travis dragged Gage into the shower with him, where they spent another few minutes together. Nothing sexual, only love this time. Only one heartbeat to another in a moment that would give them the strength to make it through one more day.

Chapter Eighteen

Sunday, February 21, 2021

GAGE AWOKE SLOWLY FOR THE FIRST TIME in more than a month.

From the moment his brain came back online, he was aware of where he was and who was wrapped around him. He felt stronger this morning, more complete. The exact opposite of every morning since that fateful day.

"You awake?"

He shifted, answering Travis without words.

Warm lips caressed the back of his neck and his body came alive.

He had missed this. The intimacy, the connection. Sure, they'd been fucking like rabbits for days on end, but it had been a distraction, not a mating. Gage had used Travis as an escape, desperately trying to get through one more minute of one more day, to convince himself that his entire world wasn't shattering because they'd lost the woman they both loved.

He felt different this morning. Not altogether whole, because he knew he would never be that way again, but he was definitely on the path to mending. Or moving in the direction of it, at least.

Gage was aware of Travis moving, rolling away from him, then back. He didn't have to open his eyes to know what the man was doing. They'd spent numerous mornings just like this, coming awake together, seeking pleasure to start the day. Sometimes with Kylie, sometimes when she had taken a turn with the kids in the morning.

"I need to be inside you," Travis whispered in his ear, his body moving up tight behind him.

Gage pressed back against the big, warm body that was so familiar, so comforting.

When Travis reached down, Gage moved higher on the bed, adjusting their positions so Travis could lift Gage's leg and slide his cock along the crack of his ass. He didn't have to do more than that, because Travis took control, sinking inside him in one slick, controlled move, filling him completely.

Gage felt the weight of Travis at his back as he pumped his hips, slow, gentle, bringing them both awake fully, together, as one.

But as was the case whenever they came together like this, their bodies knew what they needed, and slow and gentle ceased to exist as lust and passion took over. With Travis behind him, his hard, hot body and those desperate grunts, Gage blanked his mind and let the pleasure consume him. For the first time in weeks, Gage felt … hope.

He would take it.

If only for a little while.

Many hours later, after they'd kicked the day into high gear, getting the kids moving, feeding them, then cleaning up the mess they'd created during the week, Gage's thoughts drifted to that letter. The one Travis had in the top drawer of his desk. After he'd learned about it, he had pulled it out a couple of times. Never opening it because he hadn't been ready for that, but today he was.

"You look like you're lost in thought."

He turned to see Travis standing in the doorway, shoulder pressed to the doorjamb. Gage put up the coffee mug he'd just pulled out of the dishwasher.

"You still wanna read the letter?" he asked, not looking at Travis.

"I do."

There was so much conviction in Travis's tone, Gage had to look over at him.

"I asked my parents to come pick up the kids," Travis continued. "Told 'em we needed some time to ourselves but we'd be there for dinner."

Time to themselves? Gage had forgotten what that even meant.

"Pop'll be here in half an hour. We'll get them off and then we'll read it."

Gage nodded, reaching back in the dishwasher to pull out another clean cup. "Okay."

Half an hour.

Funny how thirty minutes could feel like thirty years.

By the time they helped Curtis get the kids loaded up and off down the road, a full hour had gone by. But even additional time hadn't eased Gage's anxiety a single bit.

"We can do this," Travis said, his tone once again reassuring, stronger than it had been in a while.

Gage looked at him, wondering if he was imagining it or if they really had made progress last night.

When Travis took his hand and tugged, Gage had no choice but to follow. Into the living room, sitting on the couch. His mind blanked as Travis took a seat beside him. And then there they were, shoulder to shoulder, the sealed envelope in Travis's hand.

They stared at it for the longest time. Gage traced the gentle sweep of Kylie's handwriting with his eyes over and over again.

"We both know it's not gonna get any easier the longer we wait," Travis said, his voice gruff.

No, it wouldn't.

Shoring up his nerves, Gage took the envelope from Travis's hand and slid his finger under the flap, tearing it open.

Travis pulled a single sheet of white paper from inside. For another brief moment, they stared at it until finally Travis unfolded it.

Gage's chest hitched when he saw a page full of words written in that same lovely handwriting.

Knowing he couldn't put it off any longer, Gage started reading.

Dear Travis and Gage,

If you're reading this, it means I'm no longer of this earth, and I have to hope it's after we've lived a long, happy life together. After my babies have grown up, graduated high school, college, gotten married. But if for some reason it's not, then you should know that every second I had with the two of you and the five of them made for a life more complete than I ever thought possible.

If there was some unfortunate event that took me from this world, then there are some things I need you to do for me. Things that might be difficult because, if nothing else, I know exactly who my men are. I know how you both think, I know how you both love. And I know without a doubt that the two of you will retreat because you think it will benefit the other in some way.

First of all, that's complete nonsense and you should move forward remembering that every single day. While I have never doubted for a single second how much I am loved by both of you, I also know how much you love each other. If I have a say in the matter, Travis, you won't be stubborn, and Gage, you won't let him be. You will both suck it up and move forward, hand in hand, where you belong.

Provided these still make sense, here are the things I need you to do for me:

> *~ Take my wedding band and my engagement band and have them melted down, along with both of yours. But don't worry, I don't want you to be without them for long. From those, have new bands made, one for each of you. That way you will both have a part of me with you forever. After all, the three of us are stronger together, even if we aren't all there.*

> *~ Now for the diamonds. They don't melt, so I would like you to take the diamonds in my rings and make them into necklaces for our daughters. One for Kate, one for Avery. I want them to have a little part of me with them always. You can give them to them whenever you feel is the right time.*

~ *For Kade, Haden, and Maddox, I've set aside some things that belonged to my father, things he has given me over the years. There's an old compass that belonged to his grandfather. One of them might like that. There's also the toolbox my Dad gave me when I first moved out on my own. Nothing fancy, but I know Kade has enjoyed helping me with projects. Also, the miniature airplane collection. I'll let them or you decide who gets what. Hopefully there won't be any fighting.*

~ *As a family, I would like y'all to plant a tree for me. More than one, preferably. Yes, even now I want to help the environment. Hopefully, if this time ever comes, the kids'll be old enough to select one they know I would've liked. I leave it to both of you to decide where. But if you're having a hard time, I think a magnolia tree would look lovely in Curtis and Lorrie's front yard.*

~ *And last but not least, I want the two of you to get married. It's what I've always wanted, although it was never an option. We did things our way, the three of us, but now it's time for the two of you to move forward. Together.*

I hope you both know that I love you with my whole heart. I am truly blessed to call you both husband. Sure, it might mean that I've had to complain about two pairs of socks on the floor or ask twice before someone agrees to take the trash out, but in return I've received twice as much love as most women get. I wouldn't trade our life for the world, and no matter what happens, or when, you should both know that I've had the best life anyone could be lucky enough to have.

Love always and forever,

Kylie

TRAVIS READ THE LETTER THREE TIMES. EACH time more tears streamed down his face as he heard the lovely cadence of Kylie's voice in his head.

Beside him, he heard Gage's breathing change, knew he was also dealing with the overwhelming emotions that came along with reading her words, knowing they would never see her again and that she had prepared for that.

He should've expected this. Should've known that their wife would think ahead, help them to deal with the worst possible scenario. That was who Kylie was. Thoughtful, generous, selfless, but most importantly, she'd loved them with her whole heart.

When Gage sobbed, Travis lowered the letter and turned, pulling him into his arms. They sat like that for the longest time, holding one another, protecting one another as the emotions won out.

And when his eyes dried, Travis read through the letter one more time, focusing on the things Kylie wished for them to do.

"We can let the kids plant the trees next weekend," he said aloud, his voice hitching with emotion.

Gage nodded, his hand sliding into Travis's. "Okay."

"And the rings…?" Travis wasn't sure what to think about that.

Gage turned his head. "I'd like to do that part if it's all right?"

"Sure. I'll get the stones put into settings for the girls."

It seemed so simple. Speaking it, at least. Travis wasn't sure how easy it would be for Gage to hand over Kylie's wedding bands knowing they would be melted down. That seemed like the most difficult part although he understood her reasoning.

"We should have Jessie go through her stuff, too," Gage suggested. "See if there's anything she wants. Joe, too."

"Yep," Travis agreed, nodding because he didn't know what else to do.

Then they were silent again, minutes ticking by.

"She loved us," Gage finally whispered.

"With all that she was."

And they had loved her the same.

Chapter Nineteen

One week later
Saturday, February 27, 2021

TRAVIS HAD SPENT THE PAST WEEK FOCUSED on his family and his business.

He went to work every day, as did Gage. But rather than mope as he had been for weeks, Travis engaged with others, checking on things himself rather than leaving it to everyone else to figure out. He even managed to have lunch with Kaleb and Sawyer, the three of them talking about surviving the snowpocalypse.

With the winter storm behind them, school was back in session, the kids returning to their routine. He alternated taking them to daycare to give Gage a break, and he picked them up the same. He helped Kate with her homework, although he still didn't understand why she had it. She was six. There were plenty of homework years ahead of her. No sense stressing out a first grader.

And when they were settled in at night, Travis ensured it was time well spent. He didn't stalk Brantley or Reese, and he didn't comb through the internet looking for possible news updates. He left it to them to deal with, trusting that when the time came, they would let him know. Instead, he avoided his home office, opting to be where Gage and the kids were.

But today was the day they'd set to check off one of the things on Kylie's list. With the weather warming up nicely, and quickly, they decided it was the perfect time to plant a tree. Or rather multiple since, yes, Gage had liked the idea of helping the environment, too.

"Where're we goin', Daddy-O?" Kade asked when Travis helped the kids buckle into their seats.

Kade, Avery, and Haden were with him, while Gage had taken Kate and Maddox to run a couple of errands before they met up in a little while.

"We've got somethin' to take care of today," Travis explained.

"What somethin'?" Kade inquired, always with the questions.

Travis looked at the boy and smiled. "You're gonna plant a tree."

Kade's eyes widened, a look of confusion and concern on his little face. "Why would I do that? Trees come from the grass."

Grinning, he tapped the brim of Kade's baseball cap. "Actually, they don't."

"What about me?" Avery called out. "I wanna plant a tree."

"You're gonna help. We've got three to plant."

"Three?" Kade's shock was dramatic. "That's a buncha trees."

"It is, yes. But I figure you can handle it, right?"

"What about me?" Avery repeated, a harumph in her voice this time. "I wanna plant a buncha tree."

Travis chuckled. This could go on forever, he knew.

He adjusted Haden's seat belt, touched his nose, and made the little boy giggle.

"Where're we gonna put the trees?" Kade asked.

Travis shook his head. They had decided they would spread the trees around so that everyone had a reminder of Kylie.

Gage had suggested they show the letter to Kylie's parents, her sister, as well as Curtis and Lorrie to help them understand the significance of what they wanted to do. So they had carved out time in the evenings, which meant later than usual nights. As he'd expected, there weren't any dry eyes when the letter was being read. Travis had shed plenty through the week, rereading it over and over. A couple of times he'd caught Gage doing the same, sitting in Travis's office—the one place they could usually find privacy—his eyes glued to the paper.

Most people probably wouldn't see the letter as much, but for them it was a bit of closure. Though difficult to process, it was a part of Kylie they had when they thought they would get no more.

"Are they all gonna be at Pop's house?" Kade asked.

"Nope. One at Pop's, one at Grandpa Joe's, and one here. We'll do ours later."

"Where's Daddy?" Avery asked when Travis climbed into the driver's seat.

"He's at Pop's house already. With the tree."

Kade inhaled sharply, another dramatic effect of his. "What if he plants the tree without us?"

"He won't."

"You don't know that."

Travis laughed, briefly glancing back at them in the rearview mirror before turning his attention to the road.

"I wanna plant a *huge* tree," Kade said, demonstrating his idea of *huge* by spreading his arms wide.

"We'll have to see what Dad's picked out," he told them.

"I hope it's giganormous," Avery said softly.

"That's not a word," Kade told his sister.

"Uh-huh."

"Nuh-uh."

Travis managed to tune them out for the few minutes it took to get to his parents'.

When he pulled down the dirt drive, the first thing he noticed was all the vehicles parked near the house. It was Saturday, so he knew this wasn't a family dinner, yet he saw all the familiar ones: Kaleb's Ford Expedition, Sawyer's Chevy, Zane's F250, Jessie's Hyundai, Beau's Escalade, Cheyenne's Lexus. And a few more Travis would've been surprised to see on any given day.

"Everybody's here!" Kade exclaimed. "Yay!"

If he had to guess, his son had already forgotten about planting the tree.

Travis didn't bother reminding him as he got them out of the SUV, herding them toward the house, where his old man was sitting on the front porch, Kate in the rocking chair beside him.

"What's all this?"

"It's a party," his daughter said easily.

"A party?"

She nodded curtly. "A tree-plantin' party."

"Is that right?" Travis looked at his father.

Curtis's gray eyebrows popped once. "I'm just here for the food."

Travis laughed, then passed Haden off to his dad and went into the house. Sure enough, his brothers were all there, significant others, too, plus all the kids. Amongst them, he noticed Brantley and Reese, Kaden, Keegan, and Bristol, Mack and Jeff, as well as Joe and Melissa.

"Before you yell at us," Zane said, his face sober, "we're here for support. And because we wanted to be a part of it. We loved her, too. Thought it might be a nice celebration if we were all here for the tree plantin'."

Travis's throat tightened as he nodded. "Yeah." He cleared his throat. "Thanks for that."

"Plus, you know how we all love a good party." Zane smacked him on the back, probably a little harder than need be, but that was his kid brother for you.

Travis peered past Zane to his cousin Brantley, who was standing in the kitchen chatting with Kaden and Keegan. As though he felt eyes on him, Brantley looked up, met his gaze across the room. His first instinct was to pelt Brantley with questions, find out where they were in the investigation, why so much time had passed and nothing was being done. It would've been easy to unleash on the man. Too easy.

But he wouldn't. Not today of all days.

Which was why Travis offered a nod of his chin in greeting, received one in return before he turned and sought his husband in the room full of people. He found Gage sitting on the couch, Maddox on the floor at his feet. When he saw Travis, his eyes widened.

"I don't know what happened," he said, his voice a bit dramatic. "I got the tree, brought it here, and—" He waved at the chaos as though that said it all.

And maybe it did.

After all, this was what the Walkers did. They rallied for support, took care of one another. It was something Travis had relied on all his life, one of the things he knew his wife had loved about their life. They had this … so many people who cared.

"We've got food," Kaleb announced. "Question is, do you want to eat before or after?"

Travis looked at Gage. "Up to you."

"We should ask the kids, see what they think."

"Good idea." This was supposed to be a family thing.

He pulled Avery away from playing with Ethan's triplets, then found Kate still sitting in the rocking chair. After he told them to stay put, he searched for Kade. It took a minute to wrangle him from where he was playing with Mason and Matthew. When asked about the tree, their unanimous decision was to plant it now.

"Where're we puttin' it?" Curtis asked Kade.

The little boy shrugged his shoulders. "Where *should* we put it, Pop?"

"I think I've got the perfect spot."

Curtis carried Haden while Kate, Avery, and Kade trotted beside him down the steps and across the front yard. Travis grabbed Maddox while Gage helped Ethan and Beau by picking up Jack. The rest of the crew, adults and children, weren't far behind them.

"What about right there?" Curtis suggested, pointing to an empty spot a few yards to the left of the big oak tree.

"Yay!" Kade squealed and took off running, more kids following him.

"That way Mother and I can watch over it every day."

Travis felt his sinuses heat, eyes brimming. Because he didn't trust his voice, he nodded his agreement.

The next hour was spent with everyone taking turns digging a hole despite the fact they had the machinery to do it in far less time. No one was in a hurry though, helping the kids scoop up dirt, toss it aside, each adult also taking a turn.

"How big *is* this tree?" Travis asked as he saw the hole continuing to get bigger and bigger.

"I figured we wanted somethin' strong enough to weather anything."

Just like Kylie, he thought to himself.

Once Gage was satisfied the hole was big enough, he disappeared, returning a few minutes later driving Pop's tractor, a trailer hitched to the back and a good-sized magnolia tree with an enormous root ball strapped down.

It was when Travis's brothers went to assist that Kate came over to hold Travis's hand. He glanced down at his daughter, saw she had tears streaming down her pretty face. She was probably the only one of his kids who understood the real significance of this, and he hated that she did. He hated that they'd lost the most important person in their world.

But he hoped this would give them something to hold on to, something to remind them of her each and every day.

It took some time, but the tree was maneuvered into place, the root ball broken up some so that it would settle in like it should, then the kids were once again scooping dirt to fill the hole. Kate joined them then, a smile on her face.

"You realize there're three more," Gage said from Travis's side.

He looked over at his husband. "Three? I thought there were two more."

"I bought one for Jess. Figured we'd help her plant it at her house."

Travis squeezed Gage's hand. Leave it to him to think of others at a time like this.

As he stared at the tree, Travis sent up a silent note to his wife: *Kylie, baby, I'm definitely going to marry him. Just like you asked.*

It took the rest of the weekend for them to get the remaining three trees planted. With each one, there was a celebration and a toast, everyone coming together to celebrate the life of a woman who'd meant so much to them.

On Sunday night, after the kids went to bed, Travis moved his things back into their bedroom. He'd been sleeping in there for a week, but he hadn't quite felt committed to it. Now it felt like where he was supposed to be.

He figured Kylie had something to do with that. Even gone, she was watching over him, ensuring he did what he was supposed to. It took a strong woman to wrangle a Walker, and he'd never known one stronger, with the exception of his own mother.

He was blessed to have had the time he did with Kylie, and it was time he lived up to her expectations.

But there was one more thing they had to take care of.

Chapter Twenty

"WE'VE GOT HER!"

Brantley stared at the phone sitting on his desk. Z's words were still echoing in the room and all eyes were on Brantley.

"As in you found her?" he clarified. "Or you picked her up?"

Z exhaled, his voice calmer when he spoke again. "As in we know roughly where she is."

Roughly? Brantley didn't like the sound of that. He wanted that woman found.

Reese perched on the edge of the desk, glanced at Brantley, then down to the phone. "And that would be where, Z?"

"After we received two tips tying her to the same location on South Padre Island, we sent a guy down to scope out the area. Unfortunately, he wasn't able to get eyes on her, and he held off on askin' around because we didn't want to spook her if she was there. So I set up a grid search. We were able to scan cameras in the area and we can confirm Juliet Prince was just south of there in Port Isabel, Texas, within the last seventy-two hours."

Brantley huffed, dropping back in his chair. "Seventy-two hours, Z? Seriously? There's just as much of a chance she's back here in Coyote Ridge by this point."

"Hey, don't shoot the messenger," he grumbled. "My suggestion is you hop on that private charter RT set up to get your happy asses on down there."

He sat up again. "What time does it leave?"

"He was bein' generous and got you two hours."

Brantley reached to disconnect the call but stopped when Z said, "Take me off speaker, Brantley."

He glanced at Reese, then picked up the phone, tapped the screen to return the audio to the phone. "Yeah, I'm here."

"I know you're gonna do whatever the hell you want to do, but I'd like to suggest you keep this information to yourself."

"Meanin'?"

"Meanin' don't share it with your cousin. You and I both know it's in everyone's best interest, especially Travis's, if he stays out of this."

"You're right," he growled softly. "I *will* do whatever the hell I wanna do. Got a flight to catch, Z. We'll keep you in the loop."

Brantley tucked his phone in his pocket and glared at Reese, a silent warning for him to let it go. As much as Brantley wanted to keep this to himself, as much as he agreed with Z that it was in everyone's best interest, he couldn't do that. He had already made a promise to his cousin, and he had no intention of breaking it.

"Does this mean we're takin' a trip?" Baz inquired.

"We are." He looked at each team member. "Any volunteers?"

Charlie was the first to speak up. "If you absolutely need me, I'm there. But if you think you'll have enough without me, I'd prefer to sit this one out."

Brantley knew Charlie was dealing with some issues with her mother, so he understood her need to remain here.

"Same," JJ noted.

Brantley looked at Baz. "You game?"

"I go where you tell me to, boss."

When he looked at Trey, his brother said, "Same."

"The four of us then," he decided, turning his attention to JJ. "Tell me what we're lookin' at."

Instantly, a map appeared on the television screen.

"Port Isabel is twenty-three miles northeast of Brownsville, close to the border. You're talkin' a total area of roughly fourteen square miles, half of which is water. Plus, you've got access to South Padre Island via the Queen Isabella Causeway. From the looks of it, there's nowhere to hide but a few options for hightailin' it outta there."

Exactly what Brantley was afraid of.

But he had to think positive on this. They'd gotten further than they ever had. No sense in dooming them to fail at this point.

"We'll do what we can," he told the team. "We'll need vehicles and possibly a place to stay while we're there. Check with RT, see if they've got somethin' that doesn't stand out in or around the area. We need to go in as silently as possible."

"You think she's there?"

"There's only one way to find out."

REESE DIDN'T BOTHER ASKING BRANTLEY WHERE HE was going when the man up and left the barn. He didn't have to.

If they truly were close to finding Juliet Prince—and he prayed to fuck they were—then Brantley was heading out to tell Travis.

"You think he'll let Travis come along for the ride?" Baz asked, coming to stand beside him.

Still staring at the door Brantley had just exited, Reese shrugged. "I don't think he wants to make that decision." Changing the subject, he met Baz's gaze. "You sure you're cool to go? How're things goin' with Molly?"

He saw the instant Baz's expression fell, that mask falling in place.

Reese had been doing his best to stay out of Baz's business for the past few weeks, but he couldn't help but worry. His one-night stand was now his future baby mama, and Baz had been spending a tremendous amount of time dealing with the woman. And while Reese understood personal issues sometimes took precedence, this was one that seemed to be bogging Baz down.

"I asked about her next appointment," Baz answered, his voice lacking any luster whatsoever. "Told her I'd like to go with her if I'm in town."

"What did she say?"

"She didn't answer me."

"As in she ignored you?"

"More like she avoided the question. Changed the subject."

Ah, hell. That was fucked up.

Reese didn't say as much, but he found this woman's responses suspicious. She'd bombarded Baz with the news that she was pregnant only a couple of days after they'd slept together, yet she was unwilling to provide absolute proof. Admittedly, Reese didn't know anything about pregnancies, but he thought it took a little longer than two days for a woman to know for certain.

Not that he was questioning it. If Molly Ryan said she was pregnant, he had no reason to believe otherwise. What he found odd was the fact that she was withholding the big things from the man she claimed was the father. When Baz asked to see the pregnancy test, she refused. When he asked to go to the doctor when she got the test to confirm—something she said she was doing—she refused him. Now, when she was going into her ninth week and could get an ultrasound, she wasn't willing to let Baz be part of it? Something was off.

And fine, maybe the woman was private. Maybe she wasn't comfortable letting him be part of it in that regard. But she had no qualms texting him three dozen times a day in an attempt to see him. The woman had messaged and called him so many times, Brantley'd finally had to say something about it. She had become a disruption to their work, and Brantley asked Baz to deal with it.

For the record, it hadn't worked. The woman was relentless.

Reese didn't bother asking Baz how things were going between him and JJ. He was there. He could see that it was ... well, the word he'd use would be *weird*. Those two seemed to have become best buds in recent weeks. They were working side by side, still living together, going to and from work together. It was as though they'd never had a romantic entanglement at all.

Speaking of JJ...

"I think you'll have company on your trip," she said, speaking directly to Reese. "When I called RT for housin' options, he mentioned he was sendin' someone down there ahead of y'all. A Decker Bromwell, I think. Said he'd be waitin' at the airport."

"Good. We could use the help." Unless this was the guy who had failed already. If so, it was probably a waste of manpower.

As far as Reese was concerned, the more boots on the ground they had the better, but he preferred someone capable. Although he wouldn't stop until they found Juliet Prince, he wouldn't deny he hoped they found her sooner rather than later. As it was, they'd been at it full throttle ever since Kylie's funeral, and they had little to nothing to show for it.

Sure, Z was busy perfecting their facial recognition algorithm, and they'd compiled a list of people they knew to have associated with Juliet at some point in her life. Thanks to social media posts mostly, they'd documented quite a few people they were keeping an eye on to ensure she didn't seek their help, but so far, those had turned up nothing.

Hunting door to door was their only option. And if that didn't work … well, Reese was fairly certain it was going to come down to drawing Juliet out from her hiding spot.

Truth was, he wasn't quite ready to see what that entailed. Whatever it was, it didn't sound good. For anyone.

Two hours later, they were boarding Sniper 1 Security's private jet.

It had taken less than an hour for the team to get everything in order, another half hour to swing through and grab go-bags and whatnot. JJ and Charlie had stayed behind, agreeing to get access to the camera feeds Z was monitoring so they would know what they were dealing with.

"What're we waitin' on?" Reese asked Brantley as they sat on the tarmac.

"We've got one more comin'."

Reese sighed. "You couldn't talk him out of it?"

Brantley glanced over, frowned. "Who?"

"Travis? I assume he's joinin' us?"

Brantley relaxed again, stared straight ahead. "Actually, no. He and Gage are sittin' tight. I promised to keep them in the loop."

Reese knew his shock was evident. Never would he have predicted Travis would back off of this. Sure, the man had calmed some since Kylie's funeral, what with the tree-planting ceremonies and all, but Reese knew he hadn't stopped completely.

"You tell him where we're goin'?"

"I did."

That was the first mistake.

It all made perfect sense now. There was no reason for Travis to make the trek as long as he knew where she was. He understood Brantley's need to ensure Travis realized how hard they were working on this. After all, they all felt responsible because they hadn't caught Juliet back when she'd kidnapped Kate. However, Reese knew Travis. He figured it was safe to say he knew the man better than Brantley did. Had to do with the fact he had worked for Travis for so long, spent time with him and his family over the years while Brantley was still in the navy. And what Brantley didn't know was that Travis had gotten pretty good at keeping his hands clean in matters such as this one.

He would bet good money Travis was already on the phone with Max Adorite. Reese still fully believed that man was going to interfere in this investigation, and they'd be lucky to find Juliet Prince's body when all was said and done.

And while he didn't give a shit what happened to Juliet, he did not want to see anyone go down for it. Not Travis, not Brantley, not anyone close to them. Not even Max. Everyone who knew Max knew what the man was capable of. But just because he hadn't been caught up to this point didn't mean he'd be home free forever.

With a sigh, Reese glanced at Brantley. "Who're we waitin' for then?"

"Magnus," Brantley said so softly Reese hardly heard him.

Reese knew he shouldn't look at Trey, but he couldn't help himself. The man had no idea he was about to be thrust into a situation that might not be comfortable for him. No one knew exactly what had happened on New Year's Eve when he left Moonshiners at the same time as Magnus Storme, but it wasn't difficult to draw his own conclusions.

"There he is," Brantley announced.

All eyes went to the door, remained there until Magnus appeared, a four-legged partner with him.

"Glad you could make it," Brantley said, half standing and holding out his hand to Magnus.

"Glad I could, too." Magnus shook Brantley's hand and nodded toward the dog at the end of the leash in his other hand. "This is Adira. She's my most reliable tracker. If anyone can help us, she can."

Reese's attention shifted to Tesha, who had been snoozing on the bed Reese had brought for her. Now she was sitting, head lifted, eyes locked on the newcomer.

"Don't worry," Magnus said, as though reading Reese's mind. "She's good with other dogs."

"Yeah," he muttered. "But is Tesha?"

Clearly he heard him because Magnus answered with, "Absolutely. These two ladies were introduced long ago. In fact, Adira's helped with some of Tesha's training." He lowered his voice, commanded Adira with a single word. "Greet."

Tail wagging, Adira trotted the few feet to Tesha, then leaned in and nuzzled her nose before sitting once more.

Tesha was instantly up, her full body wagging as she whimpered at Adira.

"Home," Magnus instructed.

And just like that, Adira turned into a lovable pup, yipping and hopping like she'd been born to play with Tesha.

"I'm impressed," Brantley told Magnus.

"You should be. I'm damned good at what I do."

Reese barked a laugh as he caught the way Magnus was looking at Trey when he spoke. When Trey's gaze slammed into Reese, he clamped his mouth shut, trying to hold it in.

This was going to get interesting.

Especially since Brantley chose that moment to inform Trey that he was now partnered with Magnus while Baz would be working with Decker Bromwell.

Yep. Very, very interesting.

"YOU DID THAT ON PURPOSE."

Brantley looked over at Reese. "Did *what* on purpose?"

"Invited Magnus."

"I assure you, I had no ulterior motives," he lied, glancing back at his brother briefly.

Reese sighed, probably thinking that, of all the people he knew, he'd never expected Brantley to be such a meddler.

In his defense, he wasn't necessarily meddling. More like paying Trey back. Being older, Trey had picked on him endlessly growing up, and now that Brantley was in a position to give back, he couldn't resist.

Or it could be the fact Brantley'd seen something different in Trey recently. Initially it had been what he believed was depression. Since he wasn't a doctor and couldn't very well make a medical diagnosis, he'd been keeping an eye on his brother. And the one thing he noticed that did bring Trey out of his funk ... well, it happened to be the dog trainer.

So.

Here they were.

Turning his head toward Reese, Brantley said, "Tell me what you know about Max Adorite."

"Not a whole lot, honestly. Probably not any more than what you've read about him. Mob boss. Took over the Adorite Crime Family, a.k.a. the Southern Boy Mafia, when his father, Samuel, was murdered."

"Murdered? By whom?"

"No one seems to know."

"Not even Madison?"

Brantley saw the shock on Reese's face when he mentioned the name.

"If she does, she never said." His gaze swung to the window. "She never really said much of anything about her family."

That surprised Brantley. For whatever reason, he'd conjured up this loving, open relationship between Reese and Madison. One that involved dinners with the family, date nights, flowers, and breakfasts in bed, a lot of laughing and smiling.

Yeah, so his imagination had likely superimposed a bunch of flowery bullshit, but it didn't change the fact that Reese had asked the woman to marry him.

"I read somewhere that he owns a club?" Brantley said, wanting to keep Reese talking.

"Devil's Playground. Several locations across the country. Hot spot for the young and hip."

"You go there often?"

Reese chuckled. "I haven't been young and hip for a damn long time."

Brantley knew Reese wasn't referring to his age. Being that he was thirty-one, Reese would fall into the young category. However, it was the storm clouds in his eyes that told the story of how he'd come to live too hard, too fast. One day, Brantley hoped to learn what had happened that put those clouds there.

"This club … it a front for his businesses?"

"I'm not a forensic accountant, but I figure it's a safe bet he launders money through. Certainly a perfect cash-producing setup."

"What else is he into?"

"Guns and drugs mostly," Reese answered easily. "He's got some legit stuff goin' on, too. He's acquired more since he married Courtney Kogan."

Brantley still had a hard time wrapping his head around that one. The head of a criminal organization marrying the daughter of a private security firm that worked diligently to remain on the right side of the law. He'd been even more surprised when Hunter and Trace had spoken somewhat affectionately for their brother-in-law. Granted, he didn't think they were best buds with the man, but still.

Brantley considered all he'd just learned, then turned to Reese once more. "You think Travis called Max yet?"

"If not, then he's on the phone with the guy right now."

Yeah. He figured that, too.

And strangely, Brantley wasn't as bothered by it as he probably should've been.

Chapter Twenty-One

"YOU OKAY?"

Travis looked up, saw Gage standing in the doorway to his home office. "Yeah. Why?"

Gage's response was a quirk of his eyebrow.

"I'm good," he assured the man. "I promised I would sit on the information Brantley gave us."

"You did say that, yes." Gage didn't look convinced. "Doesn't mean you have."

Travis considered what he wanted to tell his husband. Since Gage used to be a police officer, having gone the route of undercover for a long time, he knew the man leaned more on the right side of the law. He believed in the justice system.

Travis, on the other hand, believed in taking care of your own shit. Probably had something to do with growing up in a small town. They tended to deal with their own issues, settle things between them without involving the law. Growing up, when someone wronged another, it was settled with fists, not phone calls. They didn't call the police in to deal with their problems. Sure, the sheriff's department had always had their own agenda, sticking their nose in where it didn't necessarily belong, but that didn't mean they were invited.

Gage strolled around and took a seat on the couch directly across from Travis's desk. He propped his ankle on his knee and regarded Travis carefully.

Travis could see the curiosity in Gage's eyes, knew he wasn't going to leave until Travis started talking.

"Did you call him?"

Travis considered playing dumb, pretending he didn't know who Gage was referring to. However, they were making strides in repairing their relationship, and the last thing he wanted was to cause a setback.

"Not yet." Travis held Gage's stare. "I was about to."

"What's stoppin' you?"

"I wanted to talk to you first."

And that was the God's honest truth. From the moment Brantley had informed them that they had an actual location—albeit seventy-two hours old—on Juliet Prince, he'd been itching to call Max. He knew the Mafia boss would deal with the problem, make it go away once and for all without Travis ever having to get his hands dirty.

The only thing that had stopped him was the fact Gage deserved a say in what happened to the woman. After all, Kylie was Gage's wife, too. Maybe not in the eyes of the law, no, but he was where it counted.

"Talk to me about what?"

"He can take care of her," Travis said. "All I have to do is say the word."

"I'm sure he will. But what'll you be in for? We both know Adorites don't do favors for free."

No, they certainly did not. And though Travis had asked for a few favors from Max over the years, he'd only been called on once to return it. That particular incident had required Travis to manipulate a situation, maneuvering a person to a certain spot by using his resort as the carrot.

He had no idea what'd happened after that, nor did he care to. What Max did was his business. Whether it was legal or not was also his business.

"If it ever came down to it, can the feds tie you to him?" Gage asked.

"As an acquaintance, maybe," Travis admitted. "But it'd be circumstantial at best."

Gage seemed to consider that before he said, "And what is it you're askin' him for this time?"

Travis opted for honesty. "I want him to make her disappear. Permanently."

Gage nodded, as though processing that information.

Travis wasn't sure what he'd expected, but it wasn't for Gage to slowly get to his feet and head for the door.

But what shocked him the most was when Gage turned back around and said, "Then I suggest you don't let the task force find her. It'd be best if no one ever lays eyes on her again." He started to pull the door shut. "I'll just close this so you can make that call."

When Gage left the room, Travis stared after him for a few minutes, letting his instructions sink in.

Travis should probably have worried that he didn't have a crisis of conscience when it came to ordering a hit on Juliet Prince. And that was what it was, no matter how he wanted to pretty it up and call it a favor. He was asking one human being to eliminate another.

The question he had was who would he rather do it? Did he call Max and finalize his request, or did he take matters into his own hands? No, he'd never killed anyone, nor had he actually considered it before.

Had he played a part in having some really nasty people taken care of? Yeah. When his cousin Wolfe's wife, Amy, had been running from a sadistic fuck who'd used his position of power to abuse and beat her, to kill her family and imprison her, Travis had called Max. And he'd never lost a moment of sleep for it.

And when his cousin Jared's ex-wife used her own child to manipulate Jared, to punish him for absolutely no reason, Travis had stepped in. No, Sable wasn't dead, but to this day Travis kept an eye on her, ensuring she did not come back and interfere in their lives.

Travis didn't pretend to be a saint. Never had. Nor was he going to lose sleep over the decision he had to make now.

Taking a deep breath, Travis opened his top drawer, pulled out the burner phone he'd been sent for this specific instance, and dialed the familiar number.

"Yeah?" the gruff voice answered.

"I'm finalizin' my request."

"Where?"

"Port Isabel, Texas," he stated firmly. "It's a rush job."

"Understood."

When the call ended, Travis pulled the battery out of the phone. His next order of business was to destroy it as he'd been instructed.

Still sitting, he glanced at the picture of Kylie on his desk. "It's almost done, baby. Just like I promised."

MAXIMILLIAN ADORITE STOOD ON THE VERANDA OVERLOOKING his estate.

He sipped coffee, enjoying the pleasant weather and the cool breeze. He'd been up much of the night dealing with urgent business and he was slow going today. But he didn't mind the downtime. In fact, he enjoyed what little bit of peace he could find in a day.

When Rock stepped forward, Max passed the phone over to him. "Destroy it."

"Consider it done."

Since Rock, born Taye Smith, was one of his most loyal enforcers, he knew the man could be trusted to protect him, to ensure nothing would blow back on him in the end. It was because of people like Rock that Max's family had been able to build the life they had. And it was Rock and the others in Max's employ who he would ensure were taken care of for as long as they were loyal and true.

"Where's my wife?" Max asked.

"She went to visit her parents, then she was gonna put in a few hours at the office. Said she'd be back by dinner."

Max smiled. He recalled the conversation that had taken place. The one in which Courtney had done her wifely duty of inviting him to go with her to her parents' house. They'd both known before she made the request that he would decline, yet she'd done it anyway because that was what they did.

The thing was, they were on opposite sides of the law when it came to most things. Being an Adorite meant Max's wealth was built on shaky ground—the vast majority of it having been accumulated through what most considered illegal means—while Courtney was a Kogan and her family had dedicated their life's work to protecting people through any means necessary.

It was true when they said opposites attract. And if he was being completely honest, having so much opposition on various things only spiced up a relationship. Max loved Courtney beyond measure and would move heaven and earth to take care of her. He knew she felt the same for him, which was why she could overlook some of his more illicit, and often unethical, activities.

But when it was possible to keep her out of it, Max did so. Which was why he was heading back into the house to a secure location where there wasn't the risk of the feds catching anything he might say. After all, in order for him to grant a favor to Travis Walker, he had to call one in.

As had become the basis of his existence, Max worked on trading favors, and it always paid to have someone owe him.

Especially someone with a ruthless disregard for human existence.

Chapter Twenty-Two

TREY DID HIS BEST NOT TO STARE at the man sitting across from him.

It wasn't easy.

Hell, staying away from Magnus had proved futile, despite Trey's insistence that celibacy was the only answer.

Yeah, it was safe to say it was off the table at this point. For the past week, he and Magnus had been hooking up routinely, missing only a day or two because of conflicting schedules. Their interludes were always at Trey's and they never resulted in an overnight. Sure, they would often pass out after, but Magnus was always gone by morning.

And most importantly, they were keeping their encounters on the DL. Trey did not want it to get back to his brother or anyone else what was going on. He didn't want to deal with anyone's judgment or concern. If he wanted to fuck Magnus with no strings attached, by God, he was going to do it.

As he sat there, fighting the urge to look at Magnus, Trey wondered whether or not there was any privacy at the back of the small plane. It was bigger than he'd thought it would be. A Gulfstream rather than a puddle jumper, so he figured it was safe to say there was at least one room at the back.

Did they have enough time to bang one out real quick? Would anyone notice they were gone?

Okay, so the answer to the last one was *most likely*. After all, if one person moved, everyone saw them. So maybe the better question was: would it matter if they did see? As long as they had privacy, Trey could pretend they were just chatting about the case.

Brantley would believe that.

Maybe.

Oh, who the fuck cared?

Trey figured there was only one way to find out.

Once they were at cruising altitude, Trey unbuckled his seat belt, got to his feet. He shot a heated look at Magnus before walking to the back, praying that no one else was paying any attention. It would've been hard for them not to considering their close quarters, but still Trey pretended Brantley, Reese, and Baz were too preoccupied or too uninterested to pay them any mind.

Sure enough, aside from a small bathroom, there was also a room that appeared to be utilized as an office. It was no more than fifteen square feet max, but it was more than enough room to—

Trey's thoughts were cut off instantly when Magnus appeared, stepping into the space and gently closing the door. Like their other encounters, they were instantly on one another, lips crashing, tongues thrashing.

"I take it you're glad to see me," Magnus muttered against his mouth, already ripping at Trey's jeans.

"I'll be happy to see your mouth on my dick," he countered, gripping Magnus's hair firmly in his fist.

Magnus's hazel eyes glittered with heat as Trey guided him to his knees, ensuring he held tight to his hair, wanting him to feel the pain, to know exactly who was in charge now.

Trey watched as Magnus unbuttoned and unzipped him. The man was sexy as fuck, there was no doubt about that. And his mouth... Fucking hell, he had some serious talent. Talent Trey fully intended to take advantage of.

When Magnus freed his cock, Trey exhaled heavily, then inhaled sharply when those lips wrapped around him, enveloping him in soft, wet heat. He never looked away, guiding Magnus's head, feeding his cock deep into Magnus's throat.

"God, you're fuckin' good at that," he mumbled, forcing his eyes not to roll back in his head from the pleasure of it.

He thrust his hips, fucking Magnus's face, knowing they only had a few minutes alone before the others would wonder where they were. He focused his attention on the sexy sight before him, the way Magnus's eyes bulged when Trey hit the back of his throat. He did it again and again until he couldn't hold back.

With a grunt, he pushed his hips forward and came right down Magnus's throat.

Trey didn't get the chance to linger in post-orgasm bliss, righting his clothes as Magnus got to his feet.

But before Magnus could slip out, Trey pushed him up against the wall and kissed him again. He lingered longer than before, the razor-sharp edge now dulled.

"I look forward to you payin' me back for that later," Magnus whispered against his mouth.

Trey pulled back, grinned. "You're not the only one."

He let Magnus leave the room ahead of him, then waited a couple of minutes. He glanced down to ensure his clothes weren't askew, then when he figured the coast was clear, Trey stepped out.

It took effort not to smile.

More so not to think about when they were going to have a chance to do that again.

THE ONE-HOUR FLIGHT WAS UNEVENTFUL, ALLOWING Reese to catch a few minutes of sleep when Brantley did. He figured Brantley's reasons had more to do with his training than anything. He'd once mentioned, during his time with the Teams, they were forced to catch sleep when they could during missions. A skill that was obviously still ingrained in him.

When they touched down, they found Decker Bromwell waiting.

"This is the best I could do," Deck informed them, gesturing toward a ten-year-old Ford Taurus, a seen-better-days Honda Odyssey, and what had probably once been a relatively nice BMW.

"If you were goin' for inconspicuous, you did good," Brantley told him.

"And if you were goin' for reliable, you probably failed miserably," Baz noted.

"They run," Deck assured them. "Maybe not for long, but they'll get the job done."

Reese was betting they'd crap out sooner rather than later, but for now, they would do. No one expected them to be here long, so if they were lucky, it wouldn't matter.

"Do we know where she was last seen?" Brantley asked, accepting a set of keys from Deck.

"We've got one sighting of her at the Starbucks, another nearby. Two different days."

"So it's safe to assume she's stayin' somewhere around there?"

"There's not much ground to cover, to be honest. She could be stayin' anywhere, including on South Padre for all we know."

"We're gonna assume she's here," Reese told him. "And we're gonna do a grid search accordingly. There's six of us. We go door to door, business to business. Someone's seen her. It's just a matter of gettin' to her before she realizes we're here."

"Baz and Deck, y'all can start from the south, work your way north," Brantley instructed. "Trey and Magnus, work west to east. We'll take north to south, meet somewhere in the middle."

Reese opened his go-bag, pulled out a sealed plastic bag, and passed it to Magnus. "We were able to get some of Juliet's things. If you're lucky, that'll have her scent."

"We'll see what we can do," Magnus said, taking the bag. "Adira's my best, so if she can be tracked, she'll find her."

Reese hoped that was the case. He honestly wanted this to be over.

While they were standing in the parking lot at the private airstrip, another plane came in for a landing, this one smaller than the one they'd come in on.

"Just FYI, this isn't a busy place," Deck noted. "I've been here for two hours and there've been no other planes in or out."

Now there were two in a short time.

"No sense in stickin' around to see who it is," Brantley said, glancing at Reese.

Reese agreed. If that happened to be someone sent by Max Adorite, it would be best for them to hit the ground running. Even a few minutes in front of them might help.

Still, he kept his eyes on the plane as they piled into the cars and drove away. No one exited and they didn't pass any vehicles sent to pick up a passenger. Maybe he was overthinking this. It was possible the plane was coming to pick someone up, take them to their destination.

"Let's focus on the task at hand," Brantley said. "We can't control what Max Adorite does."

"You're right."

"Plus, we should have a couple of hours on him."

Reese didn't bother to mention Max wouldn't be the one flying down here. They wouldn't be waiting for someone coming from Dallas. Knowing Max, he would call in a favor from someone local. Perhaps someone in Mexico.

For all they knew, that person could already be there.

BRANTLEY WASTED NO TIME HEADING FOR THE most populated places. He figured if they did end up going house to house, that would be their last resort. For now he wanted to focus on the businesses, mainly restaurants and motels.

He steered the BMW into the first motel they saw, pulling into a spot near the main office.

It was a single-story setup, probably two dozen rooms if he had to guess. There were a couple of cars and one motorcycle parked in spaces in front of the rooms, but other than that, the parking lot was empty. He saw no one, only a housekeeping cart stopped outside the first room behind the office structure.

Brantley walked into the motel office, leaving Reese to keep an eye out in the parking lot.

"Welcome," a man with thinning hair and a bushy gray beard greeted. "What can I help you with?"

Brantley held up the picture of Juliet Prince, pressed it to the plexiglass barrier. "Have you seen this woman?"

The man leaned in to get a better look, squinting. He didn't bother to put on the glasses that were dangling around his neck.

"She looks familiar," he said, still staring.

"She's probably changed her hair color, maybe cut it."

"Yeah," he said with a nod, standing tall once more. "Sure. That could be Mary Smith."

Mary Smith? *Very original, Juliet.*

Before the man could elaborate, the phone on his desk rang.

"Excuse me a minute," the man said, turning to snatch the receiver up.

Brantley glanced around, looking out the windows as a Ford truck was pulling into the lot. He couldn't make out the driver as it puttered past, coughing black smoke in its wake.

"Sorry 'bout that," the manager said.

Brantley turned back around. "You said this might be Mary Smith," he prompted.

"Oh, right. Yes. But her hair's red now. Pretty shade, too." The man smiled, revealing a missing left incisor. "You're the second person whose been in here lookin' for her today."

Second?

Brantley sighed. "Do you have a description of the other guy?"

"Mexican fellow. Tattoos. Didn't speak much English." The man looked skeptical when he asked, "Are you with the police?"

"No, sir. I'm with a private investigation firm."

"And what do you want with Mary?"

Brantley figured telling him the woman was wanted for murder could send him into a panic, so he opted for another logical explanation. "Her family hired us to find her." He added some sympathy to his tone. "They're worried."

That was the right way to go based on the way the man's face softened somewhat. "She does look sad sometimes. Probably misses them, too."

Because they were wasting time and Brantley didn't want to risk Juliet seeing them, he urged the man for more information. "Can you tell me what room she's stayin' in?"

"I'm sorry, I can't—"

Brantley's cell phone rang. He held up his finger for the man to wait, then answered with a gruff, "Walker."

"You've got exactly twenty minutes," the deep voice said.

"Who is this?"

"Nice to make your acquaintance, Brantley Walker. My name's Max Adorite."

Leaving the balding man and his various excuses behind him, Brantley walked back out to the parking lot, moving toward the car where Reese was currently standing.

"What happens in twenty minutes?" Brantley asked, mouthing to Reese that Max was on the phone as he put it on speaker.

"One of two things, I figure."

Brantley scanned the parking lot.

"Options, I assume?"

"You're as good as Travis says you are."

He sighed heavily, ensuring Max heard his frustration.

"If you look across the parking lot, you'll see a late-model Ford truck."

Brantley was already looking at the truck, noting the driver was still in it but it was now backed into a spot at the back of the lot.

"In twenty minutes, the fine gentleman in that truck is gonna go inside room 114 and he's gonna deal with some business. For him to do so, it would be ideal for you and your friends to head on over to the Starbucks, where there are security cameras. Those cameras are gonna record you and your friends buyin' coffee."

Brantley looked at Reese. "Or?"

"Or you've got *nineteen* minutes now to go to room 114 and do whatever you feel is necessary with the heinous bitch who's inside at this very moment."

Max Adorite was giving them the choice of apprehending Juliet Prince or providing them with an alibi.

"It's your choice, Brantley."

"Does Travis know about this?"

"At this very moment, Travis and his husband are at the resort where they are bein' caught on camera going about their daily lives, runnin' their business. He's well aware of the options and he informed me to leave the decision-makin' to you. Like I said, your choice. Eighteen minutes and counting."

The call ended, leaving Brantley to look at Reese.

He wished he could pretend it was a no-brainer, that they needed to storm that motel room and call the police. But the truth was, that wasn't Brantley's first thought.

However, he was leaving the final decision-making up to Reese because, when it came down to it, Reese's conscience was clearer.

Neither of them said anything for a moment, then Reese pulled out his phone, dialed.

"Hey, Baz…"

Brantley waited, holding his breath.

"Meet us over at Starbucks in fifteen. Let's regroup."

Exhaling heavily, Brantley avoided looking at room 114 or the older-model Ford truck with the not-so-kind-looking gentleman behind the wheel. Instead, he walked around to the driver's side, slid into the car.

A minute later, they were backing out of the parking lot, Reese making the same call to Trey.

JULIET WAS BEGINNING TO ENJOY HER TIME in this small port city.

It was too bad she had to leave. If it weren't for the fact she'd felt as though someone was watching her, this would've been the perfect place to settle in for a while. Well, mainly for the reason that it wasn't too crowded. Aside from that, it was a dump. And maybe also, despite the fact most of the people were desperately lower class, they were polite to her, which made them easier to tolerate. She could almost see herself interacting with them for a little while. Until she could get her new identity established, at least. At that point, she wouldn't be caught dead in a place like this.

Although the news story about the reward for her capture had died down somewhat, she knew there were still people out there willing to jump at the chance to get their grubby hands on that money. For them, the story would never die. Which meant she had to keep moving, preferably somewhere that didn't get the local news.

Until that time, a few days in one spot was all she could afford. This was already day five, and she knew she was pushing her luck every extra minute she was here. She'd originally intended to be in Mexico by now, figuring they wouldn't care much about what was going on in the US, certainly not in some Podunk little town. She could sip margaritas for a while before venturing back to the States to finish her business with Travis Walker once and for all. Only she knew she couldn't simply walk in through a checkpoint.

But the good news was, just a little while ago, she'd finally found someone willing to fly her into Mexico, no questions asked. It had been pure luck she'd been having lunch at the only restaurant in town when she overheard a man on the phone. At first she hadn't understood him because he spoke in Spanish, but then he had started talking in heavily accented English. If it wasn't for the fact he was talking about a charter plane, she never would've approached him. He was not the sort she would talk to on a good day. He was obviously not American, and all those tattoos … they'd given her the creeps.

But Juliet had sucked it up out of necessity.

Of course, he'd been more than willing to do her bidding when she'd offered him money. Juliet had seen the gleam in his eyes. The guy was lowlife scum, probably worked for one of the cartels and would take any tiny crumb she threw his way, so she'd made him an offer she knew he wouldn't refuse. Two thousand dollars to fly her over the border. He hadn't even batted an eyelash before saying yes, only asking for half up-front, the other half when he picked her up to take her to the airport.

As much as she despised the idea of being anywhere near the guy, it worked in her favor and that was all that mattered. She just needed a few months off the grid, some time to catch her breath. At that point, she would pick up where she left off. Eventually Travis Walker would move on with his life, forget she was a threat. At that point, she'd have him right where she wanted him.

A knock sounded on her motel room door as she was tossing the rest of her stuff into her bag. She wanted to leave a few things behind, to let the people looking for her know that she had been here, right under their noses. Juliet was beginning to enjoy this cat and mouse game as much as she enjoyed this little town.

"Señorita, we must go," the muffled voice said through the door.

Juliet smiled. That was her ride to the airport.

She glanced around the room one last time, hand on the knob.

Yes, she had everything she needed for now.

She opened the door and stepped back, ensuring she didn't accidentally touch the loathsome man. Pointing to her bag, she instructed him to get it as she put her sunglasses on her nose. No sense risking someone recognizing her now.

"Of course, señorita," the man said, his tone harder than it had been before.

There was a niggling at the back of her neck, a warning that she probably should've heeded before she allowed him to come into the room.

By the time she realized there was a threat, it was too late.

She didn't even have enough time for one last thought before the bullet hit her right between the eyes.

No one ever even heard the shot.

Chapter Twenty-Three

Friday, March 5, 2021

"I STILL CAN'T BELIEVE THAT WAS A dead end," JJ bitched, leaning against one of the empty desks, arms crossed over her chest.

Brantley watched her, not looking over at Reese, which would've been his first instinct.

It had been three days since their quick trip down to Port Isabel. When they'd come back empty-handed, JJ hadn't taken it well. Every day since, she'd been grumbling, continuing to pore over data in an attempt to find out where Juliet Prince was staying.

"It happens," Baz said, sounding equally bothered by it.

"But Mexico?" JJ grumbled. "How'd she get a flight out of the country?"

"It happens every day," Reese said, passing Brantley a cup of coffee.

"We'll get her," Trey promised. "One day, her crazy will have her comin' back and—"

Brantley's brother stopped talking when a breaking news story flashed on the television screen. The news desk reporter appeared, along with a caption on the bottom that read: *Victim believed to be Juliet Prince, wanted for kidnapping and murder.*

"Turn it up," Brantley barked.

JJ grabbed the remote, hit the volume button.

"We're bringing you a breaking story out of Port Isabel, Texas. On scene is our very own Michelle Bentley. Michelle, can you tell us what's going on down there?"

"Yes, thanks, Michael." The woman standing in front of a motel sign stared directly into the camera. "You might remember the story we brought you nearly two months ago. Coyote Ridge resident Kylie Walker was run down and killed by this woman"— an image of Juliet Prince appeared on the screen—"Juliet Prince, only a few months after she allegedly kidnapped Kylie's daughter, Kate. We brought you this story when Kylie's family offered a one-hundred-thousand-dollar reward for any information that would lead to her capture.

"Just a few hours ago, we learned that Prince's body was found in a motel room here in Port Isabel, Texas, a small town about twenty miles north of Brownsville. I'm on scene now, and as you can see behind me, crime scene techs are still working.

"I spoke to local officials earlier, and they informed us they will continue to investigate Prince's death but are stating they believe it to be an attempted mugging gone wrong. Along with several false IDs, police recovered close to two hundred thousand dollars in Prince's motel room. They believe the perpetrator fled the scene after the altercation. If we learn anything more, we will be reporting to you first."

The news desk reporter returned. "Thanks, Michelle, for that update." He glanced down at a tablet on his desk, then back to the camera. "We also wanted to mention that when we followed up with the Walker family just a few minutes ago, they informed us they had utilized the services of Sniper 1 Security to aid in the investigation, and they expressed their gratitude for everyone who assisted in the search for the woman. We reached out to Sniper 1 Security for a statement. They told us they regret that the family was unable to see her brought to justice but are grateful the threat to the family has been eliminated.

"And while the one-hundred-thousand-dollar reward will not be paid, the Walker family will be donating it to the National Center for Missing and Exploited Children."

JJ clicked off the television and all eyes turned to him.

As much as Brantley wanted to pretend he was surprised by the news, he couldn't. At the same time, he was unwilling to divulge any information to the rest of the team. Brantley would keep it so that he and Reese were the only ones who knew about Max Adorite's phone call that provided them with the alibi they needed. If the investigation made it far enough, he knew they would be called in because they were in the area at the time of her death. Hence the reason they had gathered at the local coffee shop for their brief team meeting, in which Brantley relayed that they'd gotten intel that Juliet had crossed the border into Mexico. They had gone straight to the airport after, catching a flight back home.

"She's dead," JJ said, her eyes wide. "I know it probably makes me a bad person that I'm happy about it, but it's true."

Brantley figured there were a lot of people who wouldn't lose sleep over the woman's death. She had put Travis's family through hell, and they'd lost far more than anyone should have because of her vendetta.

JJ flopped into a chair and exhaled heavily. "What do we do now? I mean, we've spent so long workin' on this…"

"I've got a suggestion," Trey said, stepping forward.

All eyes shifted to him.

"My family's got a beach house and spring break is comin' up. Maybe we take a couple of days, head down there, clear our heads."

"A week," Brantley decided.

Heads turned back toward him.

"We'll take a week to regroup," he repeated.

"Before we spend several in Dallas," Reese noted.

"Dallas?" JJ frowned. "Why would we wanna do that?"

"Because we've got some trainin' to do."

JJ sighed. "Damn that Sniper 1 training."

And just like that, the tension dissipated.

TRAVIS PULLED UP TO HIS HOUSE FEELING different.

When he'd gotten the call this morning from the news investigator, he'd had to feign surprise when the man officially informed Travis of Juliet Prince's death. It hadn't been difficult since it was the first time he'd actually heard it.

Sure, he had suspected since Brantley and his team had returned from Port Isabel without Juliet and he had seen nothing of her arrest on the news. Yes, he'd taken that to mean she had been dealt with accordingly, but he hadn't had confirmation.

However, his relief had not been pretend. If it made him a monster that he was glad the bitch was dead, so be it. He wouldn't want it any other way. The woman deserved far worse than a bullet between the eyes.

Travis pushed the button to kill the engine. Grabbing his cell phone and the smart key, he climbed out of the SUV. If he was lucky, his phone would not ring for at least eight hours, preferably ten.

As it was, he had spent the majority of the day at the resort with Gage taking phone calls from family and friends, all following up on what they'd heard. He couldn't count how many times he confirmed that she was no longer a threat. Even though he'd repeated it, it hadn't really sunk in until just now, as he was walking into his house.

His empty, quiet house.

Kate and Avery were at his parents' with Ethan and Beau's daughter, Kiera. They had promised to help Lorrie with the baby in return for chocolate chip cookies, popcorn, and another showing of *Frozen*.

Kade was at Kaleb's playing with Mason, Kellan, Barrett, and Gabriel. Travis figured if Kaleb and Zoey were brave enough to request one more boy in their midst, who was he to deny them?

Haden was with Jessie and Braydon, spending the night with Rhett, Zachary, and Waylon. From what he'd heard, Brendon and Cheyenne would be hanging out so Remy and Thad could play, too.

And last but not least, Maddox was with Zane and V, playing with Theo and Dustin, but only because Sawyer and Kennedy had taken Zane's two oldest, Reid and Asher, to their place. Sawyer insisted they managed better when Matthew and Brody had other kids to keep them company.

Travis knew it was all a ruse to give him and Gage some time alone. It wasn't easy for any of the parents to get a break with so many kids, but they all pitched in when it was necessary to help out. And tonight Travis appreciated it more than usual.

He tossed his keys into the bowl near the door, then followed the scent of garlic coming from the kitchen.

His stomach rumbled in response, a not-so-subtle reminder that he'd had a granola bar for lunch and that had long since burned off.

"What're you makin'?" he asked when he pushed the door open to find Gage standing at the center island.

"Lasagna."

"And garlic bread?" he asked hopefully.

Gage pointed to a baking pan layered with Texas toast coated in butter and garlic.

"Figured we'd have dinner, then maybe watch a movie."

Travis was more than willing to do whatever Gage wanted to do tonight. "As long as we're naked while we do it."

"Which part? Dinner or movie?"

"Both?" Travis chuckled, moving toward Gage. "I don't care."

Unable to help himself, he cupped Gage's face and leaned in for a kiss. It wasn't urgent, not even sexual, really. Just a gentle press of lips to lips, a comfort he knew he would never be able to live without.

When he pulled back, he smiled. "I have somethin' for you."

Gage's eyebrows lowered. "I'm not sure how energetic I'll be until *after* we eat."

Travis let the words sink in, then he barked a laugh. "I wasn't talkin' about sex."

"Well, that's a first."

"Look who's talkin'."

Gage rolled his eyes.

Travis pulled a piece of paper out of his pocket, drawing Gage's attention to it.

"What's that?"

"A confirmation."

"Of?"

Travis passed it over. "Read for yourself."

When Gage took the paper and began to unfold it, Travis lowered to one knee before him.

"March twentieth. Three o'clock," Gage read.

Travis reached up, pulled Gage's hand down so he could look in his eyes. "Marry me, Gage. Marry me on March twentieth at three o'clock."

Gage smiled as he grabbed Travis's wrist and pulled him up. "I'll marry you any day, anywhere, any time."

Travis kissed him again, this time a bit more urgently. "Good."

"Where's this gonna take place?"

"At my parents' house."

Right by the tree Kylie had requested they plant.

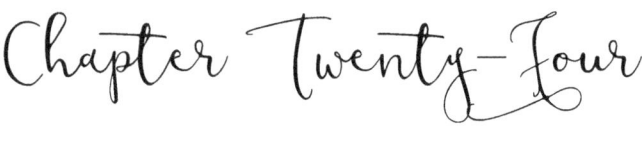

Chapter Twenty-Four

One week later
Thursday, March 11, 2021

THEY'D BEEN AT THE COAST FOR NEARLY a week. Five days to be exact. They'd made the trek on Sunday and would be leaving on Saturday, which as far as Trey was concerned was both not long enough and too long at the same time.

Oh, it had nothing to do with the relaxation. That had been incredible. Five days of nothing to do but sit down by the water, catch a nap in the warm breeze, or walk along the beach. That had been pretty much all he'd done, having promised himself he would unplug from the real world, just like his brother requested.

It had been just what the doctor ordered.

And the company wasn't half bad either.

Trey reclined in one of the many lounge chairs they'd scattered over the sand, beer in hand. Baz, JJ, Charlie, Reese, Brantley, Holly, and Luca were sitting around the campfire, laughing at the stories they'd coaxed out of him.

It was Brantley's fault. If his brother didn't react so dramatically, Trey wouldn't find so much amusement in telling them.

"Then there was this one guy," he continued, locking eyes with Brantley.

"Do not go there," Brantley growled.

"I don't even remember the dude's name," he lied. No way could Trey forget Danny Musket, but it was more enjoyable this way. "Somethin' like mustard, or muscle."

"Musket," Brantley grumbled.

"Yes!" Trey lifted his beer in a mock toast.

"Danny Musket!" JJ shouted. "Oh, my God! I forgot about him. Y'all were all up in each other's business."

"We were not," Brantley denied.

"Oh, they were," Trey confirmed. "One night, I was on duty—"

"Fuckin' mall security," Brantley hissed. "Not a cop."

"Anyway. I stopped in at E-Z's for a cup of coffee—"

"Pork rinds and Dr. Pepper," Brantley corrected, exactly as he always did.

Trey grinned. He loved how easily Brantley denied but always made the proper adjustments to the tale.

"—when what did I stumble upon?" Trey laughed. "There I was, mindin' my own business, strollin' through the parkin' lot—"

"Checkin' out the beer delivery guy," Brantley noted.

Yes, yes, he had been checking out that guy. Never did get anywhere but Trey had found him rather impressive. Tall and layered with muscle. Yum.

"—when somethin' caught my attention."

"It was Danny's Toyota truck," Brantley said quickly. "You claim it was rockin', but I call bullshit."

"My story..."

"Your lies," Brantley groused, taking a pull on his beer.

"Wait," JJ interjected. "Danny worked at the convenience store, right?"

"He did." Trey glanced around at all the faces. "And that particular night he was gettin' some action—exactly his words—while on his break."

"He did not say that," Brantley huffed.

"It's very possible he did," Trey said. At this point, the story was so convoluted, he had no idea if it was really Danny Musket. However, Brantley seemed to recall the incident, so Trey was apt to go along with it.

"I never knew you got busted makin' out in a parked car," JJ said, laughing at Brantley.

"What about you?" Brantley said, turning his attention to JJ. "I remember the time—"

JJ reached over, smacked her hand on Brantley's mouth. "Don't you dare! I mean it."

Brantley, in a quick and easy move, flipped JJ around so she fell in his lap, his arms banding around her so she couldn't hit him.

"She and Dante were havin' sex under the bleachers at the homecoming game," Brantley blurted.

JJ shouted, wrestled out of his hold, and smacked him on the arm.

Trey laughed along with everyone else. Yeah, he was glad they'd decided to do this.

It had been a difficult few months, and it was nice that they could kick back and enjoy a few days off.

"By the way, for those of you lookin' to tie one on tonight, don't," JJ warned. "We *are* goin' to the aquarium tomorrow. No matter what. It's our last day here and I am not gonna miss out."

"I'll go with you," Trey promised at the same time Baz and Charlie did.

"What about you two?" JJ asked Holly and Luca.

"We're in," Holly answered for both of them, laughing when Luca grunted.

"It's gettin' late," Reese said. "I think I'm gonna head in."

"Me, too," Brantley said as he got to his feet.

Trey was content to sit right there, the breeze off the ocean fanning the flames, keeping it relatively comfortable.

It wasn't long before everyone opted to go inside, leaving Trey to douse the blaze. Once he was sure it went out, he trudged through the sand up to the house.

He had to admit there was only one reason he was eager to get back to the real world, and it had nothing to do with his house or his job. It had everything to do with the sexy man who'd been taunting him via text message all week. Holding his ground, Trey had refused to text him back, holding out until he thought his head might explode. It had been a couple of hours ago that he'd given in to the temptation and told Magnus he was looking forward to seeing him on Saturday.

He had just made it to the small room he'd commandeered as his when his cell phone rang, an unfamiliar tone.

Yanking it from his pocket, he peered at the screen and frowned.

A FaceTime call?

From Magnus.

Trey considered ignoring it, but something compelled him to answer.

"What?" He glared at the screen as Magnus's too-handsome face appeared.

"I figured why bother waitin' till Saturday."

"You've got zero patience, you know that?"

"You havin' fun without me?"

"You're not here?" Trey rolled his eyes. "Didn't even notice."

"I doubt that. I'm sure your cock's well aware I'm not there to service it."

His fucking cock heard that statement loud and clear, thickening immediately in notice.

"I'll show you mine if you show me yours," Magnus dared.

Trey laughed, a choked sound that lodged in his throat. "You're not serious."

"No?"

Trey's eyes were locked on the screen as the camera panned away from Magnus's face, moving slowly down his... Oh, fuck that was his bare chest, his washboard abs.

Ah, hell.

His breath hitched when he saw Magnus's cock fisted proudly in the man's hand.

It only lasted a second before Magnus's face once again crowded the screen. "Your turn."

Trey looked around the small room, his eyes pausing on the bed.

"Come on, Trey. Live a little."

"Live a little, he says." Trey took a deep breath, met Magnus's gaze on the phone. "Fine, but this is your party."

"Strip first. A party's no fun with clothes."

Feeling bolder than usual, Trey stripped out of his clothes and crawled into the bed, phone still in his hand.

"Now show me yours," Magnus insisted.

It took a second for him to shore up his nerve, but Trey finally turned the camera toward his dick. He didn't have to touch the damn thing, it was standing up proud and tall all on its own.

"Holy fuck, do I miss you."

Trey chuckled, returning the camera to his face. "Do you?"

"Oh, yeah. And I'm lookin' forward to makin' your acquaintance all over again." Magnus's eyes were hooded. "Now stroke yourself, Trey."

As awkward as it was, Trey did as Magnus requested. Several minutes later, the awkwardness disappeared, leaving him with nothing but lust singeing his nerve endings and making him sweat.

"When you get back, we're gonna pick up where we left off."

Trey shook his head but didn't say anything. He knew this shouldn't be happening, knew he should invoke some sort of rule that said he could never see Magnus Storme again. He was getting in way too deep as it was. The only consolation was that Magnus continued to keep it solely about sex, which allowed Trey to maintain some distance.

"The next time I see you," Magnus continued, his voice gruff and low, "I'm gonna strip you down, run my tongue over every inch of you."

Trey continued to stroke his cock, fisting himself firmly.

"Then I'm gonna finger your ass until you're ready for me."

Ah, hell. Trey's asshole clenched at the thought.

"When you are, I'm gonna sink into you so deep you won't know where I begin and you end."

Trey grunted.

"You want that, Trey? You want me to fuck you hard and deep?"

He nodded, closing his eyes. "God, yes."

Magnus grunted and Trey recognized the sound. He was precariously close to the edge, too.

"When I'm done," Magnus crooned, "I'm gonna fuck you all over again. Harder. Faster."

Oh, Jesus.

"You wanna come for me, Trey?"

He nodded again, squeezing his eyes shut as his cock tunneled through his fist. He squeezed more firmly until he felt that electrical explosion within him.

"Oh, fuck," he growled, gritting his teeth as he came, barely aware of Magnus doing the same.

Okay, so maybe he could get used to this thing they had going.

BAZ LAY IN THE DARK ROOM TRYING to block out the fact that JJ was in the room next to him. He'd spent the better part of the past few days in her presence, still under the ruse of only being her friend.

Truth was, it was killing him.

Could he do it indefinitely if he had to? Yeah. Probably. But only because he couldn't imagine his life without her in it.

But it was during those times, like tonight, when she'd been laughing and joking and touching him every chance she got. Completely platonic, of course, but he couldn't seem to convince his body that was her intention. No matter how hard he tried, Baz still wanted her with a fierceness he couldn't explain.

Just like every night since they got here, he lay in the full-size bed in this small room and listened for sounds coming from her room. Every so often he swore he heard her, but he figured it was wishful thinking. Considering his overactive imagination usually turned what was a comfortable vacation with friends into something lascivious with his thoughts of her getting more erotic by the day, it made sense that his mind was playing tricks on him. His favorite fantasy: JJ would come into his room, crawl into his bed, and beg him to make love to her.

When he thought he heard footsteps, Baz glanced over at the door. Just beneath he could see a sliver of light. Was that a shadow? Was JJ at his door?

He waited.

Nothing.

Okay, so he was most definitely imagining things now.

He flopped back down, stared up at the ceiling, and heard a light creak.

The door opened an inch.

Propping himself up again, he watched the door. "JJ?"

"Yeah."

Baz pinched his arm because surely he was dreaming. *Ow.* Okay, not dreaming.

"You need somethin'?"

She stepped into the room, closed the door gently behind her.

Baz didn't move, wasn't even sure he could. When she started toward him, he was pretty sure he stopped breathing.

And then her knee was on the mattress.

"Is this okay?" she whispered.

"More than," he said, shifting over so she could join him. "Are you all right?"

"Don't want to be alone."

He understood that. It was different here, in this house. Not familiar like their apartment.

JJ settled in beside him and Baz managed to exhale. She was looking for comfort. He understood. Although she didn't talk about it, he knew she was still having a difficult time dealing with what had happened on New Year's.

"Baz?"

He turned his head toward her. Before he could speak, her lips were on his.

His body froze. He was scared to touch her, fearful if he did it would send her away. But he also didn't want to pull back, because fucking hell, JJ was kissing him.

"Is *this* okay?" she asked, her lips gliding over his again.

Baz rolled to his side, brushed his fingers along her cheek, and kissed her, this time taking control. And when she sighed into his mouth, his synapses fired, his body flaring to life.

Kissing JJ was unlike anything Baz had ever experienced.

He'd had that same thought the first time their lips met and perhaps every time since.

This woman … she didn't hold back in anything that she did. Jessica James was the type of woman who forged ahead, clearing a path in the process. He should know. He'd been bowled over by her on more than one occasion.

"I need you, Baz," JJ said, part groan, part whisper.

"JJ," he mumbled against her lips, sliding his thumb along her jaw. "Are you sure about this?"

"Not even a little," she blurted.

Another thing he loved about her: she was brutally honest.

However, the comment didn't inspire confidence.

"Please," she said, her lips gliding over his. "Let's not think about it."

His conscience was niggling at him in warning. Baz knew the right thing to do would be to hold JJ, to comfort her without giving in to his baser needs. Too bad he'd stopped listening to his damn conscience lately. No way could he deny her.

JJ kissed him again, and this time he realized she didn't hold back, her tongue lapping at his, her palms gliding over him roughly, as though she needed something more than he was giving her.

"Please, Baz. Touch me."

She didn't have to tell him twice.

He ignored the urge to slow things down, deciding they would do this at JJ's pace. Fast and furious. That was the way she operated and sometimes it was hell to keep up. But this … this he could manage and he did. Their clothes did a vanishing act all their own, tossed haphazardly around the room as they fumbled for one another.

Baz kept his hands on her, loving the feel of all that smooth, silky skin against his palms, her soft moans as he touched the right places.

"We've got all night," he whispered when she whimpered, rutting against him.

"Then we'll do it five more times," she said on a rush.

Five? Who did she think he was?

"It's been … months, Baz."

"Trust me, I know." As soon as the words were out, he prayed she didn't think about the last time *he'd* had sex. Even if he couldn't remember much of that night, it hadn't been quite as long for him.

"Condom," she said, nipping his lower lip.

Right. Condom.

He fumbled for his wallet on the nightstand. As would be the case, it fell to the floor, requiring him to pull away to retrieve it. But he finally managed to get the condom, only to have JJ yank it out of his hand.

Baz rolled to his back as JJ straddled his hips. She wasn't gentle when she rolled it over his iron-hard length, dragging a ragged moan from him.

"Did I hurt you?"

"Not even a little."

He'd barely gotten the last word out when JJ sank down on him.

"Fuck," he groaned as her silky heat surrounded him, her hair tickling his shoulders as she loomed over him.

God, she was so fucking hot like this. Out of control, desperate.

With his hands on her hips, he guided her as she rocked forward and back, her tight sheath dragging more ragged moans from his chest. Pure, unadulterated pleasure rocked him as she rode him like they'd been made just for this.

When she sat up, arched her back, Baz cupped her breasts, teased her nipples, admiring her sensual sounds, while mentally, he was hanging on for dear life, praying she was not going to regret this tomorrow.

"Baz… yes." She sighed and whimpered, clearly chasing that elusive release.

Rather than let her take all the credit for the hard work, Baz pulled her down to him, rolled them both so that she was under him. He didn't separate their bodies, sliding his arm beneath her, holding her tightly as he pumped his hips, driving into her hard and deep.

She bit his lower lip, crying out as they soared higher, aiming right for the precipice.

Baz pulled back so he could meet her gaze, stared into her eyes as he continued to drive into her.

"Oh, God, yes." JJ's knees clamped on to his hips as she met him thrust for thrust. "Don't stop, Baz. God, don't stop."

He gritted his teeth, impaling her deeper, faster, until her pussy squeezed his cock as she cried out his name again and again.

It was then that he let go.

As he came, he couldn't help but wonder how long it would be before she realized what they'd done.

Baz woke, having rolled over to find JJ's side of the bed empty. A quick glance at the bedside clock told him that night was fading away, but it wasn't quite morning.

And he was alone.

He should've figured as much. Last night had been incredible, which meant JJ was likely coming up with a million excuses as to why what they'd done was wrong, and so many more about why they couldn't be together.

But JJ was in for an argument because Baz had spent the past few months coming up with reasons why they *should* be together, and he was more prepared than ever to fight for what he wanted. Sure, there was another obstacle they had to deal with, but Baz loved her enough to make it work.

Baz managed to sit up, shook the rest of the exhaustion from his brain as he pulled on his shorts. He padded barefoot down the short hall to the living room, finding JJ sitting on the couch in the dark. She was wearing his shirt, one shoulder bare, her long, silky hair hanging over her shoulders.

He looked around, ensuring no one else was moving about. From the sound of it, the rest of the house was still asleep.

When JJ looked up at him, he saw her fear, felt his heart clench in his chest.

Her gaze swung away. "I don't know how to do this, Baz."

Well, at least she hadn't called him Detective.

Hoping she would elaborate, Baz stepped around the coffee table, took a seat beside her, but not too close.

"Ever since that night…" She held her knees tighter. "Ever since then, I've been scared." JJ paused, shook her head. "No, terrified. I don't want to be alone, terrified someone's gonna hurt me again."

He didn't move, didn't speak, wanting her to continue.

"I hate it. I hate what it's turned me into." JJ glanced over at him. "I've got no one."

"You've got me, JJ. You've always got me."

"And you've got Molly."

Baz sighed, hating that those few words diminished everything they'd ever had.

"You know it's not like that."

"I do know that." She was still watching him. "I do. But even if we had a second chance…"

Hope burned hot in his chest.

"Even then, I've never had a successful relationship in my life, Baz."

He wanted to tell her that wasn't true. To remind her of her relationship with Brantley, a friendship that had survived time and distance.

He wanted to tell her to think about all the people she interacted with on a daily basis in Coyote Ridge. They all cared about her and she cared about them, which made them more than acquaintances.

"My mother hates me; my father pretends I don't exist." Her tone remained quiet as she continued. "The only person I ever felt close to was my brother. But he obviously didn't care enough about me to stick around."

Baz couldn't imagine losing her brother had been easy. And because Jeremy James had taken his own life, he understood why she would think he had abandoned her. It was difficult for people to lose loved ones to mental illness.

"I'm sorry about your brother."

Her gaze swung to him slowly. "That was bad enough, but then my parents blamed me."

That was something he hadn't known. "Why?"

JJ shrugged. "They needed someone, I guess. After all, it wasn't *their* fault. Couldn't be. Saint Mom and Dad, the greatest parents on the planet." She sighed. "Since I was the only one left, I got the honor of being responsible for pushin' him to the point of no return."

Damn.

"Don't you dare feel sorry for me," she said, although there was no force in her words.

Baz didn't respond, knew telling her she wasn't responsible wouldn't do any good. Not right now.

"And all that's just proof that I can't do this." She stared back at him. "You deserve better than me, Baz."

Unable to stop himself, Baz scooted closer, put his arm around her shoulders, and had her relax against him. He kissed the top of her head, brushed her hair back. When she leaned into him, he took it as a good sign. Twisting so he could look down at her, he lifted her chin with a finger, tilting her head back.

"I don't want anyone else, JJ. Since the day I met you, you're the only one I can think about."

She didn't say anything, but Baz could practically hear her thoughts. There was no way Molly's name didn't pop into her head.

"This *is* a relationship," he said softly, firmly, continuing before she could interrupt. "I'm not goin' away. You and I both know that's not what you want. We deserve that chance."

Her green eyes were glassy once again, and he held her gaze for long seconds before he leaned in, pressed his forehead to hers.

"I love you, JJ. You might not want me to, you might not even believe me, but I do. And I'm gonna continue lovin' you even if you push me away."

She sniffled, but her head tilted, her mouth moving closer to his.

"I don't expect you to love me back," he managed. "Not yet. But you will."

Again, he knew she was thinking about Molly, and it made his chest ache.

"For the time being, let me love you and you just be content with that. Let's keep doin' what we're doin'. This friendship ... it's important. And while we're doin' that, let me show you what it means to be in a relationship, show you that you're better at it than you think you are."

"But—"

"Let me, JJ," he said sternly, pulling back to look down into her face. "That's all I'm asking. One day at a time. It doesn't have to be difficult."

Her eyes were wide, but he could see hope there. Possibly for the first time since he'd met her, she wasn't poised to argue with him.

"What do we do on the first day?" JJ whispered, and those words made his heart thump harder.

"Well, I suggest we go back to bed, you let me hold you for a few hours so you can get some sleep. That's all, JJ. I just wanna hold you. Then tomorrow we'll see how it goes."

"And go to the aquarium?" she asked hopefully.

"Whatever you wanna do. Aquarium, beach, whatever."

"That sounds like a full day."

"It can be."

"Okay."

Baz cupped her face, smiled. "Yeah?"

"Yeah. But one day at a time."

"As promised."

When she let out a giggle as he was lifting her into his arms, Baz knew this time would be different. It would require effort, but the one thing he knew with absolute certainty was that JJ was worth it.

So very worth it.

Chapter Twenty-Five

Friday, March 12, 2021

BRANTLEY RAN ALONG THE WATER'S EDGE, TESHA keeping stride beside him. He focused on the feel of the sand beneath his feet, the salty breeze on his face, his body having found its natural rhythm, giving him the ability to focus his mind.

He'd come out this morning before anyone had woken in an attempt to get some perspective. He knew the coming weeks were going to put pressure on the team. The change alone was going to cause some tension, and he would have to deal with all that plus the challenge of proving their worth to Sniper 1 Security.

They had spent the past six months on the hunt for Juliet Prince, and while it hadn't been their sole focus, it had taken a significant amount of their time. That was over. Done. There was nothing to fall back on, no excuses to be made. It was time for the next chapter in their story to be written. Was he ready? Absolutely.

Yet there was still the matter of the choice he and Reese had made in that motel parking lot in Port Isabel. They had left Juliet Prince to die, and while he didn't regret that she was dead, it wasn't a decision he'd ever seen himself making. At some point, along with all his other demons, Brantley figured it would rear its ugly head and he would have to deal with it, too.

Brantley ran through the wet sand until his thighs screamed and his lungs burned, but he couldn't seem to outrun his thoughts.

Tesha let out a bark then took off at a sprint, leaving Brantley behind.

Up ahead, he saw Reese walking toward them at a leisurely pace. Brantley closed the gap quickly, slowing as he approached, wanting to catch his breath before he said good morning to his man.

As he walked, his muscles cooling, he had another thought. Brantley wondered what the next chapter in *their* story would entail. He smiled to himself, realizing he didn't know the answer, but he was looking forward to seeing where it took them.

"You didn't wake me," Reese said, squatting down to pet Tesha.

"I didn't," he agreed, continuing to move so his muscles didn't lock up. "Thought maybe you'd sleep in."

"I tried, then JJ waltzed right into our room, tryin' to talk me into goin' to the aquarium with them. Figured I better hightail it before I did somethin' stupid." Reese smirked. "Like say yes."

"What? You don't wanna go check out the sea turtles and dolphins?"

"Prefer not to, thanks." Reese stood tall. "But she did manage to wrangle everyone else into makin' the trip."

"Everyone? Even Luca?"

Reese fell into step with him. "I think he's lookin' forward to it. Big bad Luca Switzer's got a soft spot for sea life."

"When're they leavin'?" Brantley asked.

"She didn't say. They were startin' breakfast."

"Please tell me they're makin' eggs and bacon."

"What is it with you and eggs and bacon?"

"They're mornin' staples."

"They're pan-fried cholesterol."

"Yeah, well."

They walked for a few minutes, continuing past the house down the opposite end of the beach. Farther down, he knew there were some seaside resorts, and during the summer, it was usually crowded with people trickling out from their vacation rentals to spend time in the sand and surf. So far, they'd been lucky, only encountering a handful of beachgoers. He figured the same could not be said for next week when most were celebrating the official spring break.

"I left a message with RT."

Brantley peered over at Reese. "Regardin'?"

"What comes next."

"And?"

"And he said it's up to us, but he'd like us to spend a couple of weeks up there if possible. He reiterated the training. I told him it was already on the agenda."

"It's a good opportunity for the team." While he wasn't expecting to get anything out of it, Brantley could certainly see the benefit for some of them.

"We'll also want to leverage them for ideas on gettin' clients."

Yeah, Brantley had been thinking about that, too. "Governor Greenwood said he'd continue to refer us."

"That's good news."

"In a way. But it'll still be a matter of steppin' on toes."

They walked for a short time, then turned around, made the trek back. As they approached the house, Brantley thought about the fact everyone would be leaving in a little while.

"Did they say how long they'd be at the aquarium?"

"A couple of hours, probably. Why?"

"We'll have the place all to ourselves."

Reese stared over at him. "So?"

Brantley chuckled. "You might wanna rest up. I've got plans for you."

With that, he took off running, leaving Reese laughing behind him.

Nearly three hours later, Brantley found himself alone with Reese for the first time in six days. Only after every member of the team attempted to persuade them to come along, to think of it as team building, had they finally given up, piled into Baz's truck, and headed for the aquarium. Brantley had, of course, met every single request with a decided no. He damn sure was not giving up some alone time with Reese to walk through a bunch of oversized fish tanks. Not even a killer whale—something Trey insisted would be there—had enticed him.

As soon as Baz's truck pulled off the street, Brantley made a mad dash upstairs, where Reese was chilling on the balcony, beneath the cover of an umbrella, beer in hand.

"Beer before noon?" he teased.

"You said to rest up. I was chillin'."

"I think it's time for a shower," he insisted, not bothering to wait before pivoting back into the house and straight to the first bathroom he came to.

He flipped on the shower, ensuring it was lukewarm, then made a quick dash back to his duffel, grabbed a bottle of lubricant, and returned to find Reese already in the shower.

Brantley chuckled as he closed and locked the door—just in case—then stripped off his shorts and his T-shirt and joined Reese.

He hissed a breath and stumbled back. "What the fuck, Tavoularis?"

The water was ice fucking cold.

Reese grinned. "I'm tryin' to cool off. In case you haven't noticed, it's hot."

"Not for those of us who haven't been outside for the last hour." Brantley reached around Reese, turned the water up a few degrees, then pressed the man against the tile and fused their lips. "You're gonna have to warm me up."

"Yeah?" Reese's hands slid around him, pulling him closer. "I'm bettin' I could do that."

Reese planted his hands on Brantley's chest, pushed him back.

Without hesitation or question, Brantley let him manhandle him, shoving his back against the tiled wall, outside the spray of water. When he met Reese's gaze, he saw the lust darkening his light brown eyes, knew it had been too long for both of them.

Although they had their own bedroom, they hadn't been intimate. Brantley knew Reese was hesitant with the team nearby, so he had refrained from pushing the issue. Although he couldn't give less of a shit whether anyone overheard them, he knew Reese was more private about those things.

Reese leaned in for a kiss, lingering briefly. "I want you in my mouth."

Brantley sucked in a sharp breath at the insistence in the words. Reese still had the ability to surprise him in moments like this. The longer they were together, the more dominant Reese was becoming, and when he flexed those muscles, Brantley never knew what was in store for him.

But he damn sure looked forward to finding out.

Relaxing against the wall, Brantley let his head fall to the side as Reese's lips trailed along his neck, lower. Every so often Reese would nip his skin, making him hiss in another breath. When those teeth tugged not so gently on Brantley's nipple, he groaned low in his throat.

He managed to lift his head, watching as Reese eased down to his knees at Brantley's feet. Although it would've been easy to let Reese remain in control, to sit back as the man blew his mind with that exquisite mouth, he knew Reese enjoyed a firm hand from time to time, too. When Reese leaned in, wrapping his lips around his cock, Brantley palmed Reese's head firmly, holding him in place.

Those golden-brown eyes met Brantley's and held while he pumped his hips, holding Reese's head perfectly still and using his mouth for his own pleasure.

"You look so fuckin' good with my cock in your mouth," he muttered, still holding Reese's gaze. "Suck me. Hard."

Reese did, taking him to the root before releasing him slowly.

Brantley pulled him forward, so his cock would bump the back of his throat, then released him. Again and again, slow and deep, he fucked Reese's face as he watched every glorious second. Brantley could've easily reached the peak of ecstasy, but he opted to go slow, to drag it out, because there was no sense rushing when they had a couple of hours.

Pulling out of Reese's mouth, he helped him back to his feet, flipped their positions, then let himself be used in the same manner. He swallowed Reese's thick cock over and over, loving those guttural moans that echoed in the small space.

Looked as though Reese was on the same page, because he opted to hold back, too. For a few minutes, they focused on getting clean while their hands roamed, teasing and tormenting.

Once they turned the water off, Brantley stepped out of the shower. He caught his reflection in the mirror above the vanity and an idea came to him.

He didn't give Reese time to dry off, instead, manhandling him so that he was bent over that vanity while Brantley moved in behind him. He stroked himself once, twice, groaning from the sensation. He was hard as steel and eager to feel the heat of Reese's body enveloping him.

While their eyes met in the mirror, Brantley grabbed the lube, prepared Reese for penetration, then guided himself home. He loved the way Reese held his stare, not afraid to let Brantley see every emotion as it flittered across his face.

Brantley let himself get lost in the sensation, riding Reese hard as he was flooded with pleasure. It didn't take long before they were both grunting and groaning, Brantley slamming in deeper and deeper, until he couldn't hold back.

"Fuck," he bit out, impaling Reese one final time as his cock erupted.

The instant he'd drained himself, Brantley pulled out and dropped to his knees, urging Reese to turn around. When he did, Brantley opened his mouth, took Reese to the hilt, then accepted the punishing thrusts as Reese chased his own release.

"Fuck, yes, Brantley," Reese groaned. "Swallow me." He growled softly, thrust forward one final time, and came right down Brantley's throat.

Sated, at least temporarily, Brantley grabbed a towel, tossed another to Reese, and proceeded to dry off.

"We've still got an hour and a half. I say we grab some lunch, then do that again."

Reese's response was a grin, followed by, "We'll see."

AFTER SPENDING THEIR ALLOTTED TIME SATING THEIR urges, Reese was almost grateful the team had returned.

It wasn't that he hadn't enjoyed being used and sensually abused by Brantley. He absolutely did. But he'd been worn out after the third round and too proud to admit he couldn't go another. Not without a nap first.

As they'd done the other days, they spent the afternoon down by the water. Every now and again, someone would brave it and race in only to race back out. Reese didn't care for the water even during the heat of summer, so he opted to watch and enjoy everyone else's pain.

Now, as he sat on the back deck looking out over the ocean, Brantley and Trey inside cooking dinner while the other four took a stroll down the beach, Reese picked up his phone, opened his text messages.

He pulled up the one he'd received two days ago, read it for what felt like the hundredth time.

I heard you were gonna be in my neck of the woods. Thought maybe you'd want to grab some dinner while you're in Dallas. It would be nice to catch up. I've missed you, Reese.

Honestly, he had no idea why he didn't simply delete the text message from Madison Adorite. It wasn't like he was reading it to reminisce or because he harbored old feelings for her. He wasn't enticed by her invitation, didn't even look forward to meeting with her.

But something kept him from doing so. A feeling he got, perhaps. Or maybe it was a feeling he no longer had that worried him.

Although Reese was no longer having doubts about what he wanted, accepting that he had fallen in love with a man, he wouldn't deny he had some mixed feelings. Not about Brantley. No, his feelings for him were sound. His doubts had more to do with his own sexuality.

Basically, he still wondered how he had lived his entire life without ever having so much as an attraction to a man, yet he was now in what was proving to be a long-term, committed relationship with one. As though he was a different person entirely.

Truthfully, that—the uncertainty about what prompted his choice—bothered him from time to time.

He understood what it meant to be bisexual, to want both men and women, but Reese wouldn't categorize himself that way. And he knew it wasn't a switch that could be flipped. He loved Brantley, but at the same time, if something ever came between them, he couldn't see himself with another man.

Did that mean he was still on the fence? Did it mean he shouldn't write off who he had once been? It wasn't like he and Brantley were talking about marriage or forever. They were living together, sure, but at times it seemed more for convenience than anything.

"Dinner's almost ready."

Reese jumped, turning his phone over and resting it on his knee, hand firmly over it.

"You okay?" Brantley asked, eyes narrowed as he walked around to stand in front of him.

He picked up his beer. "Perfect. Why?"

"You get a call?"

Reese took a drink, shook his head. "Just my mother. She texted to check in."

Brantley continued to watch him closely. "She doin' all right?"

"Yep." He let his gaze shift to the waves below and lied through his teeth. "Said she looks forward to us bein' up there. Wants to make us dinner."

"Sounds like a great idea." Brantley started toward the house. "Five minutes."

Five minutes would've given him more than enough time to delete that text message.

And yet he did not do it.

Epilogue

Saturday, March 20, 2021

FROM THE MOMENT TRAVIS TOLD HIS FAMILY that he intended to officially marry Gage, they'd come up with a dozen suggestions as to how they should do it. At the church, at the resort, in the park. Full wedding party, half wedding party, no wedding party. Decorations, a big reception afterward, color schemes, themes. He'd pretty much heard every variation there was from small and basic to a wedding to rival the royal family.

As was the case with most of the debates with his siblings, there'd been some arguing and bartering, maybe a little bit of bribery thrown in. Admittedly, Zoey was pretty good at that, but Travis had stood his ground.

In the end, his idea was simple: him and Gage by the magnolia tree at his parents' house. He gave them the option of getting on board with the idea or making themselves scarce for the big day. They eventually gave in, realizing he wasn't going to back down.

Travis wasn't looking for some grand gesture; he only wanted to fulfill his wife's wish, and he wanted his husband to know he was committed for the long haul. As far as he was concerned, no one had to attend except for Gage and Pastor Bob.

Although his sisters-in-law had been disappointed that they wouldn't get to plan a big to-do, they had rallied behind him. But he should've known putting his foot down didn't necessarily mean he would get everything he wanted. They'd snuck in a few things without his consent, but since they'd kept it simple, Travis could honestly say they'd had the right idea. And they were all there, seated behind them in rows of chairs. Kaleb and Zoey, Zane and V, Ethan and Beau, Braydon and Jessie, Sawyer and Kennedy, Brendon and Cheyenne, plus all twenty-three of their kids. His mother and father were also there, as were Kylie's father and stepmother.

For Travis, that would've been plenty, but someone had slipped in a few additional invitations. Several of Travis's cousins, aunts and uncles, and some good friends were also in attendance. There to help keep the little ones in line during the ceremony, or so he'd been told.

And fine, perhaps it was better this way. His entire family there to witness them pledging their love to one another.

But there was one attendee he hadn't expected. According to Gage, the magnolia trees likely wouldn't produce flowers for years. While they were already several years old at this point, having been transplanted from whatever farm they were grown on, it would still be a while before their flowers made an appearance. Yet there it was, a single bloom on the magnolia tree, the flower open fully as though seeking the warmth of the sun. As far as he knew, the other three trees had yet to produce a single flower, and Travis couldn't help but think it was a sign.

So, beneath the warm Texas sun on a beautiful spring day, Travis and Gage exchanged their vows.

Nothing elaborate because, again, it wasn't about the pomp and circumstance. He held himself together, kept a smile on his face throughout. But it was when the rings were brought forward that Travis got choked up.

At their wife's request, Gage had taken their rings to a jeweler in the neighboring town, along with Kylie's, and had them melted down together and two new rings created. The result was two platinum bands, each with three tiny diamond chips across the center. While the largest diamond and the other smaller ones had been saved for the girls, Gage had decided the three diamonds— signifying the three of them—would be a reminder that even without Kylie with them, she was still in their hearts, still part of them.

When Pastor Bob proudly pronounced them husband and husband, Travis kissed his groom and held on to Gage for long minutes afterward.

Today was a day he would always remember, a good day. And while they were still grieving, would be for quite some time, these were baby steps to moving forward.

Stay Tuned

I hope you enjoyed the fifth installment of the Off the Books Task Force. As you can imagine, this one was the hardest one for me to write. I shed more tears than I can count through every page, but that doesn't surprise me since the Walkers have kept me on an emotional roller coaster all these years.

There's definitely more to come for Brantley and Reese, JJ and Baz, Trey and Magnus, and the rest of the task force. Each book in this series is a full-length novel involving a new case and the continuation of the relationships between them all. And I promise not to keep you waiting long for each installment.

If you enjoyed *Alibi*, please consider leaving a review.

ABOUT NICOLE EDWARDS

New York Times and *USA Today* bestselling author Nicole Edwards lives in the suburbs of Austin, Texas with her husband and their youngest of three children. The two older ones have flown the coup, while the youngest is in high school. When Nicole is not writing about sexy alpha males and sassy, independent women, she can often be found with a book in hand or attempting to keep the dogs happy. You can find her hanging out on social media and interacting with her readers - even when she's supposed to be writing.

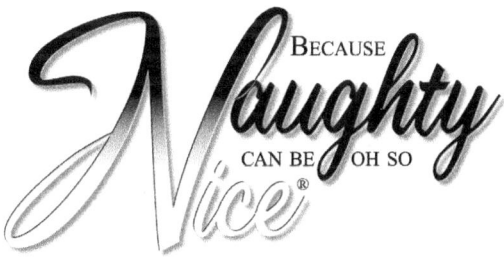

CONNECT WITH NICOLE

I hope you're as eager to get the information as I am to give it. Any one of these things is worth signing up for, or feel free to sign up for all. I promise to keep each one unique and interesting.

NIC NEWS: If you haven't signed up for my newsletter and you want to get notifications regarding preorders, new releases, giveaways, sales, etc, then you'll want to sign up. I promise not to spam your email, just get you the most important updates.

NICOLE'S HOT SHEET: A couple of years ago I produced a weekly hot sheet that gave a summary of what I'd done and what I had in the works, and I have decided to bring it back. This is a more personal newsletter that I send out for those who are curious about me, my family, my dogs, and all that goes along with the daily author life.

NICOLE'S BLOG: My blog is used for writer ramblings, which I am known to do from time to time. I will keep these separate from the newsletter updates or what I post in the Hot Sheet so that I don't duplicate in your inbox.

NICOLE NATION: I created Nicole Nation on my website to provide exclusive content to my readers including, First Look notifications, sneak peeks, A Day in the Life character stories, exclusive giveaways, cards from Nicole, Join Nicole's review team. It's free and gets you access to exclusive content you won't find anywhere else!

NN ON FACEBOOK: Join my reader group to interact with other readers, ask me questions, play fun weekly games, celebrate during release week, and enter exclusive giveaways!

INSTAGRAM: Basically, Instagram is where I post pictures of my dogs, so if you want to see epic cuteness, you should follow me.

TEXT: Want a simple, fast way to get updates on new releases? Sign up for text messaging. If you are in the U.S. simply text NICOLE to 64600. I promise not to spam your phone. This is just my way of letting you know what's happening because I know you're busy, but if you're anything like me, you always have your phone on you.

NAUGHTY & NICE SHOP: Not only does the shop have signed books, but there's fun merchandise, too. Plenty of naughty and nice options to go around. Find the shop on my website.

Website:	NicoleEdwardsAuthor.com
Facebook:	/Author.Nicole.Edwards
Instagram:	NicoleEdwardsAuthor
BookBub:	/NicoleEdwardsAuthor

ACKNOWLEDGMENTS

Of course, I have to thank my wonderfully patient husband, who puts up with me every single day. If it wasn't for him and his belief that I could (and can) do this, I wouldn't be writing this today. He has been my backbone, my rock, the very reason I continue to believe in myself. I love you for that, babe.

Chancy Powley – You were the guinea pig for this book, the one who read a concept I've never written before. Because I know you'll give me your true, unbiased input, I didn't know what to expect. When I saw your response, I was overwhelmed in the best possible way. Thank you for not only being a wonderful beta reader, but for being my friend.

Jenna Underwood — Because you continue to be my friend despite the fact that I am the world's worst friend. Thank you for always being there for me and for the postcards. They make me smile.

I also have to thank my street team – Naughty (and nice) Girls – Your unwavering support is something I will never take for granted.

I can't forget my copyeditor, Amy at Blue Otter Editing. Thank goodness I've got you to catch all my punctuation, grammar, and tense errors.

Nicole Nation 2.0 for the constant support and love. You've been there for me from almost the beginning. This group of ladies has kept me going for so long, I'm not sure I'd know what to do without them.

And, of course, YOU, the reader. Your emails, messages, posts, comments, tweets… they mean more to me than you can imagine. I thrive on hearing from you, knowing that my characters and my stories have touched you in some way keeps me going. I've been known to shed a tear or two when reading an email because you simply bring so much joy to my life with your support. I thank you for that.

By Nicole Edwards

THE WALKERS

ALLURING INDULGENCE
Kaleb
Zane
Travis
Holidays with The Walker Brothers
Ethan
Braydon
Sawyer
Brendon

THE WALKERS OF COYOTE RIDGE
Curtis
Jared (a crossover novel)
Hard to Hold
Hard to Handle
Beau
Rex
A Coyote Ridge Christmas
Mack
Kaden & Keegan
Alibi (a crossover novel)

BRANTLEY WALKER: OFF THE BOOKS
All In
Without A Trace
Hide & Seek
Deadly Coincidence
Alibi (a crossover novel)

AUSTIN ARROWS
Rush

Kaufman

CLUB DESTINY
Conviction
Temptation
Addicted
Seduction
Infatuation
Captivated
Devotion
Perception
Entrusted
Adored
Distraction

DEAD HEAT RANCH
Boots Optional
Betting on Grace
Overnight Love
Jared (a crossover novel)

DEVIL'S BEND
Chasing Dreams
Vanishing Dreams

MISPLACED HALOS
Protected in Darkness
Salvation in Darkness
Bound in Darkness

OFFICE INTRIGUE
Office Intrigue
Intrigued Out of The Office
Their Rebellious Submissive
Their Famous Dominant
Their Ruthless Sadist
Their Naughty Student
Their Fairy Princess
Owned

PIER 70
Reckless
Fearless
Speechless
Harmless
Clueless

SNIPER 1 SECURITY
Wait for Morning
Never Say Never
Tomorrow's Too Late

SOUTHERN BOY MAFIA/DEVIL'S PLAYGROUND
Beautifully Brutal
Without Regret
Beautifully Loyal
Without Restraint

STANDALONE NOVELS
Unhinged Trilogy
A Million Tiny Pieces
Inked on Paper
Bad Reputation
Bad Business

NAUGHTY HOLIDAY EDITIONS
2015
2016

www.ingramcontent.com/pod-product-compliance
Lightning Source LLC
Chambersburg PA
CBHW060153180626
46813CB00007B/2729